Natalie –

We all …

and behind every mask,
there is a story.
Make your story compelling
by living your dream!
Hope you enjoy the book!

Phantom: Edge of the Flame

Kristine Goodfellow

K Goodfellow
Sept. 2017

Published by Bird-in-Hand Books
Manufactured in the United States of America
Cover art by: Denys Prokofyev/Dreamstime.com
ISBN 978-0-9884251-0-1

This book is a work of fiction. Names, characters, places and incidents are either products of the author's imagination or used fictitiously. Any resemblance to actual events, locales, or persons, living or dead is entirely coincidental.

Edition: May 2017

DEDICATION

Dedicated to my husband. Thank you for your belief in me. You've always supported my desire to be a writer and you've diligently helped me reach my goal of publication. You are my insight into true selflessness, leadership and compassion. It's by your example that I can write passionate heroes and honorable gentleman. Thank you mom and dad for encouraging my wild imagination. You've always supported my writing dream. Thank you both for your examples of perseverance and commitment. Thank you to my sons who never questioned my need to sit at the computer and write for hours, days, weeks and eventually years. Your tolerance and patience of my writing obsession amazes me. I am grateful to have sons like you. I love you with all that I am. Most importantly, thank you to my Heavenly Father for sending His son to save us all.

CHAPTER 1 - THE MISANTHROPE

ERIK:

My wretched carriage driver seemed determined to hit every rut and crevice in the muddy road from Paris to the countryside. I wondered if he derived some sick pleasure from tossing his master around like so much cargo on a transport wagon. On more than one occasion in the last six years I daydreamed about killing him. However, *permanently* solving his ineptitude would require hiring a new driver. The gratification didn't seem worth the aggravation of the task.

He hit another bump and I lunged forward, my knees hitting the seat in front of me. He'd reached my leniency limit.

"Watch out! How big does a hole need to be before you find it worthy of missing?" I yelled at him from inside the coach.

"I'm trying my best, Monsieur."

"Trying your best to do what? Kill me?"

A sudden pull of the reins pushed me back against the tufted velvet seat.

"Why are we stopping? What seems to be the problem now?" I stabilized myself once again, planting both feet upon the Persian rug beneath them.

"There's a carriage in the road. Looks like they've run into some trouble."

"Highwaymen?" My irritation turned into interest. Dusk—the favored time of such perfidious endeavors. My senses on high alert, I peered out my window while gripping the handle of my weapon—ready for trouble. Taking the lives of a few thugs might make the trip tolerable and of course, it would make the roads safer. A delightful synergy of public service and a worthwhile activity in which I could express my hostile mood.

As the stranded coach came into view, the driver answered, "No, sir. It appears they've broken down."

"Thank you for your explanation. I could have never deduced such a conclusion from the lack of a wheel on one side. Your attention to detail is invaluable, as is your elucidation of the obvious."

"I'm not the one who asked, sir."

I opened my mouth to address his impertinence, but a most extraordinary scene struck the diatribe right out of my head. In the moments between daylight and dusk, a woman stood with the splendid sunset over her shoulder. The evening sun's rays deepened her blue traveling suit to indigo. The light caressed sections of the fabric and made her white collar look like a moonbeam on water. The vibrancy of the scene rivaled any painting in the Louvre. She turned toward our approaching vessel; the soft hues of the setting sun fell upon her auburn tresses.

Her sophisticated hairstyle framed an appealing oval-shaped face that expressed apprehension. A delicate beauty with rosy cheeks and big eyes looked toward my coach. Her striking presence against a surreal backdrop of a crimson sky almost made me disregard the instinct to conceal myself. Realizing the precarious situation of possible discovery, I drew away from the window before we approached any closer.

I sat back in my seat, letting go of my weapon and once again clutching the silver handle of my walking stick. In direct opposition to my intrinsic desire to remain hidden, I leaned forward. I had to observe the beauty of that woman one more time. I'd never be able to forget such a strange, ethereal sight.

Upon hearing my coach pass, she stepped back and landed ankle-deep in mud. Her driver dropped his tools; he grabbed her by the elbow in an effort to steady her stance. His filthy fingers left a handprint upon her velvet sleeve. Instantly, my peril-honed intuition triggered danger warnings through my head. Maybe it was the thinly veiled depravity in his vermin-like eyes. Or, perhaps one murderous lunatic can identify another. Whatever the reason, I knew that if I left her there, she would not live to see another sunset.

My heart pounded with forceful beats; I had to make an instantaneous critical decision. My potent desire to stay concealed within the coach made me consider journeying onward and leaving her at the mercy of fate.

"Driver, stop! Ask if the lady needs a ride," escaped my lips.

With restless anticipation, I leaned forward to glance at the scene once more. We hit a rather large furrow in the road which knocked me off balance. My left temple smacked into the rosewood edging around the window knocking my mask askew and launching me sideways into the seat. A massive wave of fury flushed through my body. I adjusted the mask and then rubbed the developing welt on my head.

"Confound it, man! Are you blind to road obstacles?" I straightened my cape, tugged at my collar.

"I'm pulling to the side of the road, sir. You did order me to stop, did you not?"

"Have you no sense, at all? Where did you acquire such abhorrent driving skills? A dim-witted child would know to avoid the trenches."

The driver jumped down onto the lane and sloshed through the mud as he approached the open window. I turned my head away resisting the urge to say more about his driving abilities and thus prolong his dallying at the carriage door.

"Monsieur? I thought—"

"You thought? I'm not paying you to think, am I? For if I were, you'd owe me. Now, go on, ask the lady if she would like to share my ride. We'll take her back to the city."

"Yes, sir. I wanted to make sure I heard you right—or I had not misunderstood like a dim-witted child. You've always preferred to be alone. You've never shared your ride before."

"You heard me correctly. Is something wrong with your hearing, too? Now go. Be off!"

He'd scoffed and mumbled under his breath while heading to where the stranded carriage took up half the lane. "Nothing wrong with my hearing. I'm sure they heard you down the road. Doesn't mean I understand you. Mr. High and Mighty, big-word-using-imperialist pain in my backside."

The man couldn't be more surprised by my offer than I was.

The last of the sun's rays glinted off the onyx buttons within the tufting on the empty seat across from me. I realized exactly what I'd done, so I pushed back in my seat, found a shadow and pulled up the hood of my cape to conceal myself even more.

I planned to take her back to the city. From there, she could hire a brougham to reach her final destination.

After experiencing the miserable condition of the roads, I lost my desire for traveling to the slate quarry anyway. My sculpture would have to wait.

The lady approached the door. I held my breath so as not to alert her to the sound of my quickened, nervous breathing rate. I turned my head away but watched out of the corner of my eye as the driver helped her into the coach.

"You will be all right, Madam?" he asked as she settled in across from me.

"Yes, thank you, Monsieur."

"Very well," he said. "I'll go help tie your trunk and bags onto the boot."

Heat crept up the back of my neck. I shifted in my seat and loosened the top clasp of my cape.

She turned towards me. "Bonjour. Thank you for—"

"Bon*soir*," I interrupted, hoping she'd deduce from my tone she need not address me again. I dared not call any more attention to myself.

"Thank You for—"

"You're welcome." Once again, I hoped she'd infer from my abrupt tone I was not one for simple niceties.

Moving her bags from one carriage to another took the drivers a few minutes, but we sat in silence. Upon completion of this task, her driver rode away on his horse and my driver remounted his station.

After we were on our way, she spoke to me again. With heavily accented French, she thanked me for my kindness and hoped I would not be late for my engagement on her account. Her rough mangling of the language assaulted my ears, but her voice had a melodic undertone.

To prevent further verbal destruction of my native tongue, I said, "You're welcome. I speak English. I'm in no way inconvenienced by turning around and going back to the city." *In order to be late to an engagement one would have to engage.* I had one less worry than most.

The driver continued up the lane toward the quarry. I deduced he must've been looking for an adequate place to change directions. The recent storm left the narrow road laden with mud and debris.

Although almost dark, I pulled my cape hood further down over my brow. Surely, she stared at me with either anxiety or morbid interest. If she had not exclaimed or sucked in her breath due to well-bred restraint, then she might be the type who would ask me *why* I wore a mask. The questions gathered in the air.

"I'm on my way to visit my cousin. It's been quite a horrendous journey. I think I'll extend my stay longer, so I don't have to make another trip again so soon."

I trusted if I did not respond she would address me no further. English was not a graceful language to begin with, but American English sounded needlessly belabored and dramatic. Nevertheless, something in her tone suggested she had not seen my mask and considered her host nothing more than a congenial gentleman. The sun had vanished beyond the horizon. Darkness engulfed us and I began to relax a little. Just a little.

"Why did your cousin not send a man to fetch you? Why are you traveling alone? I fear, Madam, had I not happened upon your carriage you may have found yourself in more trouble than you realize."

"I travelled with a trusted servant. The poor fellow fell from the carriage. He was unable to complete the journey with me. I set out on the last segment of the excursion alone rather than wait for my cousin to send another escort. Retrospectively speaking, traveling alone was a poor choice. I agree."

"So, you were left in the care of the driver?"

"A hired driver. Indeed." She leaned closer to me which made me draw back. "A very unsavory character he was, too. Swore like a demon and had a most deplorable habit of spit— Forgive me." She sat back again. "A lady shouldn't speak of such things."

I found the boldness of Americans refreshingly unpretentious when they didn't cross the line to impropriety.

"No need to apologize. It was he who had the appalling habit not you." Then I added, "Or, perhaps I judge you too soon. We've only met."

Her laughter filled me with fear. Not the usual fear of someone shrieking with horror after they'd caught sight of what lay beneath the mask. No, when she expressed genuine amusement over something I said, I wanted the conversation to continue and *that* disturbed me a great deal.

"How long is your holiday to last?"

"I'm not here on holiday." She sighed. Whatever brought her to Paris didn't seem to be a pleasant tasking.

"Forgive me. I had not intended to pry."

"No, it's fine. I'm here to take care of some personal matters. The undertaking could take a few weeks or a couple of months. I have no definitive answer to give you, Monsieur."

"I require no definitive answer, Madam."

"I'm Mrs. Weston. Olivia Weston. I should offer you my hand, but in the darkness, I wouldn't be able to tell if it was your hand I was shaking."

I chuckled both at what she said and her sharp intake of breath once she realized the possible misinterpretation.

"Madam, due to the unusual circumstances in which we find ourselves, I will not require such a formal introduction. I wouldn't want you shaking anything you hadn't meant to shake."

"Oh!" She tried to repress a giggle, but failed.

The carriage sloshed through the mud as the driver continued to look for a suitable place to turn toward the city again. I felt so unlike myself. Sitting cloaked in darkness—that part felt right. However, sitting across from a lady and having her neither avert her eyes nor stare at my mask in vulgar curiosity left me quite unprepared for the sensation. I rather liked the new terrifying feeling.

We lurched to a stop and she grabbed my knees to keep from losing her seat. Her touch shot through me in a flash of panic and excitement like lightning followed by thunder.

"What is going on out there?" I yelled to the driver.

"Sir, I fear I won't find a safe place to turn around. The trenches on the side of the road run deep with rain and mud. If I try to turn around, we might get stuck."

"What are you suggesting?"

"Do you know anyone out here in the country, sir? Someone who might welcome you on a night such as this? Perhaps a friend or relative will offer you a place to rest and some supper. Do you know anyone at all?"

His brazen questions grated on my tolerance. "I do not!"

"Well, sir, what shall I do?"

"Turn around as instructed."

"Yes, sir." He mumbled a curse at me and with a short snap of the whip we began again.

Admitting I had no one in the country who would take me in during an emergency made me flush with awkwardness. A well-bred gentleman should have plenty of friendly estates in which to retire for an evening. I wondered what she made of my confession. Then, I wondered why her impression of me mattered so much.

"How do you like that?" I asked her in English.

"Well, forgive my limited French, but from what I gathered he suggested we not turn around and—"

"And?" I thought she hesitated because she didn't know how to phrase her disappointment about my not having even one friend or relative in the country. No family. No friends. What would she make of *that*?

"Well, Monsieur, it sounded as though he asked if you've eaten a friend for supper. To which you replied you hadn't any. I'm not sure if you meant any friends or any supper or which of those you hadn't eaten."

She amused me in a way I had never been amused before. "You are correct. That's what was said. Your French is not as limited as you alleged. Just for clarification, I have *not* eaten any supper…or any friends."

"What did you say, honestly?"

"I told him to turn the carriage around at once. We need to get you to the city."

The carriage tipped to the right and then left and then right again before settling. With the two right wheels swallowed in mud and wedged in a crevice next to the road, our progress stopped.

The driver grabbed his lantern and jumped down. He walked to the side of the carriage where he discovered his first inclination had been correct. He released a horrible string of obscenities aimed first at the mud, then at the wheels (which he gave a sound kick) and then at me for insisting he turn around.

Madam Weston kept very still as I stuck my head out the window and informed him if he should utter any more profanity in front of the lady, I would take the hide from his bones before the light of day.

I pulled my head back inside. My face and neck warmed with self-consciousness about my threat. "Be thankful your French is not so good or your ears would burn with the profane use of language our driver has chosen to force upon us."

"Monsieur, I'm schooled in enough French to understand the majority of what he said. Off-color words are easier to memorize and less tiresome than conjugating verbs. He's quite angry with you. He believes you to be…either a gluttonous scoundrel or a hungry fiend. Which would be correct?"

Her words, her voice, her mere presence enchanted me. I chuckled. "A more accurate interpretation for his French description of me might be a wicked devil in a man's body."

"A wicked devil? Are there any other kind?"

"A charming one perhaps."

She giggled. "Ahh, yes. The most dangerous kind. However, charm aside, he'd still be wicked."

"Touché, Madam. Wickedly charming. Very dangerous."

"No, Monsieur. Even more dangerous…charmingly wicked."

Chapter 2 Stranded

ERIK:

In a moment of frustration, the driver flung open the carriage door, but he must've remembered whom he'd be addressing and collected himself.

"Excuse me, Monsieur, but as you can see we're stuck. I'll have no choice but to ride a horse back to town and return with help." The gritting of his teeth betrayed his seething anger, but his modicum of self-control saved him from any future repercussions. The man had a decent amount of intuition and enough self-preservation instinct not to cross me with overt contempt. Others who lacked such acumen lived only long enough to regret their pitiful shortcomings.

"We haven't passed a town in quite a while. Shall you and I try to push the wheels from the mud first?"

He snorted. "We'd never be able to push this beast by ourselves." Anger negated his ability to remain civil; for he seemed to overcome his innate fear of me. "You, sir? You don't look like you could push a frog through the mud."

"Indeed!" I yanked the door from his grasp and pushed him back with the end of my walking stick. "Off with you then."

He splattered through the mud as he grumbled to himself on his way to unharness one of the horses. I fought to control the anger making my heart pound with want of tearing him apart with my bare hands. My cheeks burned with the humiliating way he described me in front of the lady. *Push a frog through the mud?* I'd have pushed his face through a willow tree had a divine creature not sat across from me.

He mounted the horse and began his journey leaving Madam Weston and me in a lopsided carriage. Everything leaned to my left and her right. We adjusted ourselves to keep seated upright. Without a doubt, she realized she found herself in quite another unfortunate predicament. *She must be terrified to be all alone with a strange man in the dark.*

"I assure you, Madam, I have no cause to harm you."

"I assure you, Monsieur, I'm quite prepared to use the revolver in my handbag should it become necessary."

Shocked, I didn't move a muscle. *A lady with a gun?* Americans were a strange breed. With my remarkable night vision, I saw her put one hand inside her bag. I wondered whether she honestly had the barrel of a revolver pointed in my direction. It would not be the first time I'd found myself facing down a bullet. However, I'd never been threatened by a firearm concealed in a fancy embroidered handbag with a woman's finger on the trigger.

"You have a gun pointed at me?"

"Should I need it, I shall be ready."

"So, it's not, at this time, fixed in the general direction of my voice?"

"It's handy enough."

"No doubt, Madam, however, I assure you there is nothing to fear." The irony struck me as funny. She sat across from everything most people feared—an ugly monster from the scariest nightmares. A murderer. An assassin. A man who'd been accused by his one and only ally of having a deplorable lack of conscience.

The need to laugh at our dilemma bubbled up in my chest. To my great surprise, she laughed with me.

"Monsieur, I told you my name, yet you remain this faceless, nameless man in the dark. Should I *not* be with my weapon at the ready? Perhaps you withhold your name because of your infamy?"

Oh, if she only knew. *Faceless and Infamous.*

"I think because of our unique state of affairs, Madam, let's dispense with rigid formalities. To show you I harbor no ill intentions toward you, please address me by my Christian name as though we've long been acquaintances."

"Oh, good. Then you're a Christian?"

"I was raised Catholic."

"Then you know any harm you cause me would be a sin. You would be denied entrance upon reaching St. Peter's Gate should you give me a reason to discharge my gun."

I chuckled. "Rest assured; I don't fear St. Peter." *Or anyone else.*

"Good."

"Have you put the revolver down? May I take a deep breath and know it will not be my last?"

"Yes, I have. Something in your voice makes me believe you are a refined man of honor."

Again, she made me chuckle. *My voice*. The voice was the most dangerous weapon any hypnotist possessed.

"Thank you."

"Your name, Monsieur?"

"You, my lady, may call me Erik."

"And they told me French men were stuffy."

"Who tells such horrendous lies about French men?"

"The English, of course."

Our laughter blended together in the dark night. The fresh scent of earth after a rainfall wafted through the air. I wished, at that point, the night could last forever.

"Why, Madam, it is common knowledge that English men are jealous of French men. They spread these lies so we will stop seducing their women."

"Oh, my."

The newly discovered 'charmingly wicked' part of me was pleased because I might have made her blush.

"Exactly how many English women have you seduced, Monsieur Erik?"

Her audacity to say such a thing shocked and intrigued me.

"Humility keeps me from revealing such a secret." Heat covered my cheeks, circled around to the back of my neck. I had never touched a woman much less seduced one. In fact, she was the closest I'd been to a woman in decades.

Frogs and crickets calling to their mates underscored the silence of the carriage and filled me with sadness.

"That many?" she asked when I remained quiet.

I laughed. "I fear your imagination may enhance any exaggeration I make."

The groan of wood and squeak of springs accompanied the further tilting of the carriage. She squealed with the unexpected adjustment in the mud. We'd slid over in our seats and stopped our tilt by holding onto the sidewalls.

"I better take some of your trunks off the right side so the weight may be more evenly distributed. If not, you, my lady, will find yourself coming face to face with some stuffy French mud." I moved toward the door. Just as my hand gripped the latch, she grabbed my cloak and tugged.

"No, don't leave me here."

"I'm just going to move the trunks. I promise I shall return. I'm not on my way to slay dragons."

"No." She didn't let go, but pulled me toward her a little bit more.

I didn't want to leave her even for a few moments. Sinking another half an inch convinced me otherwise. "See? If I do not rectify this problem we will continue to sink. I'm sure my American friend does not want to arrive in Paris covered in mud. Such an entrance shall set idle tongues wagging. We can't have that, can we?"

Her sudden fright prevented her from listening to me. She focused on the fact she did not want me to depart rather than the creaking of mounting pressure on wood coming from the unbalanced carriage.

"No, Erik, don't go. I hate to…I'm afraid of the dark—of being alone in the dark," she admitted softly.

"Everything will be all right, Madam Weston. I assure you."

I needed to remove her hand from my cloak in order to exit the carriage. With tender movements, I pried her fingers from the material. A warm wave of tantalizing pleasure washed through me as I held the woman's hand in mine for a fraction of a second.

Even with both of us wearing gloves, the extraordinary moment struck me dumb. Her quick intake of breath made me shudder. Humiliation stung my cheeks. My grip loosened upon infliction of the familiar pain of rejection. But, the dear woman not only grabbed my hand, but wrapped her other one around it, too. With relief and delight, I allowed her to hold my hand for a moment. Her touch energized me with hope and immobilized me with mistrust.

"Please, Madam Weston. You will be fine. I shan't be but a moment. I will return the second I balance the load. You're safe with me. No harm will come to you with me by your side. You have my word."

"All right," she said with hesitancy. "Will you talk to me? Talk to me the whole time so I know you're there?"

"I'd be happy to."

I opened the door and stepped out on the street side. The moonless night and the canopy of trees hanging over the narrow road made removing the luggage an impossible task without the aid of a light source. I found the lantern on the side of the carriage. *She's going to insist I bring the light inside when I finish.*

If I wished her never to see me, I would have to hide my face from the light while I worked. *Afterward, I'll make an excuse to remain outside on the driver's seat for the duration.*

I had my lie ready. I would tell her I needed to sleep on top to keep watch for highwaymen. She was not the only one armed.

After removing her trunks from the boot of the carriage, I set them on the least muddy side of the road right next to the remaining horse. Melancholy settled over me because our time together would soon end. I talked to her while I worked, but tightness in my throat made my voice a bit tremulous. I turned to the one thing that had always brought me comfort in my wretched life.

Music.

I began to sing. Pleasing, yet sorrowful, the song filled the air. When I finished the task, I held the lantern down at my side and approached the door.

"All fixed now." I waited for her to request the light. My plan was to hand her the lantern without getting back inside. However, she did not respond. *Maybe she's asleep. Yes,* my *lullaby put her to sleep.*

I advanced a step. She spoke to me in a soft voice. "That was wonderful, Erik. The most beautiful thing I've ever heard."

I waited for her to demand the lantern. *Perhaps she had not seen it.* I waited longer.

"Erik, are you not coming back inside?"

"Pardon me?" I set the lantern down by my feet to see if she would object.

"Why do you delay? Come back."

Something occurred to me out of nowhere. *She's blind!*

After my astonishment faded, I picked up the lantern, blew out the flame and stepped inside the carriage.

"Madam Weston?"

"Yes?"

"Are you all right?"

"I am now that you've returned."

Due to the angle of the carriage and her unexpected kind words, I lost my balance for a second. I steadied myself and sat facing her, speechless.

"Erik, you're scaring me. Why are you not speaking?"

"I…I…Madam, pardon my most ungracious manners, but I must ask. Can you not see?"

She shrank back in her seat and clutched her handbag to her chest.

"I apologize, Madam Weston. You don't have to answer my indecorous question. I meant no offense."

"You certainly are impertinent."

"Pardon me. I just wondered—"

"*You are correct*. I cannot see at night. I'm not helpless, so you can remove the pity from your voice."

"Madam, I give you my solemn pledge. You heard no pity in my voice."

Life had taught me credence should always be validated. I waved my hand in front of her.

"Monsieur, I get the distinct impression you are moving your hand in front of my eyes as we speak."

My face burned hot with her words; I dropped my hand. Silence surrounded us; guilt thickened my tongue. I wouldn't be able to find any words with which to express my sincerest apology. Regret aside, I found myself smiling. *Blind!*

I pushed my hood all the way back. “I apologize for my continuing rudeness, Madam. Normally, I’m not so discourteous.”

“No need for forgiveness.”

I leaned forward trying to observe her as best as I could.

“Why am I getting the impression you can see me in the darkness? It’s the oddest sensation.”

“Well, I’ve been told I have the vision of a cat in the dark.”

“Is that so?” After a moment, she said, “There’s no need to stare, Monsieur.”

I drew back. “Pardon me. I meant no harm. I cannot begin to tell you how regrettable my behavior has been. I recognize my conduct is unacceptable. I don’t know why I cannot maintain my manners.” Without realizing my own action, I leaned forward again.

“Why do you apologize, yet continue to stare? Tell me what you find so outright fascinating about me. Is my face not the same as yours or anyone else’s? Do I not have two eyes, a nose and a mouth? Why do you study me as though I were an exhibit in the Freak Show at the county fair?”

Intense remorse blasted through me. I was well acquainted with the brand of embarrassment she was experiencing.

“I do not think blindness constitutes a Freak Show exhibit, Madam. Forgive me if I offended you in any way.” I closed my eyes and grinned. *Blind!*

To mitigate the awkwardness of our exchange, I asked, “Where were you headed to in Paris, Madam?”

“To my cousin’s estate. Perhaps you’ve heard of the family. Chagny? Count Philippe de Chagny? I don’t mean to impress you with a family name. I assure you royalty doesn’t hold the same sway in America. In fact, I’m certain that’s why we kicked out the British. We don't care for titles and birthrights—or at least we must pretend not to."

"The Chagnys? I've heard of them. They are patrons of the arts and regulars at the opera."

"Are you involved with the opera? Your voice? Is that why—"

"No, Madam. I prefer to stay behind the scenes so-to-speak. Although, I'm proud to say I helped build the opera house. I was the contractor. Although I'm also an architect, I did not design the theatre—nor can I be held responsible for Garnier's outlandish elevation."

"What is your last name Erik? I should like to tell my cousin, so he will know what gallant gentleman came to my rescue."

"Oh, please. I hadn't meant to be gallant. You were in trouble. It's what one ought to do if one wants to do the right thing." I stumbled upon my explanation since I rarely cared if I did the right thing or not. I rambled on to make her forget the question. She did not pursue the matter of names any further.

"Thank you again, Erik. I was uneasy about what would happen with only the driver and me on the roadside. I'm armed, but for some reason I'm a terrible shot."

I laughed. Her charm, her wit, her intelligence, put me under a delirious spell. I did *not* want to leave her company. Ever. She had managed to hypnotize the hypnotist.

"May I ask you another impertinent question, Madam Weston?"

"Be careful. Don't make me shoot you, Monsieur."

"As a rule, I never anger an armed American. I've read about the Wild West."

"I'm from New York. Hardly the Wild West."

"Perhaps *that* explains your bad aim."

She laughed. "I like you, Erik. You have a quick wit about you."

I like you, Erik. The words sounded like a piece of music too beautiful for the ears to appreciate all at once. I had to experience those words. They shot through me like an arrow; their meaning spread through my veins like a soothing intoxicant. Tears stung my eyes, but then I chastised myself for being so sentimental.

"Thank you."

"Your question."

"Why didn't your husband accompany you on this journey? Why does he allow his wife to face this treacherous voyage by herself? A woman travelling alone is neither proper nor safe."

"I'm a widow, Erik."

I couldn't move or speak. When my deficiency of intellect passed, I wanted to hop out of the carriage and swing from the trees. "I'm terribly sorry to hear that, Madam." *I lied.*

"Thank you."

Hope tickled my brain like a feather. Subtle, but the sensation let me know hope had not died as I suspected. I couldn't stop smiling.

"Would you mind if I asked you to sing again, Erik?"

"Not at all."

She sighed when I finished the aria.

"That's beautiful. Is the song from an opera?"

"Yes."

"Which one? I would love to see it. Is it now playing?"

"No. It's still in production."

"What is the title?"

"Don Juan."

She giggled. "The composer must be French. You Frenchmen have one favorite subject. You're the experts on love."

"The composer is French. I cannot vouch whether he's an expert on love."

"Of course he is. He's French."

She laughed, but I didn't. In my composition of Don Juan, I faltered in the same place for years. Refusing to be defeated, I forced myself to continue composing. Her simple statement made me realize I was incapable of ever finishing. The subject matter was as foreign to me as Portuguese—a language I'd never been taught. I had worked until I could no longer see straight and my fingers cramped around the pen. Yet, I was never happy with the result. At that moment, I understood that I never would be.

"Are you asleep?" she asked after a few minutes.

"No, I was just lost in thought."

"Oh, I won't disturb you."

"You aren't disturbing me. I quite enjoy your company."

"When do you think the driver will return?"

"Very soon, I'm sure. Are you cold?" I didn't wait for an answer. I had pulled off my cape and placed the garment over her.

"Thank you. Are you going to sleep now?"

I sat back again. "No, I think I'll stay awake. I require very little sleep."

"Shall I tell you a story then?"

"What?"

"A story. To pass the time. I've been told that I'm a good storyteller."

My jaw dropped. Warmth spread through me as if someone put a velvet cape over *my* shoulders. No one had ever wanted to entertain *me*. "Madam Weston, I would love to hear a story."

The night stretched on and the longer we stayed together, the more I dreaded the time when I would take leave of her. She had a colorful way with words. I quite enjoyed the tale. Her storytelling ability impressed me.

Using every skill I had learned from years on the road with the gypsies, I concocted a fanciful fairytale for her. She delighted in my story. Her compliments fell upon my cold heart like sunshine upon frost.

After a while her breathing became slow and rhythmic.

"Madam Weston?" I whispered. When I received no reply, I lit the lantern.

I had never studied any living human's face before. I made a point not to look at men unless absolutely necessary, but I had never looked openly at a lady. Even when I hid my monstrous face behind a mask, they hated the way my eyes made them feel. I learned from an early age to look down or look away to spare myself seeing their aversion. In my later years, I avoided people altogether and thus, kept myself safe from the humiliation they inflicted. But, there in the carriage with hushed sounds of night surrounding us, I studied Madam Weston as though she were a piece of Renaissance art. I gazed with utter fascination upon an unexpected gift.

*****

What if the driver doesn't return until tomorrow? If the simpleton showed up after sunrise with a group of repulsive villagers, they would no doubt see my mask. If they, with their group bravado, demanded I remove it, there would be bloodshed.

It would not be mine.

Facing down angry men did not concern me. They'd receive no mercy as they'd likely show none to me, but there was the matter of a certain lady having to be involved in such wicked happenings. *No!* I needed to depart before the wretched Neanderthals showed up to remove the wheels from the mud.

I fixed my eyes on the glorious creature who, although in the presence of godless evil, slumbered with sweet trust. The disparity between her and me laid my spirit very low. I refused to think of our vast differences. Everything within me longed to stay in her company forever, but there was no way.

The driver had probably imbued the locals with a tale about his master—a strange man who travels alone and mostly at night. Having the superstitious villagers believe such a tale is one thing, but if the driver lost his fear of me in daylight, the idiot could continue to tell tales of a masked villain once he arrived back in Paris. That would not do. I had to leave soon.

Chapter 3 Unveiling

ERIK:

The driver tempted fate with his failure to make haste. If I wanted to spare his pitiable life for the sake of the lady, the time to take leave came as the first rays of sun appeared on the horizon.

"Madam Weston," I whispered. "Wake up, Madam, I must take my leave." She stirred and opened her eyes. In the dawn of a new day, she sat up and removed my heavy cape from her shoulders. She blinked and then looked into my eyes. We locked gazes.

How could that be?

"Erik?"

I yanked up the cloak, threw it around my shoulders and put up the hood. "It is I. It's time for me to…" Her eyes followed me as I moved back. I broke into a cold sweat; bile filled my throat.

"Erik, what's the matter?"

I turned away from her. "I must take leave. You can trust my driver to treat you in kind. I assure you, although boorish, the man is quite honest. You will be safe."

I tried to exit, but she grabbed the back of my cape.

"Excuse me, Madam. I must be on my way. You must let go of my cloak." I didn't turn around to speak.

"But…but…"

"Madam, please let go of me. I must take my leave."

"Can you not wait until the sun is higher? I still cannot see well. You are but a shadow. Please, Monsieur, wait with me a little while longer."

A frosty chill went up my spine. I closed my eyes. Without turning around, I asked, "You can see well in the daylight?"

"I told you. I cannot see in darkness. I get along quite nicely during the day once the sun is all the way up."

I yanked my cloak from her fingers. "I cannot stay."

"Just a few minutes, please."

My agitation combined with the sound of her panic brought back horrible memories of others begging for mercy. I'd showed none, but the sound of their pleas always wounded me.

"Madam, I assure—"

"Hellfire and damnation! I don't want your assurance."

Her anger surprised me. Her use of expletives surprised me more. "What frightens you? The day grows lighter as we argue. Another minute or two and you will be able to see well enough."

"Then wait another minute or two."

I sighed. "Would you feel better if I sat on the driver's seat and waited until help arrived?"

"What?"

"I can wait outside until the driver returns."

"You're not making sense. Waiting outside will not put you at an inconvenience, but waiting inside with me will? What is so urgent that you must run away?"

At first, words did not come to me. What story could bring sense to such a ridiculous arrangement? Thankfully, I am a quick-minded liar.

"Madam Weston, I do this for your benefit. My having slept inside the carriage with you isn't proper. I fear tongues may wag all over town if the driver decides to gossip. I shall await help outside and keep your reputation unsullied. Surely, you understand why I must do this."

"Why are you speaking to me with your back turned?"

"Because, Madam Weston, I am a stuffy Frenchman." I'd jerked my cloak from her hands and made my exit before she protested. A dagger through my chest would have hurt less. A knife wound might eventually heal.

Let her be angry. She will remember the rudeness not the enchantment anyway.

I waited on the driver's bench looking toward the sunrise. I kept alert for the first sight of the driver and the peasants coming up the lane, so I could slip into the woods. My journey back would be long—and one I couldn't make until dusk.

A few minutes later, the sun shined bright. I wanted to thrash the driver. *Where did he go?* I jumped off the seat and unhitched the remaining horse. Running my hand down his nose, I spoke to him. He nuzzled me and nickered. *You and I will make a hasty exit as soon as the repulsive villagers and the incompetent driver approach. Madam Weston will have to ride in the wagon they engaged to come rescue her.*

After a while, I began to think help was not coming. I needed another plan. Keeping my hood pulled low over my brow and my back toward the carriage (in case she looked out the window) I devised a way to use leverage to get the wheels out of the mud. I'd shoved a large tree branch under the right wheel and then surveyed the situation.

The carriage door opened. Madam Weston stepped outside.

I turned away from her shivering with apprehension. "What are you doing? Get back inside at once."

"Monsieur?"

"I said, Madam, get back inside where it is safe and dry."

"I don't care to. What are you doing exactly?"

I refused to face her. Nervous energy made me want to keep my hands busy, so I moved another large branch from the side of the road. "I'm freeing the wheels from the mud."

"Why?"

I stopped and tried to keep calm. "I must get the wheels free from the mud, so we may journey back to Paris should my damnable driver fail to return."

"With one horse? How do you propose to do that with one horse, Monsieur? Shall we harness you to the other side of the carriage?"

She's right. What was I thinking? I let go of the branch and began to walk to the back of the coach. The insolent woman tried to fall in step with me. I swung my cape and turned on my heel away from her.

"Why are you acting this way, Erik? If you do not face me, I will scream."

"Scream away, Madam. Perhaps someone might hear you and they will come to rescue us."

"I don't understand. Why are you so cold now in the light of day? It's as if you changed; as if you are two different men."

"I am one and the same. Now that your eyesight has returned, I'll take my leave."

"Go then. Leave me here all alone. You, sir, are no gentleman."

The insult shot through me. I am in every way a gentleman. Mostly.

Her accusation prevented me from taking another step. I couldn't tell her I would never leave her unattended. I would've hidden in the shrubs without her knowledge. If she were in any kind of danger, I would have made myself available.

"Very well, Madam. I shall stay if you get back inside. If not, this is the last thing you'll ever hear me say."

She muttered something low and under her breath unaware my ears could pick up the faintest whisper. Her words hurt. "You arrogant frog."

The carriage door slammed behind me. I spun around to make my way to the other side. The woman tricked me! I stood facing her. She didn't know what a dangerous game she played. I turned to walk away, but she grabbed my arm.

"I advise you to let go of me at once," I said with my head turned.

"Or what?"

Her question remained unanswered. I would rather kill myself than harm her. She didn't know that though. Her bravado struck me as audaciously American.

I didn't move. I faced away from her, but her fingers still gripped my sleeve—until she slid her hand in mine. The act took me by surprise. Against my natural instinct, I swiveled towards her. Our eyes met. We stood face to face in the garish morning light as a stabbing pain of raw exposure tore through my chest. I waited for her to ask me why I wore a mask like a highwayman or executioner. She continued to hold my hand and tightened her fingers around mine when I tried to pull free from her.

"You've had your see; now let me go." She still did not release me, so I yanked my hand from her grip. Now she knew why I wanted to leave before the driver returned. She played a brilliant game. I needed to guard against further trickery and deception.

I walked to the rear and sat on the back ridge of the coach. She made her way to the front.

The marvelous time we had shared the night before played in my memory. The intolerable sweetness of that reminiscence haunted me. I wished the encounter never happened. I had experienced the esoteric delight of being with a lady—an attractive woman who enjoyed my company. I was not the world-famous magician, a hypnotist, or a masked singer in a freak show. I was *me*. A chance encounter like the one we'd experienced could never happen again. The memory of such an implausible incident would torment me forever.

"Erik," she called from the front.

"What?" I closed my eyes and waited for the question.

"I will not pursue you further. You can stay back there if you wish. I shouldn't have deceived you. I apologize."

And? And? I still waited for the question. *Why do you wear a mask? Remove it. Let me see who you are.* Truth be told, I would've loved to take off the mask and let the temperate morning sunshine touch my skin. I tilted my face to the sky and daydreamed about the gentle light of a new day caressing my cheeks, my forehead.

Despite my secret desire, I would *never* acquiesce to remove the mask. Being in the company of a masked man might make her uncomfortable, but revealing myself would only turn discomfort into horror. She certainly would not be relieved if I unmasked myself. I, especially, would feel no relief.

"I'm sorry," she said.

"What are you sorry for?" I asked from my safe corner.

"You didn't wish me to see your mask, but I followed you and made you show me. I'm too old to act upon such childish displays of curiosity."

"Is that what I am? A curiosity?"

"No, you're the same man you were last night in the dark, are you not?"

"Hardly!"

"Why so? Why the anger now? In the morning you have anger you didn't have last night."

"I'm not angry." I lied. I was not angry *with her*. She just happened to be a part of the world at which I was angry.

"Don't patronize me. If you don't want to converse, then don't speak to me. The anger in your voice is quite plain. If you want peace and quiet, Monsieur, I'll remain silent."

I shook my head. She believed I did not want to carry on a conversation with her. Oh, the irony.

"I do believe we've been abandoned here," she said after another hour passed.

"I have an idea. I'll take the horse and find help."

I would need to bypass the small villages and travel back to Paris, to my comrade Daroga's home. He would have to commission a carriage to fetch Madam Weston. Not the ideal arrangement, but under the circumstances, the only plan that could be considered feasible.

"I will not permit you to leave me here by myself."

I scoffed. "And how do you plan to prevent it?"

"Simple. You will have to push me off or take me with you." I peeked around the corner as she mounted the horse by using her suitcases as a step ladder.

The poor woman underestimated me on every level. *Or did she?*

I pulled my hood down lower over my face and approached her. "You would rather starve out here? Or are you willing to be reasonable?"

"Me? *You* are the most unreasonable man I've ever met. Am *I* ready to be reasonable?" She rolled her eyes and scoffed. "Oh, please, Erik, you won't even look at me. You're a fine one to speak of reason. *Un home qui parle dans sa cape parler de; discuter de raison d'être.*"

"Madam, please, stick with English. You've just told me I talked to my cape about my *essential purpose*."

"Despite my faulty French, you get my meaning. You converse with your head down and hood up. Are you talking to the ground beneath your feet? What a rude habit."

"Habits sometimes form from necessity," I snapped.

"So, you find it necessary to speak to your muddy boots rather than address me?"

"What do you want? You want to see? Why don't you ask? It's what you've wanted all along."

"Leave me now." She flicked her wrist in a dismissive gesture. "Talk to your boots elsewhere."

I raised my head. "No, you wanted to see. I'm here. Are you afraid to look now?"

I'd show her with a little theatrical flair as I had done many, many times in my life. I was ready to fling back the hood and rip aside the mask to prove my point. *She wants a private show? Then a private show she shall have*. The woman ignited within me new and unidentifiable varieties of fury.

She refused to acknowledge me. Instead, she climbed off the horse using her trunks again. I wondered why she'd turned squeamish when earlier she'd been curious enough to pursue me like a hound on a fox.

She didn't walk away as I expected, but came towards me. With one quick motion she threw off my hood.

A spark of burning anger burst into a blinding inferno. A deep, red, rage boiled in the dark cavern where my heart should have been. I clenched my fists to control the enormous flash of scalding temper.

"So, you wear a mask."

"Indeed, Madam. I find your abrasive manner quite offensive now. I shall be on my way."

"Erik," she said softly. "You're still the same man."

My heart stopped. The force of the beats starting again assaulted my chest like a sudden barrage of rocks striking my sternum. I looked up. She met my eyes.

My anger froze and turned into ice cold shock. She smiled at me as if when she pulled off my hood she found an ordinary man looking back at her. I had a quick impulse to throw off the mask and wipe the smile from her face.

"I won't ask you to remove your mask."

"Pardon?"

"I said I won't ask you to remove your mask. If that's what you're thinking."

The woman confounded me. I could never predict her next move. All my life, I strategically kept steps ahead of anyone I had dealings with, but this woman, this impetuous woman, bewildered me. I stood blinking in the sunlight.

"Come on, then." She walked by me toward one of her trunks. "I bought some treats for my cousins. Shall we eat breakfast?"

I stood there staring after her like a dolt. "Breakfast?"

"Yes, breakfast. I don't have pastry, but I have cookies." She pulled a large square tin from underneath some clothing in her suitcase.

"Cookie?"

"Don't you like cookies?" She opened the tin and held the container out to me.

I gathered my senses. "Oh, tea biscuits." At that moment, the frail, petite woman made my natural distrust of human beings surface. Deep–rooted suspicion clawed through my surprise. *Is this all a trick? No! This cannot be a hoax.* I shoved the danger of ruin aside and let myself take pleasure in her company—however short-lived our time together would be.

"No, not tea biscuits. Cookies. Sugar cookies. That's what we call them in America."

"Oh, well, my lady, they may be cookies in America, but these are in France now. Tea biscuits are what they're called in English here."

"That's preposterous. We cannot call them tea biscuits." She chuckled.

"Why not?"

"We eat them with coffee not tea."

"Coffee? How vile. How do you stand the taste?"

"Coffee is a commodity."

"Why not drink tea?"

"I would wager most Americans prefer coffee over tea. Maybe because during the Revolution we could not bring ourselves to do anything that made us appear British or subjects of the Queen."

"The more I hear about Americans the more I find myself liking them. Petit gateau is what we call them."

"Americans?"

I laughed. "No. Cookies."

"Try one." She held the tin out to me again.

I reached inside the container and then bit into a star-shaped cookie.

"Well?" She waited for my reaction.

"Tea biscuit. This is a tasty tea biscuit."

I reached for another, but she closed the lid barely missing my fingers. "They're cookies. If you care for another, you shall call them by their proper name." Her playful smile teased me.

I chuckled. "Would *you* care for a delicious petit gateau, Madam Weston?" I pulled out three of her cookies from my cloak and relinquished them into her palm.

Her jaw dropped. "How did you do that?"

I shrugged. "Do what?" I handed her another and then another.

"That's amazing. Did you steal them all?" She opened the box. "Oh no. Some of them have been broken on the journey."

"Do they taste the same?"

"Of course."

"Then being broken has not ruined them—their appearance has merely been altered."

"True enough, Monsieur, true enough."

We climbed onto the driver's seat and put the tin of cookies between us. A small tickle of hope touched my heart again, but this time I shoved it down deep. She'd be on her way soon.

"I will have to watch you closely, Monsieur. You seem to have the gift of sleight-of-hand."

I produced a pink puff of smoke in front of her. The rosy cloud floated upward and then snapped open showering an array of colorful confetti and glitter down upon her.

"A magician! How wonderful!"

I placed her cameo pin inside her palm. "A magician, but not a thief." I wrapped her fingers around the pin.

She checked her lapel and found the brooch was indeed missing. "You are very talented, aren't you?"

"Some have claimed so."

Although I managed to engage in a civil and amusing conversation with Madam Weston, I kept expecting to see a strange look or critical glance. The woman with the bad eyesight treated me as if I looked like any other man. It unnerved me. Hiding beneath the strange new emotions she'd uncovered laid a man whose anger swelled as the knowledge of the world he'd been denied increased. A wistful hope was in danger of drowning underneath a river of seething anger.

"Were you on your way to visit someone in the country when my disdainful lack of forethought about traveling alone caused you to detour?" Madam Weston's voice had a playful tinge which resonated in my bones like a curious melody one would never tire of hearing.

"No."

"Where were you going?"

"The slate quarry. I needed some quality pieces for a sculpture."

"Ahh, a magician and an artist. Too bad a reckless American interrupted the strike of muse and inspiration."

The unquenchable desire to look upon my *new* muse left me powerless to stop my eyes from drinking in her visage. "Madam Weston, you may divert me from any undertaking at any time."

"Why did you try to leave me earlier? Because you didn't want me to know you wear a mask?"

With her words, the sun's gentle rays turned from soothing warmth into an unnatural moment of severe heat scorching my cheeks, burnishing my forehead under the mask. My mind called up gruesome images of the heated torture chamber I'd designed. I shuddered. A wave of nausea crashed over me when I imagined being trapped inside the awful apparatus.

I blinked a few times to get the imagery out of my mind.

"Are you all right?" Her voice brought me back to the present.

"I don't like people to look at me," I said before my defenses impeded my honesty.

She turned toward the road in front of us. "I understand. What about the driver?"

"Especially the driver."

"Is he not your regular coachman?"

"Yes, the worthless lout lives off my payroll."

"He doesn't know you wear a mask?"

"He's never paid attention to my mask."

Truth be told, he'd stolen sideway glances from time to time, but he was wise enough to pretend he didn't notice anything different about me. How much he'd actually seen I couldn't be sure. He picked me up at the same spot three nights a month without questioning why he couldn't meet me at my residence, but rather in such an obscure place. Should he trail me one day, he would not be enough of a threat or challenge to cause even a slight rise in my heart rate. From what I could surmise about the man, he had two skills: A way with horses and annoying me to the point of paroxysm.

"What will you do when he returns?" she asked.

"I'll stay far from the road and walk home."

"Walk to Paris? You shall do no such thing."

"Madam Weston, you overestimate your ability to stop me from doing anything."

I produced a big paper butterfly that fluttered in front of her for a moment before breaking into several smaller butterflies. They floated on the soft morning breeze for a couple of seconds before falling into her lap atop the glitter and confetti.

"How utterly enchanting." She picked one up and fingered the colorful wings. "Clearly, Monsieur, I cannot stop you from doing anything. You are correct, but perhaps there's another way. A better way."

"Pardon me?"

"When he returns, I'll tell him you've taken ill." She turned toward me, placed a butterfly in the palm of her hand and gently blew. "I'll cover you up and they'll be none the wiser." The tiny butterfly bobbled in front of me before falling.

I smiled at her ease of lie. A handy gift she possessed, too.

I longed to brush off the sugary cookie crumbs from her cheek, but I did not dare. Too many men recoiled at the thought of shaking my hand. I would hate to make her shrink from me. "Your plan might work."

"I have no doubt, sir."

A wagon with a horse tied to the back moved up the wet lane in the distance. "Look! There they are." I jumped off the bench and helped her down. We ducked into the carriage.

I reclined on the seat and pulled my hood forward. She tucked her shawl under my chin like a blanket. Before she pulled the curtains closed, she paused and looked at me. With her gawking down on me, my mind flashed back to the days of my childhood when my home was a cage in a carnival freak show. I had the urge to bolt up, push her away and make for the woods. Except—

She smiled at me. People never smiled at the creature in the cage.

"You're all set." Her grin was that of one who shared a secret. My comrade, Daroga, and I shared many secrets during the years we spent in Persia. None of those secrets ever evoked the playful expression of shared conspiracy she gave me. Madam Weston and I shared a secret which did not involve assassination or torture. She and I played a childish game together. The warmth of her smile travelled from my eyes to my heart. I continued to grin as she stepped back outside.

Olivia explained the situation to the driver and the others. The crude voices of men filtered through the windows as they set to work getting the wheels unstuck and reloading her luggage.

Before she climbed back inside the carriage, my driver asked where she'd like to go. She said, "Take Monsieur home. I'll help him inside and make sure his household knows he's ill. When he's in their hands, you may take me to the Chagny Estate."

She stepped into the coach. I sat up, tossed aside the shawl. "Why did you tell him that? He can't take me home first."

"Why not? I can help you remain covered until you go inside. Is that so wrong?"

"You've ruined everything. You cannot help me inside. You cannot come home with me." I kept my voice low so the driver would not hear the quarrel.

"Is there a reason for your secrecy of residence? Are you married perhaps? I might remind you we had no choice of overnight accommodations. I'll be happy to explain that to your wife."

Closing my eyes, I shook my head. For her to presume such a thing made me want to laugh. Or cry.

I tapped my walking stick on the roof. "Driver, take the lady to the Chagny Estate at once."

"Yes, sir."

"Pardon me, Erik, but how do you plan on getting out of here without being seen if I don't help you?"

"You might be shocked at how easily I can leave a place without ever being seen."

"That won't work. He knows you're here."

"Take this and pay him when you disembark." I pulled a small leather bag from my cape. "When I get home, I'll rush out. I won't need to take the time to give him his salary."

She held out her hand. I dropped the moneybag into her palm. The gesture exuded finality—a bargain fulfilled. The end of a transaction. I was no longer feigning illness. I truly felt ill.

*****

I moved the black curtain to peek out while two footmen carried Madam Weston's trunks inside the Chagny home. She stood at the bottom of the steps leading to the door. I fully expected her to enter the chateau without a backward glance. When she didn't move, I began to wonder if she lingered about for my sake. *Why would she do such a thing*? I let go of the curtain and drew back in my seat, chastising myself about the ridiculous presumption she hung back for me.

The driver snapped his whip. The coach moved down the lane. A deep, sad longing grew heavy in my chest. The further away we rode from the Chagny's home, the darker my mood became. The taste of some delicious dessert lingered on my tongue, but after the first bite fate snatched away the sweet delicacy, leaving me craving more.

Olivia Weston found a slim crack in my armor, let in some light and then disappeared. All my life, I'd guarded myself against the very thing I felt at that moment. Shattered.

Chapter 4 The Visit

ERIK:

Going into the tunnel leading to my home under the opera house was not safe at that time of day. Furthermore, the pleasant weather enticed the dreadful populous to emerge. City sidewalks bustled with the trite bourgeois. The wretches congested the streets with their carriages. There was no avoiding them. Someone might follow me out of curiosity and ruin everything.

"Stop! Leave me here," I yelled to the driver.

"Here, sir? Right here?"

"Is something wrong with your hearing? You mimic me like a bloody mocking bird as of late. Yes, here."

"This is the shopping district, sir. The center of trade. Are you sure you want to be dropped here?" The driver had slowed the horses and pulled to the curb.

"Yes, yes. I'm rather ill. I know of a doctor who lives around here," I lied.

The driver remained on his seat facing forward while I stepped out of the coach. I had the fortuitous advantage of standing on the sidewalk in front of two buildings with an alley between them.

"Pick me up at our regular place next week," I demanded with my head down and hood up.

"Yes, sir." He began to maneuver the horses back into the lane. He mumbled, "I can hardly wait, you miserable snob."

I swiveled toward him forgetting my precarious situation of probable exposure. "I heard that! Unlike you, there is nothing wrong with my hearing. Get your mold-filled, filthy ears checked before you pick me up again."

Whether he heard me over the din of the street I couldn't be sure. I broke into a cold sweat. I looked around, worried my outburst had caused a stir. No one even glanced my way.

The driver turned the carriage at the corner. I began to make my way through filthy alleys to Daroga's home; the only home in which I would be accepted if not welcomed. I stuck to the shadows and walked with firm intention.

The smells of human waste and greasy, peasant fare permeated the alleyways making me gag. I tried to keep close to the slick, wet walls to remain undetected. Mangy dogs skittered to and fro. Dirty, shoeless children splashed in mud puddles of unknown derivation—the contents of the puddle and the paternity of the children probably questionable.

Babies cried inside besmirched tenements where vulgar people yelled to one another through open windows above my head. A man wearing nothing but shirtsleeves and trousers ran down the alley as though the devil chased him. He stopped long enough to vomit near a fence before continuing onward. The human race disgusted and shamed me.

I banged on Daroga's door with my walking stick. I had checked over my shoulder for anyone coming or going through the front entrance of the building.

At last, the locks on the other side were disengaged. The door swung open.

"You don't live in Versailles. How long should it take a man to answer his door in a flat this small? Were you intentionally leaving me out in the hall?" I brushed by him with one quick backward glance to make sure I had not been followed.

"And good day to you, too, Erik." Daroga checked left and right before he shut the door. Retirement did nothing to lesson his instincts. He still acted like a daroga—the chief of police in Teheran. Many years ago, convinced I did not possess enough of a conscience, he appointed himself the keeper of my scruples.

Daroga and I met by the tunnel on a weekly basis, but always, *always* at night. Seeing me during the day must've shocked him.

We never discussed the terms, but we both knew them. If I killed again, he would betray me to the police. He'd keep my existence a secret if I kept my temper in check. My preferred interpretation of our pact included my own de facto—if I were clever enough to keep him from finding out, I could do whatever I wanted.

I threw my cape on a chair before removing my gloves and tossing them on top.

"Goodness, Erik, what happened to you? You're covered in mud."

He knew I hated filth of any kind. The fact I had ruined an expensive, tailored suit didn't faze me at the moment. Being covered in muck suited my foul mood.

"May I stay here until dark? I fear going home until the sun sets."

"Yes, of course. Did you, um, *have trouble*, Erik?" Suspicion dripped from his voice. He'd interpreted my disgraced clothing and foul mood as a sign of some sort of intended or realized lethality on my part. Worry wrinkled the corners of his eyes.

"Trouble? Did I have trouble? That isn't what you meant to say, is it? You cannot directly ask me what you have on your mind?" I turned my back on him and stood in front of the hearth, shivering in my damp clothing. After a moment of silence, I picked up the poker and tried to get the dying fire to flame up.

"What did you do, Erik?"

"What did I do? That is no better than 'did you have trouble'." I hung the poker on the nail next to the mantle.

"You came here to be quarrelsome? You could have waited until I had my tea first."

With his hands busy filling the kettle and his back turned, he found the bravery to ask, "Have you slipped back into your old ways?" He set the kettle on the stove before he turned to face me. "Did you kill someone?"

I banged my fists on his mantle. "I told you I would not kill again unless my life was threatened, did I not? When will you stop checking on me like some portly, obsessive mother hen?"

"When my skinny, tempestuous chick learns to live within the law."

I spun around to face him, ready to continue the argument, but fatigue prevented me from exerting enough energy to shout. I was tired of always yearning for things—and then denying that I yearned. I thought in my middle years I had stopped feeling *anything*.

*****

Daroga set the teapot down on his modest table and gestured for me to take a seat. He put a plate between us. "Tea biscuit?"

"Cookie."

"What?"

"Americans call them cookies."

"Americans? When did you have tea with Americans?"

I scoffed with bitterness. "Why, yesterday. The Emperor invited me to join him as he hosted the President and First Lady. They served cookies. Why do you ask such preposterous questions?"

"Well, now I know you lie. The Emperor is not having tea with any Americans because we no longer have an Emperor, but a President. One and the same of course, except for titles."

The look I gave him stopped his chuckling.

"If you are going to share my quarters until dark, Erik, try to be tolerable if you cannot be pleasant."

"Forgive me. I don't mean to be so rude."

"When you're ready to talk, I will be ready to listen."

"Do have any paper? I have an idea for my opera I want to write down before the mood fails me."

He pushed paper, pen and ink toward me. "If you want the mood you're in to transfer to the music of an opera, you will certainly frighten the audience. Fury is hardly the muse you should employ to entertain."

"I don't recall saying I wanted to entertain anyone."

"Why else would you be writing an opera?"

"A question that has plagued me for years. I finally have an answer, Daroga. I write the opera because if I do not finish…I will go mad."

He laughed.

"Mad—er." I corrected myself and then smiled.

He left me to work at his kitchen table. Whenever I worked, time ceased to exist.

*****

Daroga touched my shoulder. I'd whipped around and slammed him against the wall. I held him there a second before I was cognizant enough to realize what I'd done. The fear in his eyes filled me with shame.

"Erik, calm down. You shouldn't work so hard you do not know where you are or recognize me." He yanked down his jacket and adjusted his clothing. "You haven't eaten today. You must have nourishment."

"I apologize. I reacted without thought." I took a seat. I wondered how long the food had been in front of me. I had no recollection of him even being in the flat.

For all I knew, he might have gone out and come in a dozen times.

After darkness fell over the streets of Paris, I thanked Daroga for his dependable hospitality and hurried into the night. He never failed me. He never trusted me either, but I could overlook that. Who could blame the man? If anyone had a reason to fear the lunatic who lurked inside my head, it would be Daroga. He'd witnessed many gruesome murders of political and personal enemies that were ordered by the shah and carried out by my hand. He saw the creative torture chamber apparatus I invented to satiate the sultana's desire for entertainment—and her taste for blood. He observed my insane imagination and watched my madness grow.

Chapter 5 Distraction

ERIK:

My house hidden underneath the theatre became my safe haven. In six years, no one had ever passed the third basement. Five basements below ground I had built a shrine to art and music.

As Garnier and I built the opera house, I designed creative ways to ward off inquisitive intruders should they ever try to find my home. Their curiosity would most likely end in death. I, alone, knew how to bypass and avoid all the traps and snares. On the far shore of an underground lake, I possessed all the space a man could need. *A perfect place to hold beauty hostage.*

I needed a distraction, a release. Madam Weston kept pushing her way into my thoughts. I fought the memories trying to replay within my mind, but lost the battle. Losing anything infuriated me.

I'd been playing the 'interesting ghost' for the last few years. Some harmless mischief—mostly to entertain myself. Nothing too terrible after the first years when I killed to show them what would happen if they refused to meet my demands. A little extortion never felt so good.

The performers themselves did most of the work for me. If someone fell off the stage into the orchestra pit because of his own ineptitude, they blamed the Opera Ghost. If a curtain fell because of frayed rope; if someone tripped over a cordon, walked into a wall or fell down the steps, even if I held no culpability in the accident, I bore the blame with gladness.

I wasn't in the mood to play harmless ghost games anymore. A thirst for something darker settled within my soul. I wanted retribution. What did I want to avenge? The world that kept me apart.

Pacing the floor above the costume maker's workroom, I thought of ways to release some depraved tension. The muffled voices of the costumers below distracted me. They were speculating on whether someone had permission to be upstairs in the storage room.

Someone said, "It must be The Phantom."

They laughed! *When did this happen? When did I become a joke?* I hated them. I let myself wallow in hatred while I came up with something horrendous to stop their laughter.

Someone had to die.

They'd forgotten my power. I thought about the ill-fated man who I would use to teach this lesson. *So many men…how should I choose?*

*****

I waited in my secret place above the grand staircase. I had decided the next man to cross under the center chandelier would be my victim. A fair way to choose who should die—let fate decide. As I stood there contemplating *how* the unfortunate soul would meet his demise, someone stepped into the selected spot.

Raoul Chagny seemed almost eager to volunteer. He'd walked under the center point of the chandelier and stopped. *Yes. Perfect.* The Count's younger brother—the Viscount. That should stop their laughter. I clenched my fists in rage at the beauty of his youth. By all accounts a decent fellow. He was secretly courting one of the chorus girls. Behind him, Count Philippe held a woman by the arm and showed her around.

No! I gasped, unable to move from my spot. Her unexpected presence ruined my murderous concentration. An immense sadness descended over me.

Within the walls, I walked parallel with Madam Weston and Count de Chagny in order to eavesdrop on their conversation. I spied on them through false mirrors whenever they stopped.

"Olivia, they say the opera house is haunted." The Count smirked. *Grin now you fool. We'll see who's grinning at your brother's grave.*

"Surely, you tease me."

"I do not. The ghost has been seen."

"What does he look like?"

"He dresses in the finest clothes and wears a—"

"Count de Chagny, how wonderful to see you here! And who is this lovely lady?" The two fools who run my opera house, Monsignors Firmin and Armand, rushed toward the Chagnys. They fell over themselves trying to impress their patron and his guest. Introductions all around.

I longed for her to hold my arm the way she held the Count's. Nothing could purge her from my mind.

In the next instant, several distressed performers burst from the theatre and surrounded the managers. A pageboy in full costume pushed through the others. "Come quickly, Monsieurs, Señora Carlotta has fallen and refuses to get up."

"What?" the two buffoon managers chimed.

"The large banner fell from above and nearly struck her."

"Raoul, take Cousin Olivia into the office parlor to wait." Count de Chagny transferred Madam's hand to his younger brother's arm. Raoul nodded and directed her down the hall while the rest of the group rushed to grovel at the feet of an overrated diva. My curiosity made me want to follow the performers in order to hear them blame me for such a blessed event, but the urge to follow Madam Weston was much stronger than my need for amusement.

*****

"Will you be all right here for a little while, cousin? Might I take a moment or two to check on Señora Carlotta?" Raoul asked when they reached the office.

"Of course. I'll be fine."

Check on Carlotta? Bah! He wanted to steal a few minutes with a certain pretty, young, chorus girl. Their secret affair became a little bit of side entertainment for me. They were sure to be caught. I couldn't wait to witness the trouble that would ensue. If scandal didn't happen soon, I'd have to hurry the inevitable along. One takes one's droll entertainment where one can find it.

Madam Weston arranged her skirt before she sat down in the opulent office. The room boasted a chandelier, several wall sconces and an oil lamp. Armand's work area seemed to have adequate light for Madam Weston to see rather well.

Spying the big mirror over an ornate table, she walked across the room. There, she studied her reflection. I watched unable to move or even blink—inches away on the other side of that looking glass. After smoothing her hair back with gloved hands, she leaned even closer to the mirror to adjust her comb. I backed up when I realized how close she was to the glass. She walked away but returned with a small lamp from the table and began to lean closer and closer. *She knows! She senses something wrong with the mirror or maybe she saw me.*

The Count entered and called her name. "Shall we finish the tour?"

"Yes, of course."

I held my breath, afraid she'd expose my labyrinth between the walls, but she didn't say anything about the mirror.

"I'd love to visit backstage, Philippe."

If she suspected anything and planted the suspicion in the Count's ear, I'd have to vacate my home before they discovered the secret corridors and tunnels allowing me free access in and out of the opera house. I would not rest easy until she left the country and her suspicions had gone with her. My heart ripped between my opposing needs. I wished she'd leave on the next ship to New York because she may have a simple, curious notion which threatened my very existence. Yet, I wished she would stay, so I might watch her attend the opera with regularity and gaze on her beauty—remember her kindness.

But, is there another way?

I set my mind to solve a new puzzle—one needing to be solved with haste. Then there was the matter of deciding the manner of Raoul's nefarious elimination. One must take risks if the stakes are high and one refuses to lose.

Chapter 6 The Opera Ghost

ERIK:

How things often worked themselves out without any help from mortals amazed me. We dangled on the marionette strings of our master, always at his whim. My *dark* master allowed me to be the recipient of a most fortunate happenstance.

One of the scene movers decided to end his pitiful life. The wretch had been deteriorating for years. I'd been observing him—for scientific purposes, of course. The idiosyncrasies of humanity always fascinated me. I studied the illogical choices men made in order to look for a common theme to which I might attribute their odd behavior. Their actions never allowed for such a commonality to be established.

Through empirical study, I predicted the subject in question could not last much longer at his rate of decline. I had approximated the scene mover would die soon, but not by his own hand, and not in such a tremendously dramatic way.

Despite his failure as an actor, he could never force himself to leave the theatre altogether. A distasteful drunk, alcohol inflated the man's belief in his ability and augmented his arrogance. The hapless creature believed himself to be the greatest, underappreciated actor of his time. When the theatre was dark, he often took center stage to play to his nonexistent audience. Tripping over words, he badly improvised lines. He'd shout out curses to imaginary casting directors, growing evermore resentful. He'd stumble away to brazenly fondle unsuspecting women backstage. After analyzing his actions, I concluded he behaved as a brute in order to recapture his fast-fading belief in his own manhood.

I underestimated the crude man, however. He'd decided to make his last curtain call in the grandest of gestures.

The man took his life in the middle of Act IV.

He measured with precision how much rope he would need for exactly the right effect. The clever fellow made sure he finally had center stage.

I admired his sense of forethought because death is most disagreeable when people mistake how much rope they will need or do not tie the knot properly. Some fools died the same way they lived—without dignity due to their own gross errors. They leave the earth by their own hand suffering from their own ignorance. Most unpleasant to watch. Hanging is a task that is quick and clean—if done correctly. Even in death, there is no need for negligent sloppiness.

As Carlotta hit a C-Sharp, there came a loud thump, a sharp snap. Before our eyes a corpse dangled from the end of a rope two feet from our prima donna. Although a most innovative death, I could have staged his last performance better. I'd have timed his entrance at the end of a drum roll. The devil is in the details.

A loud gasp preceded screaming from actors and audience alike. Carlotta stood in silence, her mouth still open in her last note. The rest of the performers ran offstage, but she didn't move. The ostentatious ladies in the audience turned their heads away from the man on the end of the rope. He dangled with a knot under his chin, eyes gazing ever upward. A moment later the rope broke from above. He dropped into a heap at Carlotta's feet. The man finally hit his mark and minded his cue. Bravo! Perfecto!

I ran through the labyrinth between the walls toward backstage knowing what was about to happen. I didn't need to wait long.

A vicious tale spread through the performers like the plague. The gossip about the cause of the man's misfortune filled me with glee.

"A strange shadow crossed the catwalk a few moments before," a stagehand said.

"A dark form crept behind the stage right before it happened."

"He's struck again. The Opera Ghost has killed again." A young ballerina clung to her mother, the formidable box maid.

Their ignorance made me laugh. More for my amusement than anything else, I made an impulsive decision. As people tried to exit, I climbed the steps between the walls to a precise spot.

"*Stop! What's the rush, Monsieurs? I have something to say to you,*" I yelled from behind the wall designed to maximize the acoustical projection of my voice throughout the theater. The fools actually stopped. "*You will be advised not to anger me anymore with the incessant squawking of an aging diva. This casting is distasteful. The role calls for an ingénue. You sacrificed the part to a middle-aged vocalist.*"

Much to my delight, Carlotta collapsed into the arms of one of her fawning dressmakers. The audience and performers stood motionless, looking up ready to identify the source of the voice. They would never find me.

Thanks to Madam Weston, I desperately needed some distracting entertainment. A terrible and devious plan began to assemble in my mind.

"*Miss Christine Daae shall play the part of the countess,*" I demanded.

A murmur of surprise rumbled through the theatre. Raoul de Chagny would be most displeased with my casting his secret paramour. He might be able to hide a chorus girl's past. But, a leading lady of the opera? His family would disinherit him before they allowed such common blood to sully their family tree. If I did not kill young Chagny with my hands, perhaps the privileged, handsome youth should watch his dreams die instead. Soon, I would pay a visit to his pretty little lady friend.

Neither of the lovers witnessed the scene mover's death. Earlier, Christine and Raoul had made their escape to the privacy of his elaborate carriage. She didn't need to return until Act VI. The ardent lovers managed to squeeze a tryst into every performance. I'd followed them once or twice to see what new or innovative place they would rendezvous. They must've been confused when they heard the screams and chaos of the audience rushing out of the theatre. Perhaps my performance interrupted his. One could only hope.

Raoul returned against the crowd to the chaotic main chamber, his formalwear crumpled and shirt untucked. I'm sure Christine returned backstage the same way she sneaked out—through the alley door. A little ventriloquism and she would do as I told her. Miss Daae seemed to be a very simple girl—not a complex thinker. She would not turn down a role her deceased father wished her to take, would she? Her lover's reputation or her dead father's wish? Oh, the intrigue. Her above-average (but not brilliant) voice needed a little coaching before she would be ready. I refused to perpetuate mediocrity in *my* opera house.

Manipulating their lives into my personal diversion dulled my need for violence. What a shame.

"Go! Leave now before I kill again!" A mad rush of humanity pushed and shoved in their finest gowns and smartest suits to get out the doors.

The idiot managers stood at the back yelling, "Ladies and gentlemen, do not panic. It's all under control." I laughed. *It is all under control, Monsieurs. My control!*

I relished seeing Monsieur Firmin's face as someone yelled, "I expect a full refund!" A few others agreed before they stormed out. Poor Firmin, the man almost retched right there. Oh, the pleasure of one man's spectacular suicide. Pure delight.

As the crowds thinned, I made my way to Box Five. During construction of the opera house, I had managed to make my own small viewing area behind the decorative mirror *next* to Box Five. I couldn't let anyone sit in the private box since their presence would interfere with my ability to come and go through the hidden entrance. I had left strict instructions with the managers that Box Five should always be left empty. Or else.

I made myself comfortable in my favorite chair and watched the remaining patrons race out of the theatre like rats from a sinking ship.

Someone close to Box Five shouted for a doctor. Perhaps another unfortunate soul was a victim of the Opera Ghost. I laughed until I heard something that made my blood grow cold.

"Olivia! Olivia, open your eyes! Can you hear me? Someone get a doctor." The desperate plea came from the stairway leading from the boxes to the main hall.

Forgetting myself, I stepped out of my viewing room and left Box Five without checking to see if it was safe. Someone knocked into me in the hallway and roused me from my stunned daze. Through the nearest hidden door, I retreated between the walls again.

I made my way to where I approximated Madam Weston to be. Perspiration dampened my temples as I peered out from behind the mirror a few yards away. My stomach lurched and then churned. With my face dangerously close to the glass, I watched what transpired.

Kneeling, Count Philippe leaned Madam Weston against his chest. Her head was tilted back onto his shoulder; her eyes were closed. She was a ghastly pale shade.

"What's wrong? What happened?" Raoul asked when he came upon the scene.

"She was hurt in the rush to escape. She was knocked down and trampled," the Count informed him.

No! The chaos caused by my voice has hurt Madam Weston.

"Boy! You there! Go fetch a doctor, at once," the Count ordered.

"Yes, sir!" The rushed steps of youth padded under my hiding place.

"Olivia, Olivia." Raoul tapped her cheeks.

The crystal embellishments on her ball gown shimmered with the movement of Philippe, but her arms lay limply at her sides and she remained motionless.

I've killed her.

I refused to remain a bystander any longer. Perhaps she clung to life and I could save her. While traveling with the gypsies, I'd stolen books along the way to study alchemy and medicine. Their fear of me aside, there wasn't a soul in the tribe who doubted my medical abilities by the time I'd left them.

I placed my hand on the lever to open the hidden door closest to her when the young man returned. "I found a doctor, sir."

I drew back and hurried to the mirror again.

The physician had his back to me. I couldn't see what medical help he administered. Nor could I see Olivia.

After a moment, Raoul asked, "Is she all right?"

"She's coming around. Smelling salts."

"Where were you? I left you with your cousin and you abandon her?" Philippe reprimanded his brother. A blush spread upon Raoul's lustful cheeks. *Impertinent, preening, youth.*

"Don't get up. Just sit here for a minute," the physician said.

Once the doctor moved out of the way, I sighed with unadulterated relief. Olivia's eyes were open; she sat up.

"I'm fine. I think I can…" She tried to stand.

Philippe held onto her elbow, but the minute he let go she swooned back into the doctor's arms.

"My carriage is being brought around to the front. Let's take her to my office. She's bruised and might have internal injuries."

The doctor cradled Olivia in his arms. They began descending the stairs at a good pace. As soon as the group moved from my sight, I rushed to another viewing point above the staircase. From there, I caught a glimpse of the doctor carrying her down the last few stairs. The Count and his love-struck brother followed behind.

Internal injuries?

Covered by darkness, I made my way to the Chagny house.

Chapter 7 The Visitor

ERIK:

Entering the Chagny chateau unnoticed posed no problem. I gained entrance through an open window and glided through the house unfettered as everyone slept. After searching several rooms, I found Madam Weston. I backed into a corner by a tall dresser, flattened myself against the wall and didn't move. By the candlelight next to her bed, I watched her fight sleep.

A few minutes later, she stirred and opened her eyes. Despite my plan to remain silent and just take with me the assurance of her health, her name escaped my lips. "Oh, Olivia."

She turned her head toward the dresser. "Erik?"

I've given myself away. I will have to use the power of suggestion. There was very little time. I needn't be discovered hiding in a lady's bedroom in the dead of night. I moved to the side of her bed where my voice would hold the strongest sway. "Madam Weston, I'm sorry to disturb you. I shall leave at once."

"No, don't go. What are you doing here?"

My mouth dried up; my hands began to tingle as though they were asleep. "Madam, you are dreaming. I am not here. You will not remember talking to me."

"You're not here," she said groggily. But, the woman's mind broke free. She grabbed my hand. I pulled away even though I desired nothing more than to hold her hand—to sit upon the chair next to her bed and cater to her every whim. I would give her anything the world had to offer.

A creak of a door and footsteps down the hall set my senses on high alert. There was no time to suggest to Madam Weston, for the second time, that she would not remember my presence. I slid out the window into the night.

If she remembered what occurred and expressed concern, the Chagnys might tell her she had been dreaming. Sleep powders make people have strange dreams. Nonetheless, I made a decision to pay her a second visit to suggest she never saw anything. That's what I told myself. If I were truthful, I might say the next day I waited for nightfall so I could watch her again.

Chapter 8 Olivia's Story

Olivia: The grandfather clock down the hall chimed. Another hour passed and sleep would not come. Too bruised to roll over onto my side, I lay on my back with eyes closed. Forcing myself to remain still, I hoped sheer boredom might induce unconsciousness. The mantle clock in my cousin's guestroom filled the night with metered reminders of each sleepless moment. The monotony of sound became too much. I scrunched the pillow over my ears, found no relief and let it go slack under my head again.

After a thorough examination, the doctor allowed me to leave the hospital. I longed to be in my bed back home in New York, not the ornately decorated guestroom of the Count de Chagny.

Coming to Paris was not at all what I'd envisioned. Bumped and bruised, but not seriously injured, I still winced when trying to take a deep breath. I exhaled with care and willed myself to find restful slumber by giving-in and counting the incessant tocks of the annoying mantelpiece.

My eyes simply refused to stay shut. I scanned the shadowy shapes outfitting the darkened room. My gaze stopped on a shaded area by the tall dresser; one I had not noticed before.

"Is someone there?"

"Oh, Olivia."

The distinctive voice possessed a rare, unique beauty. I knew at once to whom it belonged.

"Erik, what are you doing here?"

I should have been alarmed, but oddly, his voice soothed me.

"I heard you had an accident. I wanted to see you."

"Where are Philippe and Raoul?" A tinge of pain shot through my side when I sat up. I blinked and tried to focus on the dark shape.

He came forward and stood next to the bed. "The household is asleep, Madam Weston. There's no need for alarm. You seem to be convalescing rather nicely. I shall not bother you again. Madam, listen to me. You won't remember this in the morning. You're dreaming. Sleep now."

"What?"

My eyes became very heavy, but I forced myself to keep them open. Using every bit of energy I could muster, I reached for him. I clutched his fingers in my own. The leather of his glove cooled my hand. He stepped back, pulling his fingers free.

"Don't go," I said, but he continued to back away until he blended in with other shadows along the wall and disappeared from view. I wished he'd come back, so I could hear that voice, listen to him sing. After a moment, I could not fight sleep.

I did not wake until morning when my maid, Anna, brought in my breakfast. I barely settled the tray upon my lap when my cousin,

Raoul, came in so full of life and vigor—the way only a young man of twenty could manage. He pulled back all the heavy curtains to let in the sunlight before he sat in the chair next to my bed to take his tea.

In the light of day, the furniture had form. People's faces emerged from obscurity.

Raoul and I chatted freely as I ate. "Again, I apologize for leaving you at the opera. I should've stayed with you." His eyes shined with sincerity and remorse.

"I'll be fine. Please, don't apologize anymore." I smiled. "Stop worrying."

Raoul's shoulders relaxed. He took a sip of tea. "What's living in New York like, Cousin Olivia?"

"In what way?"

"I hear Americans are very accepting." He cleared his throat. "What I mean to say is, they're, um, well, less pretentious."

I scoffed and looked at him with curiosity.

He smiled. "Well, I understand society there is quite different than here."

"I suppose when you examine any society close enough, they are quite the same." I bit into a buttery pastry.

"Yes, I suppose a peacock strutting here looks much the same as a peacock strutting there. But, they don't adhere to such strict...they allow more..." He cleared his throat. "I've heard one can start a new life in America regardless of background."

"Raoul, if a handsome, eligible, bachelor like yourself visits New York, society would greet you with open arms. Every debutante on the east coast would bat her eyes at you; their mothers would be tripping over one another to enlist you as son-in-law material." I took a sip of tea, but continued to watch him over the steam rising from the cup.

"Suppose one did not have a title? Suppose one went there with his wife and started over." He leaned forward in his chair, his eyes wide. "What then?"

"Raoul? A wife?"

"I meant—if I were to take a wife here and move there—" A sudden blush turned his cheeks pink.

"Cousin, you are in love, aren't you? Your smile outshines the sun. Who is she? Have you announced your engagement?"

He stood, set his teacup on the end table and then dismissed the maid with a flick of his hand. After the door closed behind her, he said, "You promise what I tell you will not leave this room?"

"I promise. Now tell me everything."

The way he gushed about his love affair with a chorus girl named Christine made me smile. The energy of new love, and the optimism of youth, filled me with hope. He told me his elder brother disliked and disapproved of Christine. He hinted that he might like to elope and runaway to New York when I returned. I promised him nothing, nor did I discourage him. Afterward, we talked about the opera house and he apologized for the hundredth time.

Sunlight warmed the room as I chatted amicably with my cousin, but Erik occupied the shadowed corners of my mind.

Chapter 9 The Second Visit

OLIVIA: I had no need to be bedridden. I wanted to get up, but the doctor prescribed four days of bed rest. By the evening of the fourth day, my pain dissolved into discomfort. With nothing to occupy my mind, I longed for a walk. I wanted to explore the grounds and the gardens.

"That will be all. Thank you, Anna. You may go home." I spoke French and smiled at my young maid. "I'm fine here. The Viscount will visit me shortly."

"Are you sure, Madame?"

"Quite sure."

She left me to the haze of a slightly blurry world. My thoughts turned to the story Erik told me in the carriage. I tried to remember every glorious word and put the events in the right order, but the tale lay in a heap, disordered pieces of a puzzle my memory couldn't quite put together.

My eyes became heavy with sudden drowsiness. I closed them for a few moments. The oddest sensation washed over me. As I lay in a peaceful drowse, a sweet piece of music filled my ears. I drifted further into a restful bliss.

I teetered on the cusp of sleep, but the music abruptly stopped with the whirlwind entrance of my young cousin.

Full of movement and restless energy, he came towards me. He kissed my hand and offered a brisk bow. "Good Evening, Cousin," he said with all the seriousness that one so excited could muster.

"Have a seat. Tell me about your day, Raoul. I'm in terrible need of good news. Tell me everything." He rearranged the pillows behind my back allowing me to sit up and talk to him.

With breathless enthusiasm, Raoul talked about the plans he and his sweetheart made. One problem spoiled their delightful world. 'The Phantom' insisted the understudy, Christine, perform in place of the regular prima donna.

"Tomorrow night is her debut," he said with exasperation. "I asked Christine not to perform, so we might run away together, but she wouldn't listen." His eyes narrowed a bit. A tinge of desperation echoed in his words. "She told me her deceased father came to her in a dream and insisted she perform."

"Her deceased father spoke to her in a dream?"

"A few years ago, on his deathbed, her father promised he would watch over her from above. He said someday he would send an Angel of Music to help her achieve his goal of seeing his only daughter a successful prima donna of the opera."

"Oh, really?"

"Christine says she recently dreamt of her father. He told her he would sent the Angel of Music and now was the time to rise to fame." He drew closer to me. "I hope after tomorrow night she will satisfy her need for the spotlight and come away with me."

"Perhaps she will." Something told me the little chorus girl would be *more* enchanted by the spotlight after her debut performance. I did not dash his hopes though.

A knock on the door interrupted our exchange. Dr. Fournier stepped inside.

"I'll visit you tomorrow, cousin." Raoul closed the door behind him.

"How are you this evening, Madam Weston?"

"Same as yesterday and the day before, Dr. Fournier."

"Meaning?"

"Meaning I shall never recover if I do not leave this bed, as I will become a stark raving lunatic."

He smiled at me. "Well, we can't allow that. Let me make sure you aren't exaggerating about your physical health, since you are certainly exaggerating about your mental condition."

I chuckled. "I'm telling you, I can't stay in bed much longer. I've never been one to exaggerate. Much."

He put his stethoscope to my chest. "Battered and bruised, you are still the most charming woman in Paris, Madam. And, I've never been one to exaggerate. At all."

"Ahh, flattery, Dr. Fournier, a time-honored healer for all that ails. Surely, you must be well-loved by the women of Paris."

"I don't know about that, but a lonely widower like me must at least make an attempt at charm. Too many more evenings by myself and *I* just might turn into a stark, raving lunatic."

A widower? Tall, broad-shouldered and with a touch of gray at his temples, the blue-eyed doctor became even better looking when he smiled to reveal perfect teeth and twin dimples.

"Very well. You may leave bed-rest after one more night. May I talk to you about another matter?" He walked to the dresser to return the stethoscope to his bag.

"That depends, Doctor. If my well-meaning relatives sent you on a mission to deter me from the operation, I'll tell you right now, you cannot dissuade me. Do not challenge yourself to a battle you cannot win."

"But, Madam Weston, the surgery is only experimental at best. It hasn't been done more than a dozen times." After latching his bag, he turned to face me.

"Doctor Fournier, I'm tired now. Will you please take your leave, so I may rest?" I crossed my arms.

"Surely, Madam. I'll make one more visit tomorrow."

"With intent to convince me against the operation?"

"With intent to make sure you are well enough to go through with your dangerous plan. Good evening." He left the room before I responded.

I picked up my novel from the nightstand. The words blurred in and out of focus. I struggled for a moment. The lamps in my room were insufficient; I'd have to request more. After a few attempts, I slammed the novel shut. With tears in my eyes, I threw the book at the closet in frustration. The spine hit the door. The novel landed with a thud. Books became my solace when my husband died. Years later, I wasn't a young mourning bride anymore, but I depended on novels to keep me company—until my eyesight began to fail.

*****

Later that night, I had the unnerving sensation someone looked upon me from above. I snapped my eyes open. He gasped.

In the lowlight, I recognized the mask. To make sure I wasn't dreaming, I reached for him, but he moved away without a sound like a cat.

"Erik, I demand you stay here."

A soft chuckle came from near the window. I couldn't understand how he'd managed to get from the side of my bed to the other side of the room so fast. In a blink of an eye, he stood a few feet from my bedside again.

"You demand?" he asked.

His voice! Two short words. Two melodic words. I had to smile.

"Come forward so I can see you better." I pushed myself into a sitting position, ignoring the dull ache in my ribs.

"You need not see me, my dear. I haven't changed since our last encounter."

"Please, sir. Talking to a disembodied voice is quite disturbing."

Have I taken leave of my senses? Who is this man who lives in the shadows and slips into women's bedrooms so easily? He might be a scoundrel of the worst kind—a wicked devil in a man's body.

Logic told me I should scream with all the breath I had in me, but I rarely listened to logic.

"Why are you here, Erik?"

"I don't care to lie to you, Madam, so I'll tell you the truth. I have no legitimate reason to be here."

"Then why did you come?"

"I cannot give you an answer which will satisfy you."

"Come closer. Looking at you from this angle stiffens my neck." Instead of advancing, Erik moved closer to the window. "Come back here at once."

"You demand things quite habitually. Demands mean nothing to me."

I swallowed hard. His tone switched from charming to annoyed. At that moment, I did not care for his fickle personality.

"Take leave then, Erik. Nothing is stopping you. Don't come back. For if you do, I shall scream."

"I doubt that."

"Why do you doubt my word, Monsieur? You don't believe I would call my cousin in here to remove you from my presence?"

Erik chuckled as though I said the most absurd thing.

"What do you find humorous about the sharp end of a sword or the barrel end of a rifle, sir?"

He scoffed. "If you wish me to leave, Madam, you need only to ask me in a civilized manner. I see no reason for your curt remarks, your childish demands, or your empty threats."

"Well, I see no need for your abrupt tone. You are a most ill-tempered and perverse man!" Immediately, I regretted my outburst. A thick silence told me I'd injured him. "Erik, did I insult you? I apologize." I swallowed hard. "Do you care to start this conversation all over again?"

"On the whole, I find once words are spoken there is nothing one can do to repair whatever damage they sought to do when the words left the lips."

"I'm sorry, but your tone can be infuriating. Why must you antagonize me and watch my reaction as though you're shaking a jar containing two insects?"

"Why on earth, would someone put two insects in a jar, much less, proceed to shake them?" The charm returned to his voice.

"To make them fight of course."

"Barbaric! You mean for entertainment? Perhaps Americans need more opera houses and theaters."

I chuckled. "Perhaps we need fewer insects."

"Now, I simply must ask. Have you ever engaged insects in a fight?"

"Only when the theaters are closed."

"Sarcasm is the most elemental form of humor. I do love a good retort."

"Sarcasm is acceptable insolence. I enjoy the practice myself. Will you please come closer?"

He'd stepped from the shadows and stood next to my bed.

"See? Is that so dreadful?" I asked.

"It is sufficiently dreadful."

"Why?"

"I find your question irrational. The answer quite literally stares you in the face."

"Don't be silly." I smiled, but his gaze never left his boots. "Is flitting in and out of ladies' bedrooms another bad habit like talking to your muddy boots or telling your cape about your essential purpose? Is this your normal practice?"

He laughed. "I don't need any practice coming in or out of rooms unnoticed. And, I beg your pardon, but I've never 'flitted' anywhere."

"I see. *L'homme vole soigneusement comme un voleur dans les arbres.*"

He chuckled. "I assure you, Madam, I don't 'fly carefully like a robber amongst the trees.'"

"I meant 'sneaks around like a thief in the night'. Oh, well, if anything needs practice it's my French."

"I will not argue."

"Erik?"

He lifted his head a bit. "Yes?"

"Thank you for coming closer. I don't care to talk to shadows."

"You would rather talk to masks?"

"No. I'd rather talk to you."

My words seemed to have struck him dumb. He made no motion of any kind.

Footsteps in the hall made both of us turn toward the door. Erik disappeared into the shadows before I blinked.

I whispered, "Please, come back later."

He didn't answer; the sheers over my window briefly fluttered. He was gone.

"Are you awake, Olivia?" Philippe knocked on the door.

"I am. Please, come in."

He turned up the lamp on the dresser. "Has someone been reading to you?" he asked as he sat down. My novel was on my lap.

Chapter 10 Lullaby and Goodnight

ERIK:

I did not intend to spy on the lady for so long. The threat of discovery, first by the Viscount, and then a meddling doctor, dictated I linger in the closet. I found I enjoyed watching everything she did. To watch someone when they do not know you observe them is quite uncouth, but such a vice became second nature to me after years of living between the walls. I decided to take pleasure in my compulsion.

After the arrogant doctor left, Madam Weston closed her eyes for a moment. As long as I kept to the perimeter of the room, I could jump out the window if need be. Just as I stuck my head out of the closet door, her novel sailed across the room. It came within an inch of me. Ducking back into the closet, I worried the assault had been quite intentional. I watched through the slats waiting for a scream or a curse, but she sighed and closed her eyes.

A few minutes later, her breathing indicated she slept. I stepped out again. On my way to the window, I paused to look at her face one more time. Her eyes opened. A spiky, cold sweat made me shiver.

We had a short conversation until the Count interrupted us. I leapt out the window, but not before she asked me to come back.

She invited me back!

I waited in the shrubbery by her first floor balcony until the Count bid her goodnight. He turned out the lights on his way out, leaving only a single candle burning on the nightstand. Moments later, I slipped back into the darkness of her room.

"Erik?"

I stopped. *She heard me?* I had not betrayed myself in anyway.

"It is I."

"I know."

"How do you know when I'm here?"

"I shall keep that secret to myself." She giggled.

Intrigued, I edged closer to the bed. She turned her head in the direction where I stood a moment before.

"Thank you for coming," she said to the empty air at the side of her bed.

Not indicating where I stood would be rude, so I cleared my throat. "I'm over here."

"Don't do that. You jump around like a demon in the night. It's unsettling. Are you here? Are you there? How can I conduct a proper conversation if I don't know from where the response will generate?"

"Pardon me. I understand your predicament. I will always stand on the right. Will that make conversing easier?"

"Or, instead of standing in the shadows perhaps you'd care to take a seat? Would you like me to turn on a lamp?"

"No." I swallowed. "The lamp will not be necessary. Candlelight is quite sufficient."

With much apprehension, I sat in the chair next to her bed. The sweet aroma of toilette water floated in the air around her. Noticing such an intimate detail embarrassed me. My cheeks burned under the mask, but I breathed in the lovely, delicate scent.

"Would you like me to tell you a story, Madam Weston?"

"Oh, yes! However, before you start, I will ask you to address me as Olivia."

"I shouldn't address you by your Christian name, Madam."

She laughed. "Erik, you are in my bedroom at night…alone. Shall we stand on societal dictates and wait for a formal introduction before you address me by the name my friends use?"

"You make a rather sound argument." I took a deep breath. A breezy scent of lilac filled my lungs, but I could not make my lips move or my tongue say her name yet.

Did she just call me her friend?

With the power of my words, I transported Madam Weston into a mystical, otherworldly place. She went with me willingly. Oh, so willingly.

I finished the story and she sighed. Assuming she would like to sleep, I stood ready to depart.

"Erik?" she whispered, pulling herself up on her elbows.

I loved how she said my name. I could not recall the last time I had been addressed by a female, heard my name come forward from between the lips of a woman.

"Will you sing for me?" she asked as she lay upon her pillow once again.

"I shall."

I kept my voice soft, so as not to wake the household, but I filled her ears with another song.

"Olivia?" I whispered after she had not spoken and her breathing became rhythmic. She didn't answer, so I switched on the gas lamp next to her bed. With one shaky finger, I moved a lock of hair away from her forehead. The sensation hit me like a warm wind. I smiled.

A loud thud came from the front of the house near her window. I moved from the side of her bed and stood in the shadow of the curtain. Raoul had jumped from a tree. He must've crawled from his window to the limb in order to avoid using the front door. He stood up, wiped his hands on his trousers and tugged at his jacket before he began walking with brisk strides toward the stable. As he passed Olivia's suite, he glanced toward her balcony. I flattened my back against the wall and didn't move.

"Cousin, are you asleep?" he whispered at her window. "Have you left your candles burning?"

Light never was my friend.

He climbed over the windowsill and made his way to her bed. With an exaggerated whisper, he called her name. Receiving no reply, he blew out the candles, turned off the lamp. He tripped over the chair and banged his knee on the edge of a table. I held my laughter. Watching humans stumble in the darkness always proved a worthy form of entertainment. The fools were unable to distinguish the simplest of shadows from a true threat of danger.

Raoul slapped his hand over his mouth to stop himself from uttering another expletive. He held perfectly still and waited to see if he had disturbed his cousin.

Taking slow, quiet steps, he moved toward the window and jumped out without noticing me in the corner. Sometimes man's frailty fascinated me. I shook my head and refused to let the horrible memories of my time in Teheran surface. The fragility of man should not occupy my mind with Olivia so close. She made a small noise and rolled over. Drat that boy for blowing out the candles. *I wanted to watch her longer*.

"Erik, are you still here?"

I returned to the right side of her bed. "I am. Would you like me to take my leave so you may sleep?"

She returned to her dreams with the answer still on her lips. I pulled up her blanket and tucked in the edge before I left.

*****

I dismounted my horse once I reached the opera house. He followed me to the stables.

"She's so beautiful, Barnabas. I've never seen anything so exquisite in my life." I ran my hand down his nose. "She's too kind. Ever so lovely in person and spirit. I wish you could see her." I sighed and patted his neck. "You know, I daydream about taking her for a ride with me. But, alas, the daydreams of a madman are hardly worth mentioning." He whinnied and nuzzled my face, knocking my mask to the side. I adjusted it in haste. "Don't do that, Barnabas. You would not like what you see." The animal nudged my face once more as though on purpose. "Trust me, old boy." I straightened the mask again. "One look and you'd not sleep well tonight." I put my arms around his neck and leaned my head against him. "It keeps *me* up plenty, so trust me." I gave him a pat and stabled him.

*****

By standing behind the two-way mirror in Miss Daae's dressing room and using ventriloquism, I had no trouble convincing her I was sent by her dead father as a tutor from the great beyond. She called me The Angel of Music. The irony made me chuckle, but the moniker seemed to bring the girl some comfort. She tried her hardest to please me. I coached her in safety from behind the mirror. She learned with enthusiasm.

Every member of society had waited for Christine Daae's debut performance. We were not disappointed. Because of my tutoring, the young woman sang better than she ever had.

The night of her debut, her lover watched from his family's box. He had once again disobeyed his brother's order not to see her. Three well-heeled friends accompanied the lovesick Viscount. Raoul's eyes remained glued to his paramour. His companions were less interested in what took place onstage. They whispered, laughed and consumed alcohol in great amounts throughout the performance. While the Viscount sat rock-still, silent and enthralled by his ingénue, his ill-mannered associates took to flicking tiny, saliva-soaked paper wads into the audience below, giggling and elbowing each other when the spit-wetted flecks landed on an elaborate wig of one of the patrons.

*****

A shower of roses fell at Christine's feet after the final curtain call. Her voice, my genius. A perfect combination. Satisfied, the Opera Ghost would rest for a while. The management had obeyed my casting orders and they'd left my salary of 20,000 francs in the designated spot.

I waited with mounting impatience behind a column. Too many overbearing people lingered in front of the opera house making travelling to the Chagny estate impossible. Had they no other place to gossip? The moneyed, titled, windbags and their spoiled, self-indulgent wives loitered on *my* front steps. Thoroughly rude of them. I should've expected nothing less.

I mounted Barnabas and rode down the boulevard once the streets were deserted. Due to the pleasant temperature of the night, I had slipped my folded cape behind the cantle of the saddle. With my Punjab whip coiled and attached to the pommel, I set off to visit Madam Weston.

I left my horse to wander in the meadow while I walked the rest of the way. I could not suppress the smile playing upon my lips. I hadn't gone too far when I remembered my weapon was still on the saddle. Returning to the pasture to fetch the whip had crossed my mind, but in my excitement to see Olivia, I decided against doubling back. My thoughts occupied, I did not keep up my guard. I'd just emerged from the topiary garden when I came face to face with three men going the other way.

"What masked villain sneaks around the Chagny house? A burglar? Get him boys!"

Two of Raoul's drunken contemporaries held silver flasks in their fists while a third young man gripped a candle lantern. The biggest one dropped his flask, put his head down and charged at me like a bull. He wrapped his meaty arms around the tops of my legs and let momentum carry us a few feet before he dashed me to the ground, knocking all the air from my lungs.

"You thieving devil. We'll take care of you." The big lout straddled my chest, making catching my breath impossible. I fought lightheaded confusion as my body tried to force air into my lungs. The other scoundrel held my arms up over my head. Gasping for breath, my chest burned as though on fire, desperate for oxygen. I tried to throw him off by thrusting side to side and kicking my legs to no avail.

The third villain, still holding the lantern, knelt next to my head. Had I access to my Punjab whip, they would not be around long enough to marry and become moneyed, titled windbags who would produce insufferable brats. Air trickled into my lungs in staggered excruciating doses. One of the boys ripped off my mask and tossed it aside.

"What was that?"

That!

Managing to free one of my arms, I knocked over the lantern extinguishing the flame. I instinctively put my hand over my face. They'd caught a pretty good glimpse, but in their intoxicated state, what they'd seen puzzled them. The oversized ox slid off my chest and looked down at me; a baffled expression wrinkled his face. The one who held my other arm let go and stood up, as well.

I peered at them from behind my fingers. Rolling over, I groped in the darkness for my mask, coughing and trying to fill my blazing lungs with ravenous gulps of air.

"Did you see that?"

"What in God's name was that?"

"I'll tell you what that was."

"What?"

"Ugly!"

The boys laughed.

Just as I'd grasped the edge of my mask, a solid kick slammed against my fingers sending a jolt of searing pain up my arm. The mask landed a few feet away. I curled up and covered my head.

"What's the matter? You don't want us to see you?" The large ox prodded me with his boot.

The full moon offered enough illumination for them to see too much should they manage to pull down my arms. I stayed curled up; an instinct learned from many childhood beatings.

"Come on. Show us your ugly face."

"It's shy. It doesn't want us to see."

It!

"Show us your face or else." One of them kicked me. Despite the stab of vicious pain near my ribs, I did not respond. My instincts made me hide my face rather than protect my body.

"Show us!" Another kick from the other side sent lightning bolts of pain shooting behind my eyes. A moment later, they no longer took turns when they kicked and struck me. Lying on my side and covering my face left me unable to engage in any defense. When they tired themselves out, or the thrill of the abuse waned, they stood around me passing a flask between them. They had worked up a pretty good sweat, the bastards.

"All right men. Let's go have some fun. If Raoul doesn't want to go with us tonight that's his own decision," the tall one slurred. "Let's take this thing instead. I'm sure Madam Cherie's girls would love to have their turn with this."

"Yes, but first it will learn to obey orders. It's going to show us what it hides or be very sorry that it did not." The ox nudged me with the toe of his boot. "Put down your hands!"

I did not move. The short one had grabbed my forearms and yanked until he heard the resonance of an angry horse galloping toward him. He jumped to his feet. "Forget it. Someone comes. Let's go!"

They left me injured and humiliated.

Barnabas stood next to me breathing hard; his eyes wild. Nostrils flaring, he pawed at the grass and stood guard until I caught my breath enough to unfurl from my position.

I pounded the ground with my fists, ignoring the pain radiating from my injured fingers. How I hated them. I'd rolled onto my back and lay in the grass. *They think I am not a man? It. I am an 'it'?*

The Chagny chateau stood in the distance; the soft glow of lights came from several windows. I got to my feet, fetched my hat and mask from the ground and mounted my horse. With the devil inciting my intent, I rode away from the estate with a murderous wrath affianced. Revenge would be mine.

Chapter 11 Gentlemen

ERIK:

Trailing the carriage without arousing suspicion of the occupants wasn't difficult. Young and brash, the trio of thugs had driven their own vehicle, a sleek model made for speed and bragging rights. I doubted the over-educated brutes would notice a single rider stalking them—they needn't be on alert for a masked man with murder on his mind.

On the outskirts of town, the boor maneuvered his fancy mode of transportation into a parking field. They'd exited the carriage and engaged in horseplay as I watched from atop my mount, the hood of my cape pulled over my brow.

Gaslights flickered and cast dull circles of yellow on the sidewalk leading to an aged two-story mansion near the end of the lane. I followed the rowdy young men down the street remaining unobserved by sticking to the dark side and moving from building to building.

I waited until they were inside the house before slipping through the tall, black wrought iron fence. Keeping close to the walls, I crept to an open window where I watched them through gauze sheers bracketed by faded, red velvet draperies.

The strutting cocks caused havoc for a while before the matron of the 'gentlemen's establishment' decided the girls had received enough of the privileged swine's cruel and vulgar attention.

Ebony-painted double doors burst open. I flattened against the porch wall holding perfectly still. A couple of broad-shouldered bouncers gripped the three young squires by the upper arms. A buxom, middle-aged woman followed her two muscular employees out the door.

The largest of the boys shook the bodyguard's grip from his arm. "Unhand me!"

"You can't throw us out," the short fellow said. "You don't know with whom you are dealing. You can't treat us like this."

"Adieu, gentlemen." She addressed them with hands on her hips. "Maybe you'll think twice before you injure one of my girls. I have half a mind to call the authorities."

"Call them. I dare you," the tall, thin one challenged. "My father's a judge. See how far you'll get, you old hag. Freddy's father owns half this town." He smiled at his large friend. "Maybe more than half."

"Good riddance!" She turned on her heal and reentered the mansion with the bouncers following right behind.

The doors slammed. Heavy-handed piano playing began again. Sour notes escaped through open windows. The slaughtering of the music and abuse of the instrument made my skin crawl.

I eased away from the porch; my quarry yards in front of me.

"What the hell? That tease deserved what she got." Freddy shrugged. "The first time should be a freebie. I would've gladly paid for a second and third."

His companions laughed.

"It was neither her first time nor yours," the tall one said. "You should've left her to Eugene." "You had given her more than a slap before we came in."

"Ahh, Henri," Freddy said, "leave him alone. Of course she'd be disappointed. The girl expected a branch and got a twig. Why wouldn't she start screaming?"

"Shut up!" Eugene kicked over a rubbish can sending trash into the street.

Loud and intolerable, they pushed each other and engaged in lewd conversation until reaching the field where coachmen were accustomed to wait with the carriages for their masters.

"What the devil is this?" Freddy yanked up a knife stabbed into his fine leather seat. "Someone is going to pay for this." He scanned the dim field. "What coward did this?" he shouted. Some nearby drivers and groomsmen paused their conversations. Deciding to ignore the boisterous youths, they began talking again.

Eugene pointed to the seat. "What is that?"

With the knife still in his fist, Freddy picked up the paper that had been pinned to the Italian leather. "Light that lantern, Henri. Hurry up!"

Henri held the light over the paper. The three of them huddled to read the note.

"Someone has challenged us to meet him at Leroux's Field by the footbridge." The boys laughed, but the nervous chuckle of school boys filtered through their bravado.

"Who'd do that? Have you been with someone's wife again, Henri?" Eugene asked.

"Not recently." They guffawed, carrying on as I expected they would.

"The note is addressed to all three of us. What idiot wants to challenge all of us?"

"Somebody who doesn't know Henri was the fencing champion at the academy, I suppose." Freddy scoffed. "Or that I can crush a man with my bare hands if I so choose." He smacked one fist into his palm. "Come on. Let's go!" He jumped in the driver's seat. "Hurry up, Eugene. We need to get our weapons."

"You can't be serious." Eugene sat down followed by Henri.

"Oh? You're backing out?" Freddy shot Eugene a hateful glance.

"I didn't say that. The whole thing is ridiculous. What lunatic would engage all three of us?"

Freddy snapped the reins and maneuvered the carriage onto the street.

What lunatic indeed!

I'd untied Barnabas and raced to the appointed spot.

*****

Light from the full moon reflected off a nearby stream as I leaned against a tree in the isolated field. Before long, the rumble of a carriage coming down the lane alerted me to the lads' arrival.

Showtime.

My senses were on high alert. They'd proven their capacity for ungentlemanly behavior many times that night.

"We're here, you coward! Have you changed your mind?" Freddy shouted. He tossed down the reins and hopped from the driver's seat. Moonlight gleamed off his pistol as he pulled it from its holster. The other two carried arms as well, scabbards attached at their waists. They exited the vehicle, hands on hilts.

I lit the lantern they had left behind in their haste to leave me for dead. Once they had taken a couple of steps away from their slick transport, I placed the light in front of a grove of trees and moved away. The trio turned toward the glow.

"Are you there?" Freddy strode toward the lantern. "Why do you hide, sir? You asked us here. Shall you engage your men to surround us in an unfair advantage?"

Throwing my voice, I projected it to their right. "No, I've always favored a fair fight."

Freddy turned toward my voice. "Very well. Show yourself. I'm ready."

"What about you, sirs?" My voice came from behind Henri and Eugene. They both swiveled around, weapons ready.

"Where are you?" Eugene drew his sword, held it out in front of him.

"I'm right behind you." They quickly did an about face.

The villains now looked in the same direction, but none of them took another step.

"Show yourself at once. Are you afraid?" Freddy held his pistol up near his ear, barrel pointing skyward.

That would not do at all. *He must not have his hand at the level of his eye. It will render my whip useless around his neck, should I choose to dispatch him quickly.*

"I assure you, gentlemen, I am no coward."

"Then why do you hide amongst the trees?" Freddy asked.

"You care to see me then?"

No one answered. They'd turned around to face the disembodied voice. I was having too much fun making the lads turn in circles.

"I asked if you cared to see me." Again, they turned in unison.

"Let's get back to back," Freddy ordered. "Create a triangle. He cannot trick us any further."

To distract them I shook the branches in a large oak before creeping around to the other side. I launched a fireball from behind them. The horse skittered and whinnied. The fireball disappeared before reaching the boys' feet. At this diversion, Freddy lowered his pistol and aimed into the trees. Seizing the opportunity, I unfurled my whip and yanked the revolver from his hand with a flick of my wrist. The gun sailed across the field and splashed into a stream.

"What the hell?" Freddy gaped at his empty hand. As Eugene and Henri focused on their friend, I dispatched one sword and then the other. Each weapon hurtled in a different direction, whipping through the air and landing with a clank.

"You have disarmed us. This is not a fair fight." Eugene's voice shook.

"And you gentlemen care for fighting fair?"

"Of course!" Henri backed up as if ready to return to the carriage. Perhaps to retrieve the knife I'd used to secure my invitation. The horse whinnied. Henri changed his mind and hastened to rejoin his friends.

I held my laughter and without making a sound climbed into the carriage.

"All right, then." I answered from the driver's seat. They turned to face me. "Only one of you shall engage in the fight at a time. That's fair, correct?" I lit the lantern they'd left in the carriage. I paused for dramatic effect and then flipped back my hood. They gasped and reflexively stepped backward. Mouths hung open, eyes widened at my unmasked face.

"It's him," Henri whispered, his voice shaky.

"Oh, am I now a *him*?" My eerie laughter filled the air and surrounded the boys. "Earlier this evening I was an 'it'."

"We were just having some fun. We meant no harm."

"Well, then, good sir, the night is young. Let's engage in some more fun, shall we?"

"Listen, sir, my father will gladly pay for any damage or, uh, any injury you may have incurred. You need only to tell him how much you want." Henri put up his hands, fingers splayed, as though to show me he had no weapons.

"So…" Freddy collected himself. "You're real brave, huh? You want to challenge me bare-fisted, do you?"

"Why, yes. Yes, I do. But, what shall we do with the others in the mean time?"

"We'll wait in the carriage, sir. You want a fair fight. Sure." Eugene nodded and turned to Henri. "We'll keep out of it, right?"

"Yes, of course," he agreed.

I'd extinguished the lantern and stepped down from the carriage. "No need for that."

As I approached them, Eugene and Henri backed toward the tree line, fear making their eyes watery and wide, but Freddy stood his ground.

I crossed my arms under the cape, gripping the handle of my weapon. "I'll tell you what we'll do. I'll count to five and you two can run for the woods where you shall await your turn. One, two, three…"

The two fellows turned and ran until—

A loud crack broke the stillness of the night. Something coiled around Eugene's feet, cutting through his pricey trousers and slicing his skin. A flick of the wrist and Eugene was dashed to the ground. A second sharp snap. Henri plummeted face first into the field. Gagging, they spit out mouthfuls of grass and stood on wobbly legs.

"Tsk, tsk…you boys didn't understand the instructions. I told you to wait until I counted to five. Before then, it really isn't fair. Not to *you,* anyway. The further away you are…the more force I must use. As it is, I'm sure that'll leave a mark." Their slashed trouser legs showed tinges of red around the edges where lacerations now dripped blood into their fashionable footwear.

"What about you, Freddy? Would you like to run, too?"

Freddy's eyes narrowed; he scowled. "I'm not afraid of you." The corner of his mouth twitched belying his words.

"Good, good. One should never fear what one does not understand."

"Huh?"

Eugene and Henri began racing for the woods once again.

"Excuse me, Frederick." I rushed past him.

Before they made any real progress two cracks of the whip fractured the silence. Two men came down. Their cries of pain were cut short by my shout. "Gentlemen, I suggest you don't try that again."

Freddy, obviously sensing the gravity of facing a weapon he could not see, took the opportunity, while my back was turned, to charge. I expected he would. He desired his first punch to make direct contact with my face. Dodging his meaty fist, I maneuvered around to his other side. He came at me once more. In a flash, my whip seized his hands. I yanked him to me while Eugene and Henri cautiously rose to their feet. Keeping my eye on Freddy, I shouted, "Don't move, you two. I hate to repeat myself. Next time your bloody legs will not be able to hold you up at all."

They stood like statues in the moonlight.

Freddy struggled to pull away from me, but only succeeded in binding his hands more securely.

"You are on your honor here, gentlemen. Eugene, Henri…" I tugged Freddy closer as I addressed his friends. "I'll assume you'll wait your turn. You gave your word, did you not? You agreed to a fair fight." I gestured toward Freddy. "Your big friend here—he and I have some business to attend to before I get to you." I released Freddy's hands. Blood had turned his cuffs red from where the cat-gut bit into his skin.

"You sonofa…" Freddy charged at me, head down, ready to grab my legs. I tumbled away, rose to my feet. He sailed past me. Momentum carried him a few feet before he stumbled.

I shook my head. "You just don't learn."

Freddy spun to face me, fists ready. "Who are you?"

"Who am I? Earlier you asked *what* am I."

"*What* are you, then? I'd say something from the depths of hell." Freddy snarled.

"Not originally." I smiled. "More of an immigrant, I'd say."

The two other boys barreled towards me.

I'd had enough innocent fun for one night. I evaded their attack. "I tried to be fair with you boys, but your true nature prevents you from acting like gentlemen. Now we play without rules? Agreed. It was your choice, remember." The three circled me ready to pounce. The thrill of the deadly game made me shiver with anticipation.

*****

"You'll never get away with this," Henri whined. I'd forced him to help me load his incapacitated friends into the carriage. They groaned and whimpered as we arranged them on the tufted bench. Eugene threw his head back against the seat in resignation.

Henri looked at me with wariness, one eye swollen and turning black, blood glistening on the corner of his mouth. He was the only one who had learned to follow my orders. Alas, he was the only one still standing. One last dispatch of my whip and he no longer stood. He spewed a string of curses not fit for a young nobleman, but befitting a drunken street urchin.

"That's enough. Be quiet."

"You ugly bastard!"

"Look, Henri, you seem to be the smartest of the three. You did as I asked. Now you'll find I'm done asking. Dispense with the profanity at once or else…"

He silenced his shouts.

"Thank you."

He glared at me with loathing as I tied the trio together.

I sat in the driver's seat and picked up the reins as Henri and his crude associates struggled to free themselves.

"My father will—"

"Your father again? You know, Henri, I find it quite shameful this father of yours never taught you manners." I scoffed. "Or how to fight."

I snapped the reins. The horse picked up speed as I drove toward my destination, Gaston's Point. The carriage was an amazing piece of workmanship. What a shame to waste such an example of incredible engineering.

"If you let us go, my family will pay a reward." Eugene slurred his words not from spirits, but swelling.

"I have no use for a reward, but thank you for offering."

"Freddy is really hurt. We need to get him help. Sir, if you have any mercy at all, you'll let us go." Eugene's voice shook.

"The only mercy Freddy will receive tonight is the same he'd likely show to another."

I cracked the reins again. The gelding galloped up the hill as we approached the right place. I turned around and released the end of the rope that bound the trio together. Their maimed legs would not allow for any escape. When the rope went slack, Freddy lifted his head and glared at me. "Damn you to hell."

"Hell is no threat. After all, upon my birth, I was damned to *earth*." I'd roughly pulled the rope from around them and tossed it out of the vehicle. We neared the top of the steep incline. Exhilaration made me tremble. With adrenaline coursing through my veins, I jumped onto the horse. *No sense in taking the life of such a beautiful animal.* Cool wind whipped back my cape and slapped against my face. The breeze revived me after a night of extensive physical exertion. I felt alive!

The muscles of the powerful animal flexed and lengthened beneath me. I held onto his mane with one hand while I unsheathed my sword with the other. Exerting as much vigor as I could manage, I swung it. Wood splintered and broke, separating horse from carriage. The men began shouting and moving about in panic, their injured legs rendered useless. They weren't going anywhere. Except down.

I steered the horse toward a meadow, stopped and waited breathlessly. The futile screams of doomed men preceded a thunderous crash. A moment later, more traditional nocturnal sounds resumed—night birds sang within moonlit branches, crickets chirped seeking mates; an owl hooted three times. Such a shame things had to end that way.

Chapter 12 The Willow

OLIVIA: Philippe shoved the pocket door aside and burst into the parlor. “Where is he? Have you seen him?”

I jumped from my seat by the window. “Who?”

“Raoul.”

“I haven’t seen him this morning. What’s happened?” I crossed the room still shaking from his thunderous entrance.

Philippe ignored me. I trailed up the stairs after him. “Cousin, what’s wrong?”

He flung open the doors to his brother’s suite. We peered inside. The servants had turned down one side of the brocade comforter exposing the white linen underneath. The perfect fold and sharp crease told us no one had disturbed the bed the night before.

“Oh, God, no.” Philippe covered his mouth.

“What’s wrong?” I grabbed his elbow before he moved away.

“He … There’s been an accident. I need to get to town.”

“An accident? What accident?”

We hastened down the stairs. I refused to loosen my grip until we reached the bottom. Philippe turned to face me. His face dulled to a ghastly shade of gray as he tried to explain.

"Jacques, the groom, returned this morning from an errand in town with news of a few young men..."

Philippe's eyes filled with tears and he placed a hand on my shoulder. "A carriage accident. Jacques has heard the carriage Raoul and his friends travelled in last night was found in a culvert."

"Oh dear, no! Was Raoul injured?"

"I must go!" He snatched his hat and cloak from the hall tree. Before I asked anything more, he raced down the front steps and took the reins of his horse from the groom. I scurried down the steps after him.

Philippe mounted the horse and gave him a good kick. I stumbled on a loose stone in the courtyard, but the groom caught me by the elbow.

"Madame, are you all right?"

"Jacques, you know of this accident. Tell me what you know."

"I shouldn't say anything before the Count returns." He looked at the ground.

Taking the young man by the shoulders, I shook him. "Tell me!"

"Yes, Madame Weston. All right."

With wide eyes full of tears, he said, "They are all dead."

"Who? Raoul? Are you saying the Viscount is dead?" The ground swayed under my feet.

"A runaway carriage. The horse must've broken free. The bay was found harnessed but without the constraint. They recognized the animal as belonging to Frederick Noir, so the police formed a search party. The constable found the vehicle at the bottom of a deep ravine. He said…"

"He said what?"

"He said all of them were killed. All of the men inside were crushed beyond recognition."

I clamped my hand over my mouth and struggled for breath. Images of my handsome, vivacious cousin filled my mind.

"Madame, please, let me help you inside."

Down the lane, a lone rider galloped towards us at a good pace from the opposite direction the Count had departed. As the horse approached, my stomach lurched. *More bad news?*

The boy let go of my arm and pointed. "That's the Viscount's horse!"

"Raoul?" I still could not make out the rider with any clarity.

We stood in front of the chateau stiff as statues, eyes wide in disbelief as Raoul trotted into the courtyard. Dismounting his horse with quick, confident motions, he held the reins toward the boy. Neither of us moved. Raoul dropped the reins and turned to greet me. A wide smile brightened his face, but his grin dissipated when he met my eyes.

"What's wrong? Has something happened to Philippe?"

"Master, you're alive," the groom said.

"Me? Of course." He answered the boy, but his eyes never left my face.

I threw my arms around his neck and covered his flush cheeks with kisses. "Oh, thank God. I'm so happy to see you. Where were you?"

He pulled back from my embrace with a nervous chuckle. "What is all this?"

"Someone needs to tell Philippe." I turned to the groom. "Go find him. Inform him his brother is safe."

"Yes, Madam. I'll take the shortcut through the woods." He mounted the viscount's horse.

"What's going on here?" Raoul asked.

"You haven't heard about the accident?"

"Philippe?" He watched the groom charging down the lane leaving a trail of dust behind him.

"No, your brother is fine. He's gone to look for you. Come inside. I'll tell you what happened."

*****

Raoul's pink cheeks turned alabaster when I explained what happened. I couldn't tell him the names of the others involved, but he seemed to know. He'd dropped onto the settee and held the sides of his head. I sat next to him and placed a hand on his back. He remained in a stupor for a couple of minutes looking down at the rug under our feet.

His head jerked up and he faced me. "Someone recognized the horse? But, maybe they were mistaken." His voice shook; he cleared his throat. "Perhaps the reports are wrong." He stood.

Philippe hurried through the parlor doors. "Brother!" He'd crossed the room with giant strides and pulled Raoul into a tight embrace. Raoul hesitated for a moment before he returned the hug. Closing his eyes in quiet anguish, he clutched his brother. At last, he let his emotions about his friends' deaths come to the surface.

"Philippe, tell me, are Freddy and the others really—?"

"I'm afraid so," he said softly.

I backed away to give them a moment. Their love for each other was apparent as they held onto each other in a prolonged embrace, until...

Philippe pushed his brother away making him take a step back.

"Where in hell were you? You told me you were going out with your friends. You left with them when they came to fetch you. Did you lie to me about your whereabouts?"

Raoul blinked a few times. "I, I..."

The grandfather clock struck ten as Raoul struggled to find words. He stopped and restarted only to falter again.

"You lied to me. You did not join your friends because you left them in order to see that girl. That performer. Am I correct?"

"You don't understand."

Philippe turned his back on Raoul. "Go to your room. I don't care to listen to any more of your deception. I cannot believe a word that comes out of your mouth as of late."

"But, Cousin, he's alive. We should rejoice." I held Raoul's hand. "I'm so glad you're here. I don't care why you were not with them. I'm simply glad you weren't." He smiled at me with sadness.

My older cousin scoffed. "Well, am I correct, brother?"

"You are." Raoul glared at him. "So, what?"

"Leave now. Go to your room, Raoul."

"Wait. Let's not argue. We should be—"

"Cousin Olivia, I'll thank you not to interfere in this instance. You don't understand what disgrace such a woman will bring to this house." He picked up an ivory tipped pipe from the mantel, struck a match.

"But, Cousin, now is not the time to discuss this."

"No? When is the time to discuss this? He doesn't care what happens to this family. He cares even less for my authority. Running around behind my back—making a fool of me in town." Philippe inhaled and then blew out smoke in an angry breath. "When mother and father died, you were but a child. I took care of you. I brought you up to be a noble gentleman worthy of your title. And what do you do? You sling mud at our reputation by courting a chorus girl."

"I will not listen to this," Raoul said.

"You won't listen at all. Ever!" Philippe threw the long match into the fireplace and left the room in haste.

Raoul turned to me. "Thank you for caring, Olivia." He kissed my hand. With shoulders sagging, he started out the door, but stopped short. "If he wonders where I am, tell him I've gone to town where I've possibly lost three friends. Selfish bast...Forgive me." Raoul left me standing alone in the sunny parlor.

*****

Days and nights went by without a visit from Erik. His desertion did not come as a shock. One as elusive as Erik would disappear rather than say goodbye. I hadn't told anyone about my nighttime visitor—who seemed nothing more than a fanciful dream.

No longer confined to my bed, I strolled around the Chagny Estate. The bruises on my ribs and arms from the mishap at the opera house had shrunk and turned dark.

My cousins had cancelled the welcome gala arranged in my honor due to the dreadful accident in town. No one in the household felt like celebrating.

As I walked the estate, I steered my mind away from the recent heartbreaking news and my impending operation. I tried to sing the lullaby Erik sang to me. The haunting melody stayed on my mind. The night before, the song filled my head as though he sang in my ear, but I struggled to find the right words while walking the grounds.

I wondered if I hit my head in the mad rush to leave the opera house that night. Perhaps Erik's visits were nothing more than the effects of a head injury and fantastic dreams from medicine. A little more doubt seeped into my mind every day.

A strange loss filled my stomach. I couldn't eat. Nothing held my interest for long. I closed my eyes and relished the sunshine on my face. Then—I remembered something.

Dreams included images and sound, but dreams did not contain odors or a sense of touch. Erik smelled of leather, grass after a rainstorm, and horses. My sense of smell and hearing had increased as my eyesight worsened. Sometimes Erik's pleasing and distinct scent let me know where he stood even in the darkness.

Dreams could not do that. In addition, I touched his hand, the leather glove over his long slender fingers. Should a dream be able to produce touch as well as smell? No.

Every night, I left the window open and kept a small lamp burning next to my bed. The room still had shadows in which he could hide if he chose. Every morning, I awoke disappointed in his failure to call upon me.

I walked toward the meadow. The brightness of the day allowed me to have a decent view of the flowers and trees. Their forms were a little indistinct, but the vivid colors of nature were not.

I lay under a Willow tree at the mouth of the meadow. The wispy branches swayed in the breeze as the sky played Hide and Seek behind the leaves. The movement of the lilting Willow branches and the peek-a-boo clouds relaxed me.

In my sleep, his exceptional voice called my name. Even though moments earlier the words of the lullaby had escaped me, the verses now created vibrant dream images and filled my ears with sweet song. I relaxed, wrapped within the intoxicating melody.

Someone picked me up, but I didn't open my eyes for fear if I did, the flight of imagination would end. Instead, I leaned my head against him. With the lullaby coming from his lips, and the vibration of song on his chest, I sighed with complete contentment.

Surrendering to the fantastic experience, I delighted in the scent of leather and clover. Vaguely, in the back of my mind I knew a dramatic dream didn't fill me with pleasure.

Erik did.

He cradled me in his arms and secured me within the world his music created. I had no desire to end the encounter.

My body lolled in such a relaxed state; as though my muscles didn't know how to move. I attempted to speak, but I only thought the words.

Erik, don't leave me.

As the song ended, my strength came back in gradual increments. My eyes fluttered opened. I found myself on my bed.

An effervescent energy allowed me to live *inside* the lullaby. The extraordinary sensation flooded me with yearning—a desire I had not experienced since the loss of my husband. The tremulous tingling came from deep within the middle of my being. Every nerve, every muscle, my skin, even my hair seemed to have been aroused.

My hands wandered to my breasts. Just when I succumbed to the urge, Erik's perfect voice came from the shadows. "Shhh…Madam, sleep now."

With his words, the physical sensation left my body, but the desire did not leave my heart.

*****

I sat up and looked around. The curtains fluttered in the window. Night had fallen and I had no idea how long I had slept.

A resounding knock at the door jerked me from wherever my soul wandered. The interruption had thrust me into the present with no silky remnants of the perfect calm or the euphoric longing.

"Cousin Olivia! We've looked everywhere for you. You gave us quite a fright. We feared you hadn't come back before nightfall and you might be lost and alone in the dark."

"Forgive me, Philippe. I hadn't meant to upset anyone."

"I'd checked in here earlier and you weren't here."

"I must have stepped out and returned after you left."

"She's in here," he shouted to Raoul.

Chapter 13 The Plan

ERIK:

After I had my revenge I did not have the will to visit Madam Weston anymore. I cared for her too much to take away her sweetness by drawing her into a nightmare world of my own creation. Nonetheless, I had a deep desire to visit the Chagny home—for a final gaze upon my muse so I might finish the opera.

At dusk, I walked through the Chagny garden, clinging to the shadows of trees and away from the last rays of sunlight. I planned to slip into her closet while she dined with her cousins.

A gray bundle under a Willow tree caught my eye. My body instinctively crouched into a defensive stance. I wrapped my hand around my weapon keeping my wits about me. Never again would I leave without my Punjab whip and cape. Woe to anyone crossing my path should they give me a sideways glance.

Suspicion amplified my senses; I crept closer.

Madam Weston.

I rushed to her side believing she might lay dead under the dusky sky. I knelt down ready to shake her, but she sighed. My muse slept under a tree with a smile upon her lips. She stirred. I stepped back, not wanting her to wake with me standing over her. Nevertheless, I needed to get her back home. She would not be safe by herself after sundown.

"Shhh…Madam Weston. Do not wake yet. Sleep on." I used my skill to keep her in a dream state. To be sure she would not resist my voice again; I decided to sing to her. I wanted to take my beautiful friend back to her room without her ever knowing I'd been there.

I scooped her into my arms. Apprehension bounced against my chest. My nerves pulsed with both trepidation and joy. "You'll be all right, Olivia. I have you. You're safe."

She smiled and sighed again. An extraordinary thought entered the forefront of my mind. *That expression of worry-free ease and complete trust was meant for me.* Closing my eyes for a second, I experienced the strange warmth of my own contentment. The chill of dire reality brought me back in a snap. The dear woman did not know what evil lurked under the mask. For if she did, her smile would have been a shriek.

Instead of lying limp in my arms, she conformed to my embrace. Placing her arms around my neck, she rested her head upon my shoulder. The tears stinging my throat made singing difficult. Regret poisoned my pleasure making me shiver in the warm night. This beautiful woman trusted me. *I was not worthy of such trust.*

I'd entered the Chagny home through the side door and stole into her room unnoticed. I laid her on the bed and watched from the corner knowing when the song ended she would wake. Except…

I had not meant to stimulate her mind into such a deep trance or make her body so profoundly relaxed. For when I stopped singing, she stayed in a fugue much longer than expected. A door closing somewhere in the hall roused me from my contemplation. I'd induced her into false slumber and slid into the closet before the Count knocked upon her door.

Was that smile really for me?

They departed for supper. I slipped out the window and journeyed home.

Energy I had not experienced since I was a young man rippled through my muscles as I rowed across the underground lake to my home. *She showed me respect devoid of fear.*

The foreign sensation of happiness grew stronger with every encounter. Such unexpected delight brought to the vanguard of my mind the knowledge that I would never fulfill my craving for true intimacy. How awful to know my deepest desire came not from lust, but profound affection. Every time my heart danced for joy, my soul bristled with anger and shot out warnings of the worst possible devastation.

I will never quench the yearning. The honest admission hurt more than I could bear. Rough-edged antipathy smothered my sadness.

I pulled the boat to the shore and surrendered to the hostile voice coming from my very essence. *You are always deprived of what every man takes for granted.* Goaded by such a harsh realization, I began to concoct a plan fully aware the outcome might very well destroy me.

The next night, I had to meet with Daroga. Should he connect me to the deaths of the lads, our acquaintance would have to end in his demise. It would be a shame, but I could let nothing stop me from my new objective. *I would know the secret that had always been denied me.* Wallowing in umbrage, I let the darkness within my soul consume me. I hid in the shadows of bitter resentment.

*****

I prepared myself for our short visit. Daroga must not see the monster waiting to be released. If he sensed something amiss, his suspicion would ruin my plan. I adjusted my mask and set off to meet him. Hiding my true self was never a challenge.

Daroga waited for me in a carriage down the street. I climbed inside, but kept my hands hidden under my cape in case I needed to use them.

"Hello, my friend." The former chief of police greeted me with a smile. In Teheran, he had been a submissive subject of an insufferable shah. Although he was a witness, he never participated in my lethal activities demanded by his Royal Highness. A promise to start over in Paris came with a pact to leave behind my licentious past.

"Daroga."

The carriage lurched forward.

"How are you, Erik?"

"Fine. Thank you." My tone expressed calmness, but underneath I vibrated with annoyance as he made small talk. The dark clouds covering my mind refused to part long enough to fake a pleasant conversation.

We reached the park; the driver pulled to the curb. Daroga and I walked toward the water's edge. We sat upon two rocks jutting out on the riverbank. Our usual place served its purpose, but I hated the idea of having to meet like rats in the dark, dank night. Antagonism prickled my skin. I had to restrict my anger by clenching my fists. *Why should I not be permitted to take supper with a friend in a restaurant without being studied by everyone? They'd gawk with unabashed curiosity. Or they'd stare as if they could not believe an inhuman oddity dare be present in their polite society. Or they would cast sideway glances with blatant mistrust as though wishing to vanquish the masked ghoul ruining their appetites.* Indignation wrapped itself like a coarse rope around my neck, but I maintained a cool head.

We'd exchanged enough pleasantries for me to know he suspected nothing.

"Daroga, I will not be able to meet you for a while."

"Why?" His voice dripped with suspicion.

"I'll be working."

"You've been working since the day we met. You have never failed to meet with me despite your artistic pursuits. Why this? Why now?"

"Be happy for me. I'm almost done with my opera. There is but one piece missing. Once I understand that piece, I shall put down the pen and never pick up the opera again."

"You slave over an opera for twenty years only to put your opus in a drawer? Insanity."

"Would I be sane to let the managers mangle my opera with their miscasting and terrible stage direction? They would do my work no justice, Daroga. If I can solve this problem, the end will virtually write itself and I shall rest easier. I'll have the answers I seek before long."

"What do you mean?" He shifted his weight and leaned away from me.

"Nothing. You make too much of my words. I meant to say I've almost solved my problem—with the opera."

"I understand, but why the sudden need for isolation? I fear you will become so involved in your creation you will forget to eat and die of starvation."

Although he teased, he'd brought up a legitimate fear he might have.

"I shall eat. I promise you. Here's my list. You will find I've ordered twice as much as I normally consume. Do not fear, Daroga. I will not forget to take regular meals." I handed him a list of provisions as usual. "You will find in addition to food, I've added a few other necessary items. Also, send word to my driver. Tell the dimwit I won't need his services until further notice. You will do these things for me?"

"Of course." He took the rolled-up sheet from my hands.

"Thank you." I handed him the money. "You, sir, are an honorable man. I am amazed by your loyalty."

Daroga stood up. "No need to be amazed. You had the decency to save my life once."

"You give me too much credit to attribute my act of saving you to decency." I chuckled. "That is a fascinating theory though."

"Why else would you nurse me back from death's door?"

"I needed to test my medical skills—to see if they could rise to the challenge." I shrugged.

"You cannot fool me, Erik. If I had not seen humanity in your eyes, I would've let you die at the hands of the shah the first time he tried to kill you. Working as his assassin usually means when he feels you know too much, you will become victim of his newest hired assassin. It's amazing you are still here. His plan barely failed."

"A particularly undignified death I would have suffered. I would rather not be found curled up next to my bed and covered in my last meal. Poisoning is a most vulgar and messy death."

He laughed. "The most bothersome thing to my fastidious friend would have been the mess he left behind."

"In addition, I ruined a good suit that night."

We talked until we came within earshot of the cab driver. Daroga lowered his voice. "I shall return with the items tomorrow as usual."

I entered the carriage realizing I'd put my dark plan in motion. I found myself blindly following the prescribed steps. The most disturbing part was I did not remember its development. Sometimes I scared myself.

*****

I worked on the opera at a furious pace. Once Daroga acquired the things on my list, I would have two weeks' worth of food and necessities. In that time, I might turn her fear of me into love. She would forgive me for taking her. She'd understand why it had to be this way. There was no other way. *You must have her*, a malevolent voice in my head commanded.

Chapter 14 Thwarted

OLIVIA: After dinner, Philippe, Raoul and I retired to the parlor. I knitted, feeling with my fingers where I needed to knit and where to pearl.

Philippe read while sitting in a burgundy wingback chair. He rested his feet on an embroidered hassock trimmed with golden fringe.

Raoul slumped at a desk near arched windows decorated with floor to ceiling wine-red damask drapes. He scowled as he reread the letter a messenger brought him hours before.

Earlier, he'd let me read Christine's note. I was correct in my assumption the limelight would stimulate her ambition and incite a desire for the stage which could eclipse her desire for my cousin. In Christine's letter, she'd asked him to postpone their elopement until after opera season.

Except for the clanking of my needles and a page being turned every now and then, a dreadful silence surrounded us.

Raoul tossed the note down on the desk, crossed his arms and scoffed. A mounting tension grew in the room, a continuation from the cold, forced civility between the brothers at dinner.

Since no one seemed in the mood for conversing, I hoped to break the silence in the room with literature. I cleared my throat. “Perhaps you will read to us, Philippe. Are you reading anything of interest?”

“Probably nothing as notable as what my brother has read for the fourth time in an hour. Perhaps he'll read that intriguing letter aloud to us.” Philippe filled the bowl of his pipe and struck a match. “Obviously, Cousin Olivia, he doesn't wish to share the fascinating news with us.” He'd lit the pipe and shook the match to extinguish the flame. “Did someone thwart your advances, Romeo?”

Raoul crunched the paper in his fist and tossed the wad into the fire. “You don't need to know everything. You're not my father. And I am not your prisoner.”

Philippe chuckled. “Prisoner? Raoul, I have indulged you since childhood. What little respect you've shown me recently has caused me to wonder if you would do better with some limitations both financial and social. You think you're my prisoner? Maybe I should treat you as one.”

“Unless you chain me in the wine cellar you cannot stop me from doing anything. You know what I believe? You wish the same gloomy bachelor status for me you've forced upon yourself. I won't live my life like you. You can threaten me with my inheritance if you want, but you can't stop me from doing what I please.”

Red-faced, Philippe looked up from his book and pointed at his brother with the long end of the pipe. "You are a spoiled, ungrateful young man who needs to learn his place."

"Oh? Where is that? Under your thumb?" Raoul stood, fists clenched at his sides.

"Cousin, everything will be all right. Have a seat." I dropped my knitting onto a table. I stood next to Raoul and placed my hand on his shoulder, applying a little pressure until he sat down.

Philippe blew out a stream of smoke and looked down at his book. "Under my thumb? You don't belong under my thumb. You belong in the nursery with your thumb in your mouth."

"Cousins, let's not do this, please." I tried to stop the latest row between them. I'd grown cautious whenever they were in the same room.

Raoul looked out the window instead of responding to his brother's jibe.

"Let's keep our tempers and..."

"...stop behaving like thumb-sucking children." Philippe scoffed.

"I'm leaving." Raoul shoved back his chair and stood. "I will not be insulted in my own home."

"Then go to your prima donna and be insulted in the street and behind your back if that's where you would rather be insulted."

"You don't even know her."

"Maybe I'm the only one who doesn't. You know how show-people are. She's probably had—"

In a flash, Raoul yanked his brother up by the lapels. The pipe rolled onto the marble hearth and spilled. Philippe knocked his brother's hands off his coat before shoving him aside. Raoul went after his brother once again, pulling him forward and tossing him onto the couch. The couch shifted backward knocking into a narrow sofa table. A candelabrum and a glass swan crashed to the ground. Philippe and Raoul continued to struggle with one another. Two servants, alerted by the ruckus and my shouting, separated them.

Raoul had yanked down his jacket and tugged at his shirt before he left the parlor. He slammed the front door when he exited. A moment later, his horse galloped down the lane. His destination would not surprise Philippe or me.

Shaken and frightened, I retired to my room. I pulled out the tortoise shell comb and let my hair fall down my back. Throwing myself on the bed, I sobbed. Once the tears started, all my sadness surfaced. The funerals for the young men, the arguments, the long days by myself—everything that lay in my dismal future brought forth a flood of emotion.

I only cared to see one person. I let the tears fall into the pillow as the room continually grew darker.

Then, I knew.

I sat up and pushed my hair away from my face. "I know you're here."

He answered from the corner. "What upsets you so, Olivia?"

"It doesn't matter." I twisted my hair into place and slid in the comb. Some strands hung down at the sides of my face, but I didn't bother to fix them.

"I should not have come. I apologize."

"Go then." I curled up defeated on my bed. "You're just a dream anyway. You don't exist. You're a shadow, a ghost in the corner."

"You do not lie."

His words dripped with sorrow as if there was a lifetime of hurt behind them.

"Why do you choose to live in the world of darkness, Erik?"

He seemed to be retreating because his answer came from another corner closer to the window. "My banishment to the shadows was not chosen by me, but required by all."

Sitting up, I faced the sound of his voice. "Well, *I* do not require you to remain hidden."

Nothing moved in the corner where he stood. His reply came from the other side of the room. "I wish that were true."

Tired of him trying to confuse me with his voice-throwing trick, I rose from the bed. He must have assumed I would go to where I'd heard his response generate, but he didn't fool me.

In the dim light of the lamp, I hurried to the correct corner. He swished by me before my fingers touched him. The air moved and a caress of his cape slid down my arm. I whipped around with frustration.

"Go away, Erik. Your games do not interest me anymore." In all honesty, I did not wish him to leave. Nevertheless, at that moment I didn't care for his evasive manner.

He stood in silence.

"Why are you still here?" I addressed the side of the dresser where he wished to stay hidden.

A moment of silence passed before he answered me. "You desire me to leave and I shall. I apologize for my intrusion in your life. It has been a pleasure meeting you, Madam Weston. I thank you for your kindness."

"Erik, don't leave."

Chapter 15 Go Away

ERIK:

In the dark corner of her room, with my heart pounding vibrato, I took a deep breath ready to steal her away.

Once again, she surprised me.

In Teheran, working as the shah's assassin, I had slipped into rooms full of men without any of them glancing my way before I found my victim. Oftentimes, the unfortunate man stood in a perfect spot. I would pull him to me and we'd both disappear in a blink of an eye. The other men usually continued talking without realizing anything was amiss. Depending on his rank or position, a few minutes or the better part of a day, might pass before anyone noticed his absence. I had never betrayed myself in a room full of trained killers; yet, this woman had an uncanny ability to sense me.

I tried to confuse her using ventriloquism, but failed. My trick infuriated her. She asked me to leave. I no longer cared about the plan. Brutal sadness wedged in my throat; I could barely swallow. I managed to say goodbye. I would never be back.

Just as I reached the window, she said, "Erik, don't leave."

I closed my eyes. A painful weight crushed my chest as I inhaled. "Do you desire me to stay? Or do you command me to leave?"

"Will you do as I wish?"

"I will."

"I wish you'd come here."

"Pardon?" My feet wouldn't move from where they were planted.

"I wish you'd stop lurking in the dark and talk to me like a normal person."

"I *could* turn up the lamp, Madam. I *could* talk to you. But, I could *never* be a normal person." I didn't breathe or blink. I waited….

Plaintiveness made her words shake. "Erik, you have been the one bright spot on this whole bloody expedition."

An audible gasp escaped my lips. Grateful for an unexpected respite, I said, "This must be one hellacious expedition, Madam." We both chuckled.

"You cannot imagine."

"I'm sure."

"I'm afraid I add more burden to an already tension-filled home." She sat down on the bed.

I moved a bit closer. "They don't support your decision to get an operation?"

"So, you've eavesdropped on my private conversations?" She tucked a lock of hair behind her ear.

"I overheard quite by accident, I assure you. Are you ill, Madam Weston?" I held my breath and awaited her answer.

"No, Monsieur. The operation is on my eyes."

"No!" I almost choked on the word.

"You will try to talk me out of the surgery, as well?"

"Your decision is none of my concern." *Oh, her regaining full sight was of great concern to me.* "This operation will allow you to see perfectly again?"

"I'm hoping."

"When?"

"Two weeks from now."

I took another step forward. "Two weeks? What are your plans during this interim?"

"Die of boredom in this room."

"We cannot let that happen. I give you my solemn oath." I placed my hand over my heart. "I shall never allow you to die of boredom."

"I believe you. However, I will not tolerate your trying to come in and out of this room without my knowledge. If you are in here, you must make your presence known."

"How do you know when I am here? Tell me your trick."

"A good magician never reveals her secrets."

"Touché, Madam. Touché."

Silence surrounded us for a moment.

"Olivia, come with me." My dark plan crumbled, but my hope did not collapse.

"Oh, no. That isn't possible."

"Trust me. I will bring you back the moment you request to return. No harm will come to you. You have my word."

"Where would we go? I cannot see at night. You don't understand what it's like to have your world completely dark."

Oh, if she only knew...

I'd crossed the room, stepped into the light and put my hand out for her. "Come."

Our eyes met. She put her hand in mine. We walked to the window. First, I jumped out. She sat on the edge for a moment.

"Olivia, trust me."

She jumped into my arms.

"I'm afraid to walk. I can't see where I'm going."

"Fear not, Madam Weston. I will never let anything harm you." I carried her across the estate making my way to the meadow. Once again, she wrapped her arms around my neck and leaned her head on my shoulder.

After I helped Olivia mount Barnabas, I sat behind her. Securing her against me with one arm while holding onto the reins with the other, I gave the horse a good nudge. He ran all the way home.

Once inside the tunnel, I dismounted and walked next to the horse. Olivia looked radiant with her cheeks rosy and her hair windblown.

"Never have I experienced anything like that. I imagined we flew through the night atop Pegasus, the winged horse. Thank you, Erik. I enjoyed the ride. Where are we now? I see candlelight—lots of candles—as though we were in a church."

"This is my home, Madam."

"You live *here*?"

"I do."

With a gentle grasp around her waist, I removed her from the horse and helped her into the boat. The movement of the water frightened her. She clutched me. "I don't like this. It's too dark. I cannot see well."

"Trust me," I whispered in her ear as I disengaged her fingers from my sleeve. I held her hands in mine until she stopped trembling.

"Why are we on water? Are candles floating on water? Is this magic?"

"The world is full of magic, Madam. One needs only to believe."

I rowed to the other side of the underground lake as she tried to make out the shadowy figures and shapes surrounding her. She struggled to see my world.

"There is nothing to fear here, Olivia."

"I know. I'm with you."

Her words made the sorrowful ache I'd carried since birth vanish for a moment.

We'd stepped out of the boat and she focused on the candelabras lining the path to the entrance. *I'd expected her.*

We entered my house and I led her to the sofa in my parlor. Once I finished lighting the chandelier, her full vision returned.

"Why have you brought me here?"

"Are you sorry you came?"

"No, I thought I was too old to have such a wonderful adventure."

I smiled. "Never. Your adventure, Madam Weston, has only begun if you're brave enough to continue."

Chapter 16 Art

OLIVIA: Erik showed immeasurable patience. He carried a heavy candelabrum without complaint in order for me to study the art in his house.

Inside his stone home, he'd painted incredible pastoral scenes on the walls. He'd carved flowers and trees on the support columns. Travertine benches depicted detailed fairytale scenes and primeval castles of indescribable beauty.

He allowed me to touch the magnificent wood carvings and stonework. He put his hand over mine, so I could experience the perfect lines, gentle curves and the exacting scale. The tender way he touched his work confirmed how much love went into each piece. Although Erik denied the similarity, he'd created an ornate cathedral dedicated to art.

In the music room, a large, elaborate pipe organ took up a section of the back wall. All available surfaces of the room—every table, chair and desk held stacks of musical scores in various size piles. The disarray in his music room contrasted with the meticulous order of the rest of his home. An alarming, frenzied kind of creation existed there.

Crumpled papers covered much of the rug under our feet. Each wadded and discarded sheet of music seemed to have absorbed the composer's fury at his inability to transfer the music playing in his head onto the paper. The room almost vibrated with a powerful need—as if the frustration from the failed attempts to find musical perfection pulsated from the walls.

"What are you composing?" I stepped on a few wads and nudged others away from where I walked.

"An opera."

I turned to face him as he followed behind me. "Will you play your compositions for me?"

"Perhaps another time. I haven't completed the opera yet. When I do, I promise you, Madam, yours shall be the first ears to hear the music I've created."

His voice had a different tone. He sounded delighted. His evident joy pleased me.

"Erik, why do you hide down here? You are an artist of unparalleled talent." He pushed off a few papers from the organ bench and we sat down. "If you shared your talent, the world could be yours."

He scoffed with sharp bitterness. "No, thank you. I do not want *the world*."

"You don't live like this because of the mask, do you? Genius such as this is a gift. To squander your enormous talent is a sin. You should never waste any ability God gives you. Keeping all this hidden seems incredibly selfish."

Erik stood up. "I'm selfish? You presume I waste my talent? Are you saying if others do not see what I create, it's not beautiful? Or, perhaps you believe I need others to judge my ability? I need no such validation. I create art for the sake of producing art, Madam, not to *have the world*!"

"Yes, but I admire your incredible paintings, your unbelievable sculptures. You have gifts bestowed upon you by your Creator. To keep them hidden is a dreadful act of intemperance. Not sharing such beauty is disregarding His—"

Erik crossed the room as I spoke. Suddenly, he knocked over a metal music stand with a rushed swing of his arm. He shoved over a heavy candlestick. "Why should the world be allowed such beauty? The world has shown no compassion to me! The world is a revolting place. I will not allow my work to be desecrated by the wickedness of man!"

He strode toward me with deliberate steps. "Perhaps I blatantly refuse to share any talent your God has bestowed upon me because in His providence He chose to defile the vessel with which I may bequeath it! Don't be fooled. With one hand, He consecrated me with ability. And with the other, He blighted me with this." He made an angry gesture toward his mask. "Know this for certain: Desiring beauty is not a gift. Desiring beauty is a curse! I am cursed!" Erik had picked up a stack of musical scores from the organ. With both hands, he threw the papers in the air.

Music sheets fluttered to the ground and landed all around us. I cowered at the sudden flare of temper and covered my face. As swift as his rage burst forth, it subsided.

A moment later, he tried to pull my hands from my face. "Forgive me. I didn't mean to frighten you. Please, forgive me."

I shoved his hands away from me. "Don't touch me. Take me back at once. For I believe I'm in the company of a madman," I said without thinking.

I expected my words to anger him further. My heart banged against my chest with alarm. Instead of denying my accusation or trying to calm my panic, he did a most peculiar thing.

Erik pushed off the papers covering a settee in the corner. He plunked down; wrapped his arms around his long, slender legs and rested his head on his knees. For one so tall and angular, he seemed to coil into himself.

Needing a closer look, I crept towards him. His odd behavior both worried and frightened me, but I'd never find my way home without his escort. I wondered if I should leave him alone, but my instincts drew me to him instead of away from him.

His shoulders shook with the slightest of tremors—enough to give away the fact he was crying.

More than once, something about Erik stirred a strange maternal-like response within me. Seeing him in such a state of distress hurt me somewhere deep inside.

No harm will come to you. His perfect voice in my memory soothed my nerves.

"Erik," I whispered. He did not respond. However, his shoulders stopped shaking. He sighed deeply. "I'm not angry with you, but will you take me home now?" I'd grazed his shoulder with my fingertips and quickly pulled back my hand. He'd lifted his head, unfurled his long legs and faced me with sadness and regret in his eyes.

"Yes. I should take you back now."

Without saying a word, we returned to his parlor. He put on his hat and cape. Once I finished fastening my cloak, he slid my hand through the crook of his arm to steady my steps. His hands trembled.

You are safe with me.

A strange thought flashed through my mind. *He is more afraid of me than I am of him.*

"Shall we?" He took a step, but I did not make a motion to move forward. "Madam?"

"Have you any tea? I find myself quite thirsty. It would be nice to have some refreshment before we make the journey home."

He stood very still. "You would like some tea?"

My asking for tea confused him. He seemed to try to make sense of my puzzling behavior.

"You care for tea?"

"Yes, do you have any?"

Surprise thickened his voice, but I also heard the smile he wore. "Of course. Would you care for some Russian tea with lemon or English tea with milk?"

"The English version, if you don't mind."

He led me to the sofa. "Please, forgive my deplorable lack of manners. I should have offered you refreshment upon our arrival. My mother would be mortified by my lack of decorum. She was French by birth, but was raised by very British parents. She insisted I learn how to speak the Queen's English and schooled me in all the etiquette that defines being British." *Before she hatefully abandoned me.*

"Your grandparents were English? I apologize for saying such biting things about them. You must believe I meant no ill will toward the English."

"Believe me, Olivia, I took no offense in your good-natured ribbing of the British." He chuckled. "Mocking the English is an accepted form of entertainment here in France. That is, when we are not busy hating the Prussians—or we are unable find insects for which to entice into a battle within a jar."

The mirth in his voice filled the air. His words left his mouth and danced near my ears.

Chapter 17 Home

ERIK:

I risked everything to show her my home and art. I didn't care if she knew my secret. Should she betray me, I would no longer want to live.

We had a superb time until my temper flared and almost frightened her away. After obliging her demand to take her home, I planned to return to my house on the lake and never again venture out into the world of man. I would die in the tomb I created with my own hands.

For reasons I cannot begin to imagine, she changed her mind and asked me for a cup of tea. We drank our beverage together as if we were an ordinary man and woman sitting at a bistro by the fountains. Her staying with me after my outburst filled me with anticipation. This time I could not, no matter how hard I tried, push a long-forgotten sliver of hope into the corner of my mind where it liked to hide.

"How is the tea? Care for another lump of sugar?"

"No, thank you. This is fine."

"I need to take you back while it's still dark. I wish you could stay all night, but your family will be looking for you in the morning." I wanted to bite my tongue when the ill-worded sentence left my lips. I hadn't intended to infer anything improper.

"Yes." She sighed. "They shall visit me and then disperse leaving me on my own accord and in the care of a young maid barely free from her mother's apron strings."

"Have they no entertainment set up for you? What about a party in your honor, something of that nature?"

"They had a gala planned, but the deaths of those poor young men caused its postponement."

I was unable to meet her eyes.

"Philippe promised to host another party sometime soon. To be quite honest, I would rather they leave me to my own devices than parade me around to strangers like an oddity—an insolvent relative they are obliged to care for. I don't want to become that *poor blind woman.*"

Oddity. "You will never be a poor blind woman to me."

"Thank you."

Our gaze met across the table. Quite suddenly, she began to cry. Anxious heat made my neck burn. Ladies had cried in front of me before—cried out of fear, cried out in distress, even revulsion, but never sadness.

Am I supposed to say something? Do I touch her? Pat her back? Do I let her regain composure on her own? I stood up and contemplated whether or not to go to her. I could not make myself either sit down again or journey a few feet to the other side of the table.

She covered her face with a napkin and sobbed.

Do something! Shaking with uncertain intentions, I approached her chair. "Olivia, are you all right?" *What a dim-witted thing to say. I sound like a simpleton.*

"Yes, give me a moment to…"

For a second, she seemed to regain control of herself, but she sobbed and started all over again.

I couldn't tolerate the sound of her crying. I would do anything, anything in the entire world, to make her happy again. With my heart pounding out warnings in giant beats of trepidation, I reached for her shoulder. Should she shrink from my touch, I would hurry back to my chair and wait in silent patience for the display of emotion to stop.

When my hand touched her shoulder, she startled. An agonizingly familiar expression of astonishment crossed her face. As far back as I could remember my touch always resulted in an automatic response of shock.

To my enormous surprise, she pushed back her chair and flung herself into my chest. I stood with my arms held down at my sides. The sensation slammed into me as though I'd walked into a wall and lost all my senses. I took a deep breath, closed my eyes and wrapped my arms around her. Not knowing what to do with my hands, I balled them into fists. After a moment, I unclenched them. In utter bewilderment, I placed them on her back.

I tightened my embrace and whispered in her ear, "Please, share with me what I should do to help you. I promise I will do it. Forgive me, Olivia, I'm unfamiliar with the customary expectations or the acceptable way in which I should respond in this situation. I don't know what to do."

She pulled back, quelling her tears and sniffling. "Oh, Erik. You dear, dear man. You're doing it." She pulled me to her once again.

I was doing nothing more than holding the distraught woman, so I continued to do so. In the folds of her arms, I found remarkable warmth—a comfort I did not know existed. Instead of pulling away, which I assumed she would do after she gained control of herself, she pulled me closer still.

Allowing me to embrace her in a moment of emotional weakness I might understand, but afterward it seemed she hugged me for no other reason than her desire to be in my arms. Keeping my eyes closed and my embrace firm and gentle, I found myself on the verge of my own weepy outburst. I was unable to stop my silent tears. I didn't want to remove my hands from her back in order to wipe them away.

An incredible moment passed, silent but heartfelt. She dropped the embrace and met my eyes. "Oh, Erik, I've upset you. I apologize."

"No, quite the opposite, Madam. You have shown me great kindness and given me something quite precious."

"What would that be? A pool of tears on your beautiful suit?" She chuckled and swiped her hand across my lapel.

"No, Madam Weston. You've given me the valued and prized friendship of a woman."

She stepped back. Her eyes opened wide and lips parted in shock. Alarm turned my heart feral. It slammed against the cage of my chest trying to escape the inevitable pain caused by my saying the wrong words and ruining everything. I held my breath waiting to see what she would do next. I readied myself for the demand to take her home.

"I'm privileged to be considered your friend, Erik. What an honor."

I exhaled, shaken by her words. "It is no honor I give you, Madam. Being a friend of mine brings with it no merit." *She should know you're not the man she thinks you are*. I lacked the will to tell her.

"You are too modest. To befriend such a talented man is a gift." She wiped her eyes.

"Modesty is not where my intentions lay. For you do not know who I am."

"No, I don't. That's your secret and when you are ready to tell me, I will listen."

She tilted her head. Her big, tear-filled eyes peered into mine. I had the most insane impulse. I wanted to kiss her. The urge came from the middle of my heart like a warm summer breeze carrying on its current joy and nervous excitement. I leaned forward, but quickly righted myself. The logistics of kissing through a mask had never been of issue before.

Relieved the mask stopped me from overstepping the bounds of a newly minted friendship—and embarrassing myself in the process—I turned away and began collecting the tea set from the table. “We better leave.”

“Thank you for showing me your art—your home.”

I hadn’t shown Olivia every room in my house. The torture chamber door had remained locked. Should someone manage to pass the other lethal snares guarding my residence, he would find certain death inside an apparatus of my own invention. My last line of defense.

If intruders tried to invade my sanctuary, they’d find themselves trapped inside a virtual hell. Similar to a carnival House of Glass or an amusing mirrored maze, its appearance masked an efficient death trap. Child’s play. Except for a hangman’s noose in the back.

I would *never* show her my sleeping chambers either. If she saw where I rested my head at night, she would run away in terror knowing she had shared whispers in the dark with a self-loathing demon.

Inside my bedroom, I have painted the horrors from inside my head. The images had to come out. I could not rest until I released the visions. Upon my four walls, I painted all the things which will cause me to burn in the deepest pit of hell.

To enter the room in search of rest became my punishment here on earth. My history surrounded and assaulted me upon my entrance. My past rose up in horrifying scenes from which I’d never escape. The victims, whose faces I remember, watch me from their portraits. Night after night, they surround me with their death stares. They accuse me and condemn me with their eyes. And they are not silent. I hear them scream and beg for mercy all night long.

A completed requiem rests on a music stand at the foot of the bed. Music created to end an ugly life of an ugly man.

Chapter 18 The Contraption

OLIVIA: The next morning at breakfast, Raoul sat alone in the dining room. He didn't seem to notice when I joined him.

"Good Morning." I sat at my usual place across from him.

He stood and gave me a weak smile. "Oh, Good Morning." He flopped into the chair, sighed and pushed food around with his fork. His usual enthusiasm and youthful buoyancy hid behind an expression of miserable contemplation.

After the maid had poured our tea, he dismissed her and closed the dining room doors. He sat in the chair next to me. I swiveled in my seat to face him. He held my gaze for a moment, looked away and then once again peered into my eyes. His cheeks flushed.

"Raoul, what bothers you so?"

"I have a favor to ask of you. Ordinarily, I wouldn't involve you, but I'm desperate."

"What do you need?"

"I would not ask this of you, Cousin Olivia, if there were any other way, but..."

"Yes, go on."

He lowered his voice. "Christine and I are engaged. We're keeping our betrothal a secret."

Icy fingers of trepidation touched my neck upon hearing that word come out of his mouth. *Betrothal.*

"What about the note she sent you? Did you two reconcile?"

"Yes, of course. She was confused, but now we know exactly what we're doing."

"Why is it a secret?" I picked up the teacup trying to remain calm, not show my dire intuition.

"Philippe will not listen to me. He won't make an effort to like her. Our plans must remain a secret."

"I understand. I've been in love before, but you need to slow down." I set the teacup on the saucer. "If you make a mistake—"

"No, Cousin Olivia. Two fully-grown people want to get married. This isn't a mistake. We're in love."

"Maybe if you wait a while, Philippe will relent."

"He won't. My brother insists on planning my future as though I were his puppet."

"What do you want me to do? Talk to him?"

"No, all we need is time to…" He scanned the room as if to make sure we were alone. "…I know this is a great deal to ask, but Christine and I came up with a plan."

He held my hands in his and leaned toward to me. "There is a two week break between operas, so we need to elope now. By the time anyone finds out, we will have been together for a fortnight. Philippe won't force us to annul our marriage after such a long period."

"How am I involved in this?"

He gently squeezed my hands. “I need you to tell Philippe you’ve asked me to take you on a sudden expedition—a holiday. If Philippe believes I am to escort you on this journey, no one will look for me nor will they suspect I’m with Christine.”

“Oh, Raoul, I cannot accompany you.”

“I shall take you anywhere you wish. You can have your maid come with us. Or, I can hire another servant, as many as you need to attend you. We’ll make our honeymoon a pleasant little holiday for you.”

I gazed into his imploring blue eyes. Love had blinded him to any repercussions his actions would bring. “I want to help you, but not in this way. I’ll talk to your brother. Maybe I can get him to change his mind.”

He released my hands, disappointment apparent in his change of countenance. “No, please, don’t say anything. I understand your reluctance to go. However, you won’t betray us, will you? If we run away, you won’t tell anyone?”

“Never.” I kissed his cheek. “Rest assured.”

After Raoul left the dining room, my thoughts turned to Erik. I chided myself for such irresponsible behavior. Leaving the house without telling anyone and following a masked man into the night seemed uncharacteristic of my nature. Nonetheless, I couldn’t talk myself into using more stringent cautionary actions concerning him. I found myself smiling, unable to conceal my excitement over having such an incredible escapade. Under Erik’s rage, I sensed a soul wallowing in hopelessness, but longing for compassion. Instead of concentrating on his flare of temper, I replayed how tender and vulnerable Erik seemed afterward.

He lived in another world. I had to let him visit my world whenever he desired. I could not force any preconceived conventions upon him.

*****

Late into the night, I sat in the chair next to my bed, dressed, waiting and hoping. Just as my knitting needles clanked together, the two gas lamps on either side of my bed flamed up to the highest setting. A little fluttering noise came from above me. Something soft touched my head.

I thought pieces of paper fell from an unseen source—until the fragrant, powerful scent of roses filled the air. I cupped my hands to catch the petals as they fell. Soft, white petals touched my face like tender wings of a butterfly.

The cascade continued, swaying and swirling in a gentle whirlwind before falling all around me. When the petal shower stopped, I found six red roses upon my knee.

"Thank you, Erik. That was so beautiful, like a dream."

The flames in the gas lamps turned back to the lowest level. He came forward and stood at the edge of the shadow where the illumination from the lamp stopped. In an instant, he knelt on one knee before me and picked up my hand. "Will you come away with me tonight, Olivia? I have a surprise for you."

"You've bestowed a wonderful surprise on me already. Am I to receive more?" My cheeks grew tight from grinning, but I couldn't hide my elation over his visit.

With strange somberness, he said, "I would love to surprise you every day for the rest of my life."

The night brimmed with exciting possibilities.

I'd picked up the red roses, but when I stood, all the white petals and my knitting fell at my feet. The ball of yarn rolled across the floor and under my bed leaving a stringy red trail.

"Come with me." He put out his hand.

"Yes, I will go."

*****

We journeyed to his home once again. As soon as he led me inside, he said, "Please, sit down. Let me get you some refreshment."

"Oh, don't cause yourself any trouble."

"No trouble, at all. I should like to join you." He pulled out the dining chair for me.

He'd removed his gloves and suit jacket before he gathered dishes from a china cabinet to set the small table. Not long afterward a most delightful aroma filled the air.

"Coffee? Have you made coffee for me?"

"Yes, however, we'll have to make do with tea biscuits, my dear." He set a plate of cookies in the middle of the table.

"Oh, you are too kind."

"How do you take your coffee? Cream and sugar?"

"Yes, one lump, please."

He returned with the coffee service on a silver tray. His long, slender fingers always moved with such grace. They possessed an elegance I'd never seen before.

Several black bruises covered the back of his left hand. I hated the thought of Erik being hurt in any way. I wanted to know what happened, but dared not ask.

He pushed back his sleeve to pour the coffee. The bruising continued up his arm and disappeared under his white shirtsleeve. I had no doubt Erik kept a secret which necessitated his withdrawal from everyone, but he wasn't ready to tell me yet.

After he finished pouring, he took a seat across from me and sipped his coffee.

"Well, Monsieur, what do you think?"

"I think, well, I think I shall stick to tea."

I smiled. "Coffee's an acquired taste."

"That's imperative information for those who desire to acquire a taste for caustic beverages."

I relished the flavor. "Finish the first cup. By the end, you'll crave another."

He'd taken a sip before he dropped an additional lump of sugar into his cup. "I wager the only thing I will crave is a cup of tea with which to wash away the taste."

After we finished our coffee, he said, "You are right. I may try another cup."

"Now?"

"No, one cup of bitter a day is plenty."

He came to my side of the table where he presented the crook of his arm for me to take. I slid my hand through—as I had done many times before. This time, without his glove, his bare fingers touched me. The sensation sent a tremor through my body starting at the top of my head and flashing down to my feet. A sheepish grin tugged at the edges of my mouth.

I thought we would visit in his parlor, but he continued to his library instead.

"I have something for you." He opened the door.

On the desk in the center of the room, something the size of a marketing basket was covered by a silky, crimson cloth.

"For you, my lady."

With all the flair of a seasoned performer, he brandished his hand above the gift. The silk jumped into his palm with flourish revealing an odd contraption.

"What is that?"

"Please, sit down."

I settled into the chair. "What are these levers for? What goes in the slot here at the top? Does something come out over here?" I touched the machine with my fingertips.

"Does the lady want me to explain the engineering or does she prefer to have the device demonstrated?" His voice contained a playfulness I had not heard before.

"Am I a laboratory rat you've enlisted to test this for you?"

He chuckled. "I know it works. There is no need for tests or apprehension."

"You're absolutely right. I trust anything you built would never harm me." I turned from the machine to face him again. He sucked in his breath at my words.

"Erik?"

He snapped back from wherever his mind retreated for a moment.

"Here we go." He placed a large, rectangular sheath of papers, bound at one end, in front of me.

"What is this?"

"Uncle Tom's Cabin." He stood behind my chair.

I opened the ledger book and found the pages blank. "What is the meaning of this?"

He held his palm up. "May I have your hand?"

"What for?"

"To teach you to read."

"I know how to read." I chuckled.

"Trust me, Olivia."

I gave him my hand. He put his fingers over mine before placing them on the page.

"Do you feel that?"

"Yes."

"Those are words. Words you can read with your fingers."

I pulled my hand away and looked at him with curiosity before turning back to the ledger. A regular book sat on the table. *Uncle Tom's Cabin.*

Erik turned to the first page of text. He placed both my hands on the bumpy page in front of me. As he pulled my fingers across the tiny pricks, he read from the novel.

"What is this?" I yanked my hands from under his.

"You learned to read by putting the letters together with your eyes to make words. A brilliant Frenchman by the name Louis Braille has come up with a way for you to do the same with your fingers. I 'borrowed' this book from the blind institute here in Paris to show you."

"Not even the doctor in New York spoke of this. How can this be?"

"An American doctor might not know about the Braille method yet. Or, perhaps he assumed you knew. Did you talk with him at length about your eyesight?"

"No." At the time, I couldn't wait to get out of his office. I spoke very little to him once he told me what would happen in the future. "But, Erik, I couldn't learn how to do this. I can't learn to read again. Not this way."

"Nonsense. Let me show you the alphabet. Braille works with six different combinations of dot placement. I'm a very quick learner. I'll teach you."

"I'm a fast learner, too."

"I've studied for a couple of days now. I'm still a beginner."

Something told me although he claimed to be a novice, Erik already had a firm grasp on the concept.

"I appreciate what you're trying to do, Erik, but even if I learned how, I'd only be able to access the texts from institutions for the blind in France. I don't plan to attend such a place."

"Ahh...see. Here is where my invention will help you. The levers here..." He pointed to the six arms protruding out of the box. "...they correspond with the dots. Six combinations make up the letters of the alphabet. I push the lever; the machine punches the holes. The letters, the dots, are raised onto the paper which will allow you to read the text with your fingers."

I stared at the contraption. *He invented this for me? What kind of intellect does he possess? How did he invent such a useful tool in such a short amount of time?*

"Olivia, I can turn any text you wish into this Braille method. Go ahead; pick a book from my library. Any book at all."

"You would do that for me?"

"It would be my pleasure."

"You would sit and punch holes into paper until you've transcribed an entire novel for me?"

"Madam, I would transcribe the entire library for you."

Tears filled my eyes. My hand rested on the raised punches of Uncle Tom's cabin. I ran my fingers over the page. *I won't have to stop reading.*

"How did you know reading is the one thing I will miss the most?"

"Are you pleased?"

"I am most pleased. Thank you." I wiped my eyes.

The prospect of reading with my fingers filled my mind. I had the solution—the means to escape into fiction at my fingertips. My world seemed much less bleak than a few minutes prior. Erik had given me the gift of hope.

"Thank you." I leaned toward him. "May I hug you?"

He didn't move. He stared at me through the mask. Fear flashed in his eyes.

I drew back. “I apologize. Forgive my forwardness.”

He threw his arms around me with enthusiasm and childlike eagerness. With little effort, he lifted me into his embrace.

“Should you ever wish to hug me, Olivia, you never need ask,” he whispered in my ear. His voice swept through my body making me come alive with the need for physical consolation—more than that—the need to be with a man again.

Chapter 19 Power of Suggestion

ERIK:

During the time I worked as a magician and performer, even when I stood center stage in front of a packed house, my soul craved the comfort of a place to hide. I'd lived my early years alone in my mother's attic and lived my later years alone in the cellar of a theatre. The dark beckoned me. I feared if I did not stay within its borders the light would expose me for the monster I am.

Olivia had always lived in the sunlight and daytime. She feared the gradual darkening of her world. We spent time together between dusk and dawn—like Phlox and Primrose our relationship bloomed under the stars and moonlight.

*****

We sat side by side on a bench in front of my fireplace. I wished I could gaze at her face rather than stare into the flames. I turned to look at her every so often. For her next visit, I planned to take away the bench and move two chairs in front of the fire—two chairs facing each other. A smile spread across my face when I realized there would be a *next time*.

A lace embellished candy box sat between us on the bench. Olivia bit into a piece of chocolate, leaving a smudge next to her lips. She laughed at something I said. Without much forethought, I wiped away the smudge with my thumb. She stopped mid-giggle and turned to me with wide eyes. I yanked my hand back expecting her to jump from the bench. Just like Icarus—the fool who flew too close to the sun, I had become too bold.

"Forgive me. There was a…I was removing a…you had chocolate on your—"

"It's quite all right. I'm not made of glass. I won't break."

Her words caused me to shiver. But before any frightening memories clawed their way to my consciousness, she placed my hand on her cheek. "See?" I closed my eyes, relishing her warm skin underneath my palm; the tips of my fingers grazed her hair.

"You don't mind my touch upon your face?" I meant for the words to stay in my head, but they ended up springing from my lips.

"Why should I mind?"

My body turned ice cold. I wanted to run away. For if I continued touching her, I feared my emotions would burst forth, embarrassing me with their magnitude.

"Thank you." I removed my hand.

The room fell silent except for the crackling and snapping of the fire. I needed to stop my heart from beating with unnatural rapidity before the pace killed me. I did what came natural.

I turned to music.

With quick strides, I made my way to the piano. "Would you like me to play for you?"

Her eyes brightened. "Oh, yes. Please."

She sat next to me as I sang and played my most soothing and beautiful pieces. The songs I'd chosen had the ability to captivate entire audiences. Sometimes the music had brought tears to both the ladies and gentlemen in attendance. I filled each note with the passion I had always been denied.

She began to shed silent tears. Noticing the effect, I removed my hands from the piano and put them in my lap.

She sighed deeply and leaned her head against my shoulder. "I love being here with you."

"I shouldn't use music to elicit such strong emotion from you."

"It's not the music. It's you."

My spirit started to soar, but a hurtful little voice in my head told me I had her hypnotized—what she said meant nothing. *What kind of demon am I to use such a horrible form of deceit?* I stood up from the bench and slammed the keyboard cover shut. She startled and caught her breath.

"Time to go, Olivia."

"No, not yet."

"Oh, God, what have I done? I shouldn't have brought you here. I've deceived you."

"You deceived me? How?"

"Time to go, Olivia."

"Why are you angry? What happened?"

"You poor woman. You have no idea what's been done to you."

"Nothing has been done to me. What are you talking about? You aren't making any sense. Why this sudden change of mood?" She stood up and faced me.

"We must leave now." I reached for her hand, but she pulled away from me with a scowl. "I said we're leaving, Madam. Give me your arm." I reached for her again, but she stepped away from me.

"What will you do if I refuse? Will you have another tantrum? You want to throw something? Here, throw this." She grabbed the score from the stand, held out the music sheets, taunting me.

"You don't understand, Olivia. You shouldn't be here."

"Why not?"

I sighed. No answer would make sense to her. "Because I'm not the man you think I am."

"The man I think you are? I don't know who you are. How can you *not* be the man I think you are if I have no idea who he is?"

"Madam Weston, please. I cannot stand here and take this. I must take you home at once."

"You can't stand here and take what?"

Turning my back to her, I closed my eyes and tried to hold my passion, disappointment, and rage inside. I clenched my fists and found the courage to do the right thing. "You only think you want to stay here. I have suggested it and you have believed it. It's what I do."

She stayed silent, but I still couldn't face her and witness the pain my duplicity caused. I waited for her to demand an explanation. For when she did, I would tell the truth. I was not only a skilled magician, but also a magnificent hypnotist. A dishonest man with a dubious past.

"You, sir, give yourself too much credit."

I shook my head. "That is untrue, for I deserve no acclaim. I deserve to live in the hell I've created."

"Turn around. I loathe talking to your back. How many times do I have to tell you?"

"Fine, but I will stand here and wait for you to gather your things so I may escort you home."

She scoffed. "Why don't you 'suggest' I follow your commands? Try to make me do something. Use your magic."

"I haven't any magic."

She approached me.

I stepped back and forced words from my throat. "We must leave now."

"No." She giggled. "You're being silly."

Her mocking of me hurt more than any beating I'd ever endured. I didn't possess enough strength to fight the world any more.

"Are you telling me I'm under your spell?" Derision dripped from her voice.

"That is exactly what I'm telling you."

"I've heard of these things before. People who claim to make you do things against your will."

"Precisely!"

"If you can make me do whatever you suggest, make me want to leave."

Making her want to leave would be all too easy. One practiced movement and the mask would fly off revealing the face of death. She wouldn't be able to leave fast enough. The painful truth filled me with despair.

"I haven't any proclivity to play games with you, Olivia. If you won't gather your things to leave, I will pick you up and carry you."

She put her hands on her hips like a defiant child. "You wouldn't dare."

I avoided her eyes to escape the confirmation of my fraudulence. A moment later, she still had not moved. I stepped toward her, but she slid by me.

I did not want to rough-handle her. I couldn't lay a hurtful finger on her if my life depended on it. "Why do you tease me, Olivia? Can't you tell I don't care for these games? I have asked you, as a gentleman, to let me escort you home."

"If I were under your 'spell' there would be no need to argue with me, correct? Now that I have made my point, I shall gather my things and allow you to escort me home."

"Why do you try to provoke me?"

She stopped smiling, tilted her head. "Provoke you? I'm sorry, Erik. Provocation was not my intent. I don't understand what I did to elicit your strange and sudden change of emotion. I shall go with you now, but I'd like an explanation, if you don't mind." She picked up her cloak and gloves.

Could it be true? Did she want to stay of her own volition?

"If aggravation was not your intent then please forgive my accusation. I wish I understood why my moods sway thusly. The only explanation I can offer is to admit to a terrible temper—a disadvantage which has caused me nothing but difficulty since the day I was born. One would think by my age he would have control over his emotional flare-ups. Are you ready to leave now?"

"I think I know why you're upset."

"I doubt that."

"You believe whatever you hide behind the mask will prevent me from seeking out your company."

Her directness surprised me. She spoke the truth, but the simplicity was illusory.

"I can tell by your silence. I'm right. You're worried an almost blind woman will not like what she sees. Do you not grasp the irony, sir?"

"*Almost* blind, but not totally blind."

"Not yet." She looked down.

I shivered when I registered her meaning. "Is this a progressive sight loss, Madam Weston?"

"All right. I'm ready. Let's go."

I didn't move. "Olivia?"

"Yes, now you know. I shan't get better. Only worse." She began to button her cloak.

"What about the operation?"

"I'm not having any operation."

"Why not?"

She paused for a moment before continuing with her buttons. "Yesterday, I visited the doctor—the ophthalmologist. He won't perform the surgery. It's not the right operation—or it's the wrong kind of blindness. Either way, I've travelled to France for no reason. The whole thing was nothing more than a folly. A false hope."

"Why didn't you tell me?"

"I didn't want to tell anyone. The Count and Viscount still believe I'm a good candidate for the surgery. The truth is—I'll never see well again. I will become totally blind! There. Are you happy now?"

Her angry tone made me take a step back. I wondered whether I should be immensely happy or immensely sad because I was both.

"Let's go now, Erik. I can't look at you."

"Pardon me?"

"I cannot tolerate the pity in your eyes. Take me home."

"Oh, Madam, I assure you, what you see in my eyes is not pity."

"What do I see?"

"One very stupid man who almost made a very critical mistake."

"What mistake?"

"Not telling you how I feel."

"How do you feel?"

"I feel as if I will die right here…" I swallowed hard. "…if you shan't give me permission to embrace you."

She smiled through her tears and I wrapped my arms around her. She whispered in my ear, "Should you ever wish to hug me, Erik, you never need ask."

"I love you," I whispered back. I had never uttered those words before.

Chapter 20 The Chairs

ERIK:

I'd returned to the opera house and found myself unable to stop smiling. I hummed as I opened the hidden doorway into the manager's office. Armand had a disposition more suited for the stage than a management position. Temperamental and dramatic, the slightest issues became monumental to him.

His partner, Firmin, had grown accustomed to drawing him back before he hit the heights of hysteria. In the tedious days before Olivia, I enjoyed pulling Armand's marionette strings. I often sneaked into his office to hide the document on which he'd been working. After watching him search with mounting anxiousness and enlisting every available employee to help him find the paper, I would set it back in the very spot he left it. Someone else would find the document sitting in plain view on his desk. He would accuse the finder of either lying or being mistaken about where the item was found.

I'd witnessed employees move the article to where Armand himself would find it and, therefore, bypass the diatribe. The accessibility of an ego so easily toyed with could supply endless entertainment for a bored specter.

*****

I pushed open the secret entrance and stepped into his office. I picked up one of the new chairs from in front of his desk. Armand had taken months to find the right chairs to keep in style with the flamboyant décor of his private office. I set the first chair down in the passageway and returned for the second. However, I did not come empty handed. That would be rude, so I made the man a trade. I'd found two suitable seats in the prop room with which to replace the ones I obtained.

I spent the night planning for Olivia's next visit. First and foremost, I moved the bench from in front of the fireplace and put Armand's chairs close together and facing each other just as planned. Afterward, I had a few other tasks I needed to finish before sunrise. Idle hands are the devil's playground.

Later that morning, as I walked between the walls near the offices, I heard Armand's most predictable curse words.

"Ca me fait chier!"

I hurried back to get the best view of Armand's performance.

"Fiiirmin! Come quick!" Armand stood next to his desk wiping his brow with a crisp, white, handkerchief. For such an early hour, his cheeks and nose already had a lovely red sheen.

Firmin had rushed from his office. "Are you all right? What's wrong now?"

Armand pointed to the place in front of his desk.

Firmin scratched his head. "What are those?"

"They're the wood and papier-mâché boulders from the production of Hannibal." He paced in front of his desk, rubbing his forehead. "This is atrocious! Just plain wrong."

"You are saying they are not the *correct* papier-mâché boulders?"

Armand blustered incoherently before his words came together in a way that made sense. "No, Firmin! Don't you notice anything wrong? Anything missing?"

"Oh! Your new English chairs?"

"Yes, my chairs. My new George Bullock chairs have been stolen."

"Someone has replaced them with props?" Firmin stifled a chuckle and placed his hand over his mouth, trying to hide his amusement.

"This is not funny. I shall find whoever is responsible for such a childish prank and he will rue the day."

"Armand, where are you going?"

"To the prop room where the devilish prankster has most likely stashed my new chairs. If I should find one scratch on them, I'll…I'll…I'll do *something*!"

He continued to screech until he was out of my earshot.

Chapter 21 Lies

OLIVIA: "Nonsense Olivia. You will not inconvenience me. I escorted you to the hospital for your last appointment and I shall do the same today." Philippe sat at the breakfast table awaiting the food.

"Thank you. I appreciate your help, but—"

Raoul walked in at that moment.

"But, Cousin Philippe, Raoul promised to take me today."

My young cousin paused before making his way to his seat at the long table.

"Isn't that what you said yesterday, dear cousin? You would escort me today?" I gave him a slight nod of my head. I could not make out his expression from such a distance.

He cleared his throat and then lied for me. "Yes, of course. Why, I almost forgot. Forgive me. I'll call for the carriage."

"Not until after breakfast, Raoul. The appointment is for *after* breakfast, remember? Please, join us."

"Well, fine," Philippe said. "But, I hope you'll still meet me for luncheon? I've some business at the opera house. Why don't we meet each other about one o'clock?"

"Yes, that would be lovely."

He turned to his brother. "Raoul, will you escort her to Firmin's office at one?"

*****

After breakfast, Philippe left the dining room. Raoul rounded the table and took the seat next to me. "What's this? Do I detect some clandestine affair you would like to keep from my brother?" He smiled brightly. "The roses in your room are beautiful. You obviously have an admirer. Who? The good doctor?"

My cheeks flushed; I looked down. Anna came in with the teapot and refilled our cups saving me from answering him.

Later, Raoul helped me board his carriage. "I apologize for lying to your brother and making you lie to cover my lie."

He sat down in front of me. "Philippe is rather ignorant about affairs of the heart. Since father died and he inherited the title of Count, he's too busy for romance. He means well, but wishes me to yield to his commands without my own thought."

"Be patient with him. Being the head of the family is difficult."

"Christine and I love each other. Why doesn't he try to understand?" He sighed and then smiled at me. "Where are we *really* off to?"

"To town. I need to make it appear I've kept my doctor's appointment before meeting Philippe at the opera house."

Raoul opened the door and addressed the driver. "We won't be going to the hospital. Take us to the square instead." He sat back down. "So, why are you not keeping your appointment?"

"I no longer plan to have the operation."

"I can't say I'm not more than a little relieved. But, what made you change your mind?"

I told Raoul the doctor refused to do the surgery. I fully trusted he would keep my secret. "Please, don't treat me differently because I'm going blind."

"You shall always remain the same person to me." He grinned. "You will always be my favorite cousin. Let's go make a wish in the fountain. From the look on your face this morning, I dare say I am not the only one smitten. I'm happy for you even though you choose to keep your suitor a secret from me."

His words wiped the smile off my face. *Smitten? Am I smitten?* Whenever I thought of Erik during the day, warmth of friendship surrounded me. I always wished the hours to pass with haste so I could once again be at his side.

My mind continually traveled back to visits to Erik's beautiful home. He'd started transcribing a novel for me during the day and helped me learn Braille at night.

The tedium during the long hours between visits tormented me. A terrible notion crowded the edges of my thoughts. In the United States, there wouldn't be nighttime visits from a stylishly dressed, talented, sweet, and funny admirer.

"I fear we've been neglecting you, Cousin Olivia. I've been so caught up in my own life. Philippe and I have left you at home with nothing to do."

I held Raoul's arm as we strolled around the plaza. "Don't feel guilty. Enjoy yourself while you are young. Go everywhere. Do everything. You shouldn't be shackled to a thirty-one, soon to be thirty-two-year-old relative."

"When?" He grinned.

"When what?"

"When is your birthday? We shall throw a big gala for you."

"I don't require such an extravagant celebration. Thank you for thinking of me. You're very—"

"Nonsense. You tell me when your birthday is or I shall have to find out myself. Save me the trouble of snooping. Tell me."

"Friday."

"Great. Friday we'll mark the anniversary of your birth with a fantastic celebration."

Despair kept me from holding my smile for long. The one person I'd want to invite to my birthday would never be able to attend. Unless—

"Raoul, I have a marvelous idea. Let's make the party a masquerade ball. We should all wear disguises and cover our faces with masks."

"What a grand idea. I'll talk to Philippe at once. Perhaps we should hold your party at the opera house. Invite all our friends and—"

"And Christine Daae perhaps?" I grinned.

"My brother will never allow her to attend. He would forbid me from inviting her."

"One never knows who hides behind a mask, Raoul. Your brother will not recognize the girl with whom you dance."

"Thank you, Cousin Olivia." He tilted his head and gave me a sad smile. "I'm so sorry about the operation." He kissed my cheek.

"You won't tell anyone, will you?"

"No, I'll not betray your confidence, Olivia."

He'd keep my secret. I would keep his.

Chapter 22 The Invitation

ERIK:

Olivia stood behind me as I made our coffee. "I have a surprise for you, Erik."

"The lady surprises me every day." I put sugar and cream on the tray.

"Friday at the opera house…"

I spun around to face her, heart pounding with the mention of my secret location. "Yes, Friday at the opera house what?"

"You shall join me at a gala my cousins are throwing to celebrate my birthday."

I turned my back again and continued setting up the tray. No response came to me. No words to either lie or refuse her wish. I tried to keep my voice from divulging the horror that made me shudder. "I cannot possibly attend."

"Yes, you can."

"No, Madam, I pray your indulgence in this instance. Although, I would love to celebrate your birthday, I cannot attend your party."

I tried to walk past her to set the coffee service on the table, but she took the tray from my hands and set it on the counter. Holding my arms, she looked into my eyes. "My party will be a masquerade. Don't you understand? You *can* come."

"I've…I never…I can't."

"Monsieur, I've invited you to a simple birthday party. No need for such panic."

"I've never been to a birthday party before," I mumbled. "I don't care to."

"Never been?"

"Never." I shrugged.

"Not even your own?"

I hated the pity in her voice. "Not everyone has birthday parties. Celebrating such occasions is by no means mandatory."

"Oh, Erik." She stepped toward me. "I didn't mean to upset you."

I avoided her eyes. "I hate birthdays." I tugged at my shirt cuffs, straightened my waistcoat. "I've never needed such a tradition to mark the passing of another year."

"I'm sorry. I didn't realize you felt so strongly."

"No, of course you didn't." I put my arms down at my sides with my hands clenched in fists so she would not discern how a mere suggestion of a party made me shake.

Before I had a chance to control my emotions, she'd pushed up my left sleeve and ran her fingers over fading bruises. The memory of that night coupled with the sensation of her caress on my bare skin left me lightheaded. I closed my eyes.

"Who are you?" she whispered. "What happened to you?"

"I am an illusion, Olivia. None of this is real."

She embraced me. "You are not an illusion. You're right here in my arms."

I wished she could hold me like that even after she knew what horror existed beneath the mask. For a quick moment, I imagined her truly loving me. The real me. *That will never happen.*

"Come." I pulled away from her and picked up the tray.

If she remained in my world, she would endure more than refutation for attending a party. I swallowed the guilt-induced lump in my throat. I'd started a relationship knowing our association could never end in happiness.

I offered my arm, but she stepped back and studied me with a strange look. "I'm sorry. I should not have insisted you come to my party."

"I hope my refusal to attend didn't anger you." I set the tray on the table and faced her.

"No, I quite understand. I'm not angry."

"What's wrong, Olivia?"

"Why don't you trust me yet?"

"I trust you." A bristle of heat encircled my neck and continued down my back. I studied my shoes to avoid her eyes.

"It's not only your face you hide from me. I know that. I had hoped before I left France you wouldn't want to hide anything from me."

"I'm not hiding. I'm right here."

She crossed the room, bypassed the table and sat on the sofa.

"Your drink will get cold, Olivia."

"I don't care for any coffee at the moment. Thank you."

"Have I done something wrong?"

"No, I wanted to speak to you." She patted the place next to her on the divan.

My palms began to perspire. *What had I done to push her away?* "What's the matter?"

"I've decided to return home soon after my party."

I didn't respond. She continued, "I worry if I wait much longer, I will be completely unable to see. I need to make arrangements when I arrive home. Set my affairs in order. Do you understand?"

I knelt in front of her taking her hand in mine. "I wish you never had to leave. If you stayed here with me, I would take care of you. I promise I'd do everything and anything you require. I would make all your requests my duty to fulfill." The words came out before I had thought them through. I clung to the last hope of a normal life—afraid if she slipped away, I would be lost to the world forever.

"You are sweet. I can't expect you to take on that responsibility. I have talked to the doctor since you and I spoke last. He's told me about places in the United States where blind people learn how to make things."

"Why would you want to go to such a place? Make things? Like what?"

"Well, the example the doctor gave me was brooms." She chuckled. "I'm sure he gave me a poor example. Given more time, he might've thought of another."

I didn't find humor in the situation at all. *What will happen to her if she's at the mercy of someone else?* The thought terrified me. The vermin-like eyes of her driver flashed through my mind.

"Make brooms? You cannot go to a place like that. Are there no relatives in America who will take care of you?"

"If I relinquish my husband's estate to his cousin, his family will ensure the manor and the property would remain as beautiful as they are now. Erik, I simply cannot maintain the upkeep of my home in New York—even if I had all the help in the world. If I can't see, how can I run a large household? I'm sure my husband's cousin would allow me to continue living there, but I wouldn't be comfortable doing so. Don't worry, I'll find myself somewhere suitable. But, I'll not be a burden on anyone."

I wrapped both of my hands around hers. A pain in the middle of my chest left me short of breath. “Don’t go, Olivia. Stay with me, please. I have another bedroom. I don’t mean to infer any impropriety. I believe you are a lady of highest integrity. If I have out-stepped my bounds, I apologize, but the thought of you leaving puts me at great odds.” My passionate plea surprised both of us.

“What are you saying?”

“I’m saying…” I took a deep breath and put my happiness on the precipice. “I love you. I will do anything you ask if you stay here with me.”

“I can’t. That won’t work.”

“Stay for a week. No! Two weeks. Just stay with me. Let’s see if the arrangement will work.”

“I’m sure if I told the Count I plan to hole up with my mysterious friend for two weeks, he would agree in no time. He’d give me his blessing to carry the family name into the ground.”

“Or under it,” I muttered.

Her words gave me hope. She didn’t say she would never consider my suggestion. Nor did she jump up horrified. In fact, the hesitation in her words made me think she might be considering the invitation even as she declined it.

“Come, let me show you the guestroom.”

“Guestroom?”

“The furnishings belonged to my mother. After she passed away, I brought her things to my house on the lake. I had no reason to set up the furniture, but I couldn’t stand to leave the room in disarray. Let me show you.”

“All right.”

I led her to the room off the parlor—the one I’d prepared just for her only weeks before.

Chapter 23 Accommodations

OLIVIA: Erik had stepped inside his guestroom and turned on a lamp. A white, cutwork lace runner draped down the sides of the marble top dresser. The stone floor was covered with a creamy rug with magenta roses and golden fringe. An elegant white iron bed had blue roses painted on porcelain finials.

"Look here." He opened an etched glass music box revealing a bride and groom turning in circles as though they waltzed. I couldn't speak as the pitch-perfect chimes filled the room with Chopin. He set the box down on the dresser before crossing the room. He rushed from one side of the bed to the other to turn on matching lamps. Ornamented with rows of dangling tear-drop crystals, the lamps' soft pink shades cast a dusky glow inside the feminine room.

"Come in. Please."

I didn't move. He hastened back to me. Before a single word came out of my mouth, he spoke with breathless excitement about how staying with him *would* work. He placed my hand on his chest. "Please, think about my proposition before you answer."

His heart banged against my palm in rapid, excited beats.

I sighed. "There might be a way."

He threw his arms around me and rocked with slow motions to a song he alone heard.

"I cannot bear to be apart from you," he whispered.

I met his gaze and had the oddest urge to kiss him, but kissing with the mask between us was not an option.

"I'll provide everything you need. You shall have whatever you desire, my lady. I promise."

"I don't need much. A little coffee, some nourishment and most of all, I must be kept entertained," I teased.

"As luck would have it, Madam, you are looking at one of the greatest entertainers who ever lived."

"And one of the sweetest men who ever lived. If I do this I need to lie to Philippe."

"Yes?"

"I'm not saying I will take you up on your proposal, but, what about this..." I led him back to the two chairs in front of the fire. "My young cousin, Raoul, is in the throes of his first love. He's consumed with adoration for a young soprano."

"Christine Daae."

"Yes! How did you know?"

"I'm sorry. I didn't mean to interrupt. Please, continue." He leaned forward in his chair, folded his long fingers under his chin. I finished telling him Raoul's wish to run away for two weeks under the guise of taking me on a last minute excursion.

"This is sheer providence, my lady. Let's begin this plan at once."

Chapter 24 Masquerade

OLIVIA: The opulent opera house made a vibrant backdrop for my celebration. Enormous golden sculpted angels with raised hands holding lamplights shone on either side of the horseshoe-shaped staircase. Cherubic and Romanesque statues of gold sparkled from pillars and alcoves. Crystal chandeliers glowed in a parade down both sides of the grand hall leading to a colossal, three-tiered, chandelier hanging in the center of a colorful cupola.

I checked my butterfly mask in a massive mirror—one of many, lining the entry hall.

"You ready?" Philippe offered his arm.

"Count Philippe de Chagny and his cousin, Madam Weston." They announced us and we descended the stairs.

Philippe nodded indicating the orchestra should begin playing. Waltzing couples circled the glistening, inlaid marble floor. Wonderful music filled the room mixing melody with merry conversation and laughter.

Philippe turned towards me. "Do you care to dance, Olivia?"

"Not right now." I smiled. "But, I would love to watch you. Perhaps a young lady is waiting for an invitation from you."

"Are you sure you don't mind? I would rather accompany you than leave you by yourself."

"No, please. I would take pleasure in watching you."

Philippe escorted a graceful young lady to the floor and added to the colorful crowd. Philippe and Raoul requested to have an enormous amount of lighting so I would not struggle to see.

I admired the majestic architecture of the room. My fingertips followed the sculpted lines in the column at my side which bore striking resemblance to the work I'd seen in the columns of Erik's home. *He did say he was the contractor, but...*

"Madam Weston, is that you?" A voice from the opposite side of the column startled me out of my contemplation.

A dazzling smile bracketed by deep dimples gleamed below the silver-edged half-mask of Apollo.

"It is I, Dr. Fournier. Might I wish you the happiest of birthdays, Madam."

"Thank you. What a lovely party they've thrown."

"Only one thing could make this night better."

"Oh?"

"Would you do the honor of dancing with a most humble physician?"

"Oh, that's very kind. I'm afraid it's been a long time since I danced and I might not remember how."

"Then it's been too long. You must brighten up the dance floor. You are the brightest star in the night sky. You cannot hide behind columns. Shine forth, Madam Weston. The sky awaits its jewel." He bowed and held out his hand for me to take.

A gifted dancer, Dr. Fournier waltzed me around the floor in graceful elegance. I floated along with him, directed and led by his flawless ability.

"You are a most beautiful addition to the opera house, Madam Weston. I'm happy to have made your acquaintance even though it took a disaster to bring us together. You seem to have healed just fine."

"I had excellent medical care." I smiled at him.

"Are all Americans as beautiful and charming as you?"

"You flatter me, Doctor."

"Yes, but is it working?"

"Indeed." We laughed and continued around the dance floor.

The music stopped. He lifted his mask, pulled a handkerchief from his pocket and dabbed his forehead. I stopped his hand when he went to pull the mask down again.

"I like seeing your face, Doctor. Apollo stares at me. I'm wondering if he thinks I'm too heavy-footed of a dancer."

He laughed. "I don't know about Apollo, but the man beneath the mask thinks you are a divine partner. He'd like to ask you for another, but he doesn't want to keep you from the dozens of suitors who've signed your dance card. That wouldn't be fair." He pulled his mask down over his face. "But, I am Apollo! I care not for rules. I shall dance with the beautiful woman once again if she will have me."

He flipped the mask up to the top of his head again. "Are you brave enough to defy the gods, Madam?"

I chuckled. "I had better not. France doesn't need another plague."

The orchestra had started again. "Shall we obey the deity?"

"Oh, yes. The god of medicine has smiled upon me while I visited France. I owe him." I put my hand in Dr. Fournier's. He left the mask perched on the top of his head. I relished the opportunity to look into a striking face and the bluest eyes I'd ever seen.

After each musical piece, he would pull down the mask and have Apollo either poetically demand or suggest with flattery that we continue *or else.*"

Delighted in his ability for witty conversation, we danced several waltzes in a row. During the orchestra's intermission, he led me to a chair. "Let me get the lady some refreshment."

"Thank you."

He returned with two flutes of champagne. I drank mine a little too fast. A pageboy walked by with a tray of drinks. Dr. Fournier swapped my empty for another full one. After the third flute, we stepped out onto the dance floor to continue our glorious momentum.

"Are you tiring, Madam Weston?"

"Not tired, but a little warm."

He offered his arm. "There's a wonderful breeze and a beautiful full moon is out. Let's take a stroll on the front steps, shall we?"

"Yes, I could use some fresh air."

"By the way, I arranged to hang the moon for you, Madam Weston, hoping I could impress you."

We walked down the steps where other couples strolled and took in the beautiful Parisian night.

He pointed to the moon. "Ahh, there she is. Casting the glow of romance upon unsuspecting couples everywhere."

We'd gone too far from the gaslights. The world became too dark. I shivered. "Take me back, Doctor. Let's go back."

"You don't want to walk a bit?"

"No, please, take me back to the party."

"Of course. Are you all right?" He stepped in front of me and held my hands. "Are you ill?"

"No, I simply want to return, that's all."

He offered his arm and we went back up the steps.

"I shall get you a cold beverage. Perhaps I've tired you from too much dancing." His voice sounded more serious than only moments before.

My nerves calmed once we returned to the foyer. I didn't want to concern him. "I'm fine. Honestly. I'm enjoying my time with you. Although, I think we might be fodder for gossip if we don't return to the party." I gave him a big smile.

"I wouldn't want that. On the other hand, if it scared away all your other suitors, a scandal might come in handy."

"I'm not too worried about gossip and scandals."

"That's what makes Americans so enjoyable. The 'devil may care' attitude is something I admire."

"This is my birthday, after all. No one should say a harsh word about the guest of honor, correct?"

"Madam, I hope you let me share in your birthday next year. I haven't had this much fun dancing in years."

Behind the cheerful conversation and laughter, I fought a wave of sadness because by my next birthday the world would be black. To keep such frightening thoughts from my mind I decided to enjoy every minute of the party. It could very well be the last birthday celebration I ever attended.

"Shall we dance or do you need to rest?"

"Let's dance."

We hadn't come very far into the foyer when we heard a scream. A moment later someone yelled for a doctor.

"I'm a doctor. What's happened?"

"A man has fallen down the staircase. Come quick!"

"I shall return in a moment, Madam Weston. Will you be all right here or shall I find the Viscount to—"

"I'll be fine. You must go care for the injured person."

"I'll be back as soon as I can." He kissed my hand before rushing away.

From behind my left shoulder a familiar voice filled my ear. "I thought that bloody fool would never leave."

"Erik!" I turned to face him.

He wore a spectacular devilish costume. Erik always had a regal, commanding air about him. His costume gave him even more of a majestic presence. He wore a luxurious red velvet cloak with a train that dragged on the floor behind him. A skeleton mask covered his face. Atop his head a large, black feather protruded from a showy red hat.

"I thought you weren't going to come. I'm so pleased you attended after all." I stopped myself from throwing my arms around him.

"You seemed to be enjoying yourself without me. I do believe Madam has an admirer. In addition, Madam is equally enchanted with her companion." We moved from the foyer into a wide hallway. "It's dreadful someone had the misfortune to fall down a flight of stairs and interrupt your cozy evening."

"Erik?" His antagonistic tone alarmed me. I wondered how long he'd watched us before he made his presence known. Thinking back, I remembered seeing the red costume in the background or right next to us several times, but thought nothing of it.

"I think you and your arrogant doctor make a most glorious couple. I shall leave you to your party, Madam Weston. I thank you for the invitation. I would like to wish you a very happy birthday. Adieu, Madam." The malice and anger in his voice made me shudder.

He turned on his heel to leave, but I grabbed him by the back of his cape. Erik always walked with a graceful and steady gait, but I caused him to take a misstep as the cloak's closure caught him at the neck. After regaining his footing, he whirled around. The red velvet sifted through my fingers. Before he could move, I clutched the cape again and held the material tightly in my fist.

"If you please, Madam, let go of my cape."

"No."

"Pardon me?"

"You wait one minute, Erik."

"You refuse to relinquish my cape? Then I shall have to—" Before he finished his sentence, I found myself holding the red velvet cape in my hand, but Erik vanished in a flash of fire and puff of smoke.

A few couples who happened to be in the same hallway witnessed his exit. They applauded.

"Excellent! Quite fascinating," one gentleman said. "Was he commissioned for entertainment? Shall we see more of him tonight?"

My fingers clutched the fine cloak. I didn't know what to say.

"Oh, we haven't missed the show, have we?" his female companion asked. "I love magic."

A commotion from the foyer interrupted the discourse. I hurried to see what occurred. I stopped behind a group of onlookers near the grand stairway. A communal gasp came from the front.

Philippe came upstream through the crowd and took my arm. "There you are. Come with me. Raoul commissioned some delightful entertainment without telling me. The magician asked for the guest of honor. Come on. Let's see what he can do."

Erik shouted from the top of the stairs. "I will not begin until everyone is silent!" Fury permeated his voice. "Ahh, here is the guest of honor. Now we can start. Come closer, Madam. The light is much brighter up here."

Oblivious and delighted, the Count escorted me up the stairs until I stood under the brilliant light of the chandeliers. I stopped two steps from the top and refused to go farther.

Erik wore a silky black cape over his costume; he had discarded his red hat and skeleton disguise. Instead, he wore his regular mask. Because people engaged in quiet conversation while they waited for the entertainment to begin, Erik shouted, "Silence!"

A giant ball of fire bounced down the steps. After reaching the bottom, it exploded into a puff of red smoke. Everyone gasped and then applauded.

Erik stood at the top of the stairs and impressed the crowd for several minutes without even looking at me. I wondered if his anger subsided since he seemed delighted to perform.

Out of nowhere, an egg appeared in his hand. After a slow flutter of his fingers, the egg rose up and floated above his palm. He began descending the stairs with great showmanship.

As he paused in front of me the egg changed colors. Our eyes met. I lost any hope he'd ceased being angry. Continuing to the bottom, he showed the egg to all the people lined up near the banisters. The egg jumped from hovering above his left palm to his right. I heard people murmuring, "*Look! It's turning different colors.*"

"*That's amazing.*"

"*The egg is spinning in midair.*"

"*It changed directions!*"

When he reached the bottom of the stairs, he plucked the egg from the air and tossed it above his head. The egg cracked open. Two white doves winged their way through the opera house right over the audience.

The manager yelled, "Birds! We cannot have birds in here. Someone contain those animals at once."

This seemed to pique Erik's interest. He sauntered up to Monsieur Armand. "Is that what you desire, Monsieur? Should they be caged?"

Armand stumbled on his words. Erik towered over him and asked with menace, "Is caging the animals what you desire?"

"Yes, Monsieur, an opera house is not a place for animals to roam freely."

"No truer words have been spoken, Monsieur."

A puff of multicolored smoke appeared and engulfed Armand's head and shoulders. A few sparks snapped, a bright flash of light and Armand had what appeared to be a birdcage over his head.

The audience roared with laughter. Armand played along by opening up the tiny door across his face.

After producing a big piece of silk from midair, Erik tossed the material over

Armand's head. "No one belongs in a cage, Monsieur."

He yanked the cloth from over Armand. Although he no longer had a cage over his head, a small hen perched on top of his fancy hairstyle.

Armand let out a shriek. "Get off! Get off," he cried over the uproar of laughter surrounding him. The bird cackled with annoyance, but refused to fly away. The audience laughed with delight. Firmin had sidled up to his partner and tried to remove the hen by flicking his wrists back and forth, repeating, "Shoo! Shoo!"

The hen finally left her roost and almost flew into a few guests before finding her way to the ground. Cackling, the bird strutted down the red carpet runner delighting the crowd even more.

Turning back to Armand, Erik asked, "We can't have animals roaming freely. Will we be in need of another cage?"

"No, I would say certainly not," Armand answered.

The audience burst into applause. Erik put his hand across his chest and gave a sharp, professional bow.

"Would you like to see more?"

The spectators cheered.

"Let's ask the guest of honor what she would like to see, shall we?"

He strolled back up the stairs. "What does Madam wish from me, her humble servant?" He knelt on one knee, his head bowed in supplication. When he looked up, antagonism shot from his eyes.

Speechless, I shook my head.

He stood up. “I am here for your entertainment as you wished. I’m sure there is something I can do for you, Madam Weston. After all, I exist for your amusement and *nothing more*. I realize I am a mere diversion, a way to keep boredom at bay.” His voice dripped with controlled rage.

Unaware of his malice, the crowd cheered. I wanted to comfort him—tell him I did not expect him to perform. He was more than that to me. My mouth dried up. I couldn’t make any words come from my lips.

“What’s the matter? Cat has your tongue?”

From somewhere on the other side of the staircase came a meow. Then another. And another. Everyone looked around for the cat, but the meow jumped from one side of the room to the opposite side so fast no one could trace the source.

The guests laughed at their own silliness when they turned left and right looking for a cat they knew did not exist.

Erik called their attention back to him. “Now…a gift for Madam.”

A puff of blue smoke burst from the air followed by a flash of light. Erik held a box wrapped in bright paper with a white ribbon on top. “Perhaps the kitty cat is in here?” He put the box to his ear.

A tiny kitten mewed from inside the package. The crowd let out a collective, “Ahh.”

In the next instant, the noise from the box changed. The kitten inside grew frightened.

“Ladies and gentlemen, I do not think the little cat is alone in there.” He put the box to his ear again. “No, I think the cat has company.”

The meow of a tiny kitten became a giant roar of an angry tiger, surprising the audience and making everyone jump.

“Madam Weston, would you like to open the box to find out what is inside? A kitten or a tiger?”

I didn’t want to be part of the game anymore. “No, thank you, Monsieur.”

The audience laughed, amused at my unwillingness to open a box everyone knew did not contain a tiger.

“Oh, please, Madam. Open the box,” Erik said.

“No, thank you, Monsieur. I don’t care to.”

“Perhaps someone will assist you. How about you, Doctor?”

Dr. Fournier had just rejoined the crowd and stood at the foot of the stairs. Erik descended. “Will you open the box for Madam Weston?”

Smiling, the doctor took the package from Erik’s hands. He’d barely opened the box when a quick flash of fire flared out. The doctor slammed the top over the flame. A giant clap of thunder exploded through the grand hall frightening the doctor so much he fumbled the box a few times.

“No, thank you, Monsieur. I don’t care to open this present either.”

A sustained moment of laughter filled the room as the doctor held the box at arm’s length.

“Silence!” Erik yelled. The laughter stopped.

A moment later, Erik's voice contained charm again. "I guess that leaves me. I will have to see what's inside the box." He'd taken the present from the doctor and climbed the steps as he spoke. "I tried to give this to Madam Weston, but she declined. Rejected my gift. She did not want what I had to offer. Let's see what Madam Weston refused to take from me tonight."

After he reached the top of the stairs, Erik opened the box with flourish. A colorful display of sparks flew out followed by pink confetti that rose in a twisting motion before bursting open and cascading to the ground. A big paper heart, much like the butterfly he'd made me, floated out of the box and spun in the air.

The heart twirled and changed colors until the paper was bright red and spun at a fast pace. A second later, the heart had turned black and burst into flames. The ashes fell on top of the confetti.

The audience cheered, "Bravo!"

Erik stood tall and once again took a bow. "Before I bid you all a good night, I shall ask if you are brave enough to indulge in a most delightful piece of *dark* magic. The darkest magic you can imagine."

An excited rumble ran through the spectators. A few people yelled answers.

"Yes!"

"Show us!"

Erik stood at the center-point of the horseshoe staircase. He held onto the banister, glaring down at the people below.

"If you are brave enough—I shall, on this very night, conjure up the Grim Reaper himself. You will be able to look upon the face of death. Although, I doubt any of you are brave enough to face him for long."

A few of the men laughed. Erik's head snapped toward them. "You don't believe me? Perhaps you would rather look upon the devil himself? Are you brave enough?"

"Go on then," someone shouted. "We're not afraid."

"Are you sure?"

The men in the audience shouted answers.

"Show us."

"We aren't scared."

"You cannot frighten us."

With a flash of brilliant light, he ripped the mask from his face. "Behold! The face of death! The devil himself!"

Women screamed and turned away. Men stepped back in horror. With another explosion and burst of flame, he disappeared leaving sparks snapping on the ground.

The audience gawked in stunned silence for a moment until a loud roar of approval and thunderous applause filled the room.

I stood frozen in my spot.

Philippe appeared at my side. "A most excellent choice of entertainment. I've never seen better."

The orchestra started again. The sounds of people laughing and talking filled in behind the music. I realized I had been cradling the red cape as if holding a small animal.

The doctor made his way through the crowd to where I stood. He talked to Philippe for a moment, but I didn't hear anything they discussed. The image of Erik's face burned in my memory.

"Well, what do you say Madam Weston? Do you care to dance?"

"I don't think so."

The doctor took my hand in his. "You're shaking. Did the magician scare you? Don't let such a ridiculous illusion frighten you, Madam Weston. Child's play. Under his mask was another mask."

Philippe added, "Yes, he was very good. I must say, very realistic, right doctor?"

"A masterpiece. A living corpse if ever there was one." They laughed.

"I must ask Raoul where he found him. Where is my brother? I have not seen that boy in a good while."

The stairs rocked back and forth. The giant chandelier above my head faded in and out of focus.

The doctor caught me before I hit the marble stairs.

"She's fainted. Bring her to my office at once," Armand directed.

Doctor Fournier carried me down the stairs with Monsieurs Armand and Firmin in front of us clearing a path through the crowd.

"Make way! Step aside."

"Coming through! Move, please!"

*****

Philippe and the doctor peered down at me as I reclined on the sofa in Armand's private office.

"I don't know what came over me."

"I think you had yourself a little scare, Madam. You'll be fine. Just a case of the swoons. Should I ever get my hands on that magician who scared you, I'll throttle him." The doctor chuckled.

I blinked a few times, thinking I might have hit my head because behind the doctor, Monsieurs Armand and Firmin appeared to be sitting on giant boulders.

Chapter 25 Dark Revenge

ERIK:

Unable to bring myself to enter my house after I left the party, I lingered on the bank of the lake. Crouching down, I dragged a stick through a murky pool creating ripples at the shore. I'd tossed my mask behind me and waited until the water was still again before I studied my reflection in the candlelight. *The face of death.*

Now she knew what lay beneath.

I hadn't meant to reveal myself. The decision was spontaneous—the consequence of all the hurt I'd known in my life and a way to punish us both. I've always despised the sound of the gasps and screams from the audience when I unmasked my face. All around the world the reaction was the same. Horror had a universal language.

Olivia had seen me. I could hide no more.

*****

A few hours earlier, I drank my tea and brooded about Olivia's party scheduled to take place five floors above my home. The familiar ice cold fingers of resentment scratched the back of my neck. *Left to wander alone in the gloom of darkness while the rest of the world bathes in joviality and communion under bright lights.*

Staying at the house on the lake became unbearable. I'd pulled on my gloves and fastened my cape with haste. *Watch from behind the mirrors*, I consoled myself.

It'll be the closest you'll ever come to joining, a spiteful voice in my head mocked.

A few minutes later, I was ready to navigate through the labyrinth in search of the best place to observe. Out of nowhere a thought pushed itself forward. *She chose to have a masquerade for my sake.*

In the cavern of my stomach, all at once, a multitude of bats evacuated their dim grottos and flapped upward. Their wings brushed my insides in frantic jubilation. *She had a masquerade so I might attend. Of course!* Anxious energy coursed through my body; jittery nerves made me shiver.

I imagined attending the party with her—envisioned her on my arm as we walked through the crowd mingling with other partygoers. Dancing, drinking punch, strolling on the front steps. I imagined Olivia and me whispering to each other in the moonlight while a cool, star-kissed breeze blew her hair away from her exquisite face.

What would it be like to blend into a crowd of people? To enjoy an ordinary evening of social activity? I might talk to anyone I wish. They'll listen to my words instead of stare at the mask. I can do this.

The decision to attend had been made. I rushed between the walls to visit the costume department. The party was about to start. I didn't have much time.

Upon my arrival, the bats no longer fluttered in my stomach, but nose-dived against my internal organs, slamming into my chest with dizzying acrobatics of anticipation and fear. I paused at the top of the stairs for a moment to collect myself.

There she is!

Olivia wore a decorative butterfly half-mask that showcased her beautiful smile. I hurried down the steps anxious to surprise her. I was halfway down when the doctor escorted her toward the dance floor. She held the crook of his arm. He clasped his fingers over hers as they walked through the crowd to join the dancers.

I stiffened with outrage and shock.

Two hundred or more people at the party, but I identified her lilting giggle above the others. That little clatter of merriment tormented me. That's how she laughed when I entertained her, when I amused her—when I made her happy. *Someone else captivated her. Someone else evoked the same response.*

I couldn't take another step. People bumped into me on their way down. Others moved around me on their way up. Olivia and the doctor arrived on the dance floor. My jaw tightened like a vice. The good doctor put his hand on her back and pulled her closer. I ground my teeth.

That should be me!

He had stolen my dance. I had never danced before and an interloper took my only partner. My breath bounced off the mask in loud, fast currents. My hands clenched in fists, clutching the edges of my cape. I forced my way downward.

I'd followed them close enough to hear their conversation. She playfully touched him on the shoulder after she straightened his bow tie. He dared to adjust her mask. And when he did, his hand lingered on her hair.

Olivia did not mind his touch or his attention. I'd never seen her so cheerful. She drank champagne and danced several waltzes in a row with the foppish physician.

Every rejection from my past gathered like a storm; a cyclone of red-hot rage slammed into the middle of my soul. *Why did I think she would be different from any other woman?*

Women are creatures that crave beauty. They want to gaze upon their dance partner and find a handsome man staring back.

I had tried to break free but discovered I was shackled to my destiny.

I could've slipped away without her knowing, but my anger and pride would not let me leave until she knew I'd seen her. I wanted to hurt her as she'd hurt me. *Maybe I should make her feel as foolish as I feel.*

In the end, I could not humiliate her the way I intended. I could never hurt Madam Weston in any way. This led me to make a spontaneous and disastrous decision.

If I was incapable of hurting her, I was more than capable of shocking her.

I stood close enough and under bright lights so she wouldn't miss any of the gruesome truth. She didn't scream or turn away. She didn't even close her eyes. Truth be told, the woman did not look horrified or disgusted. If I had to name her expression, I might say confused or dismayed.

I had just let her go.

A calm sense of loathing filled my chest as I left the party. Olivia had punctured a big hole in my heart. The only way to fill the empty space was to pack it with anger. I needed to find some diversion—something to take my mind away from all I'd lost.

If the world judged me to be a monster simply by my appearance, perhaps it was time to show the world what I held back. I could let that monster out of his cage. I was too tired to change who I'd become. One cannot fool fate.

Perhaps the good doctor might have an accident. Yes! Of course!

I tossed the stick into the water, stood up from the lake's edge and picked up the mask. The party would be over soon. I wanted the best opportunity to devise a dramatic death.

*****

The pompous physician bid Olivia good night, kissed her hand and helped her into the Count's fancy coach. As soon as the driver pulled the horses from the curb, the physician rushed back into the opera house. I trailed him and waited for the right opportunity.

As the party finished, the doctor talked to a man in a clown mask. I didn't bother listening. Their conversation would be the last he'd ever have.

The two men parted company. The clown made his way through the dwindling crowd toward the stage-right entrance into the theatre. A few minutes later, the doctor walked to the stage-left entrance of the theatre. He was up to something.

My inquisitiveness distracted me. My curiosity became stronger than my urge to kill. I kept up with him until we came to the stage. I used the catwalks to trail him from above.

The rotten dandy had checked left and right before looking behind him. The clown had tossed off his mask and rushed forward from the shadows. The two men fell into each other's arms. My mouth opened in disbelief.

"I'm sorry I couldn't spend any time with you. Don't be angry." The doctor kept his voice low as he tried to soothe the other man.

"You were with her all night. Why don't you admit you find her attractive? You'd rather be with her." The clown sobbed into the doctor's chest.

"No, no. You know that's not true." The doctor held the other man's face in his hands and gazed into his eyes. "She'll be on her way to the states soon. Don't you understand? This was the perfect opportunity to throw everyone off our trail. People were beginning to ask questions, Louis. We need to be more discreet. Think of my practice. After she leaves, I'll act brokenhearted.

Every gossip-hound will be glad to assume I fell in love with a beautiful American. I'll be the poor, spurned lover. Don't you see? It's perfect."

"You promise you have no feelings for her?"

"No, Louis." He wiped his lover's tears with his thumbs. "She's a delightful woman, but my heart will always belong to you." He'd kissed the clown's forehead and pulled him into his arms. Kissing each other with passion, they began shedding clothing.

I attempted to stifle my glee, but failed. My hearty laugh reverberated through the theatre. The lovers split apart, looking around in horror. I enjoyed watching them scramble to pick up pieces of their discarded costumes. They slipped and slid in their haste to redress while running out of the theatre. The sight of their guilty struggle filled me with merriment. My maniacal laughter made them run faster. I sat down on the edge of the scaffolding. *The handsome doctor? My rival?* The man's secret saved his life.

After a moment, I laid back and stared at the roof above the stage. My hysterics had left me breathing heavy. The smile dropped from my face when I thought of Olivia. *What did I do?* I bolted upright; my heart ripped open. I'd ruined my one chance of happiness—however short-lived it might have been.

Below me, Raoul and Christine climbed out of the orchestra pit. They buttoned and fastened their clothes while looking around the theatre.

"What was that?"

"I don't know. The laughter came from up there." Christine pointed to Box Five. "The Opera Ghost!" She grabbed Raoul around the waist and turned her head away.

He chuckled. "That's a silly fable. People playing jokes on one another and blaming the Opera Ghost. He doesn't exist."

"Raoul, you heard the laughter, too."

"Someone fooling around trying to elicit some response. Come on, let's go back. We're safe. I'll protect you from any old Opera Ghost." He wrapped his arms around her.

"That's not funny. He'll get you if you anger him."

"Be careful, Christine. The Opera Ghost will get you." He tickled her. She squealed. The two young lovers ducked back into the pit. Watching them nauseated me.

Why must I always be the joker and never the lover? I was cursed with the passion of a lover, the face of a knave.

Chapter 26 Oh!

OLIVIA: Before I went to bed, I shut my window and pulled the drapes closed. I sent the maid away as usual, but this time, I turned out the gas lamps. I did not expect my nighttime visitor. I climbed between the sheets and attempted to make sense of what happened at the party. The doctor said the illusion was a mask under a mask. Erik might have devised something to scare me. He was clever enough to invent something so realistic. *But, what if it wasn't a second mask?*

I began to cry.

I thought about certain things he'd said—not liking birthdays, never being invited to any parties. The notion of why he chose to live alone and isolated from everyone tore at my conscience. My eyes grew heavy and I did not fight sleep. He'd never be back.

Beautiful violin music filled my dreams. A soft, sad tune played in the back of my mind. Sweet and soothing almost like a—

"Lullaby!"

I bolted upright in bed, wide-awake. The melody jerked to a stop. The music was not in my head at all.

"Erik?"

The closet door opened just a bit. A sick, heavy sensation lodged in my chest. I wished I wanted him to leave me alone—that I could send him away and never think of him again. But, my heart refused to let him go.

He stayed hidden in the closet, but he whispered in my ear. "I'm so sorry. Forgive me, Olivia. Please, don't hate me."

I lay back on my pillow with my eyes closed, tears blocking my throat. The face of death stared back at me from behind my lids. I held back a sob. The man behind the mask waited in my closet expecting me to send him away. I sensed it.

"Don't be afraid, Olivia. Please, don't be frightened of me."

Tension and anxiety were almost palpable; his voice had an unfamiliar waver. I turned on the lamp next to my bed.

"Why? Why did you do it, Erik?"

"Because I'm a foolish man. I acted irrationally for no other reason than the most fundamental of human emotions. I was jealous. You can't hate me any more than I hate myself."

I closed my eyes, took a deep breath. "How could you possibly know that?"

He sighed. "You're right. I cannot accurately gauge how much you hate me. I'll leave now, but I couldn't let you return to New York until I apologized. Even if you don't accept my apology, please know it was given with utmost sincerity and the most contrite of hearts. But, I beg you, don't hate me."

I wanted to say so much, but remained mute. My heart pounded with heavy sorrow. The incessant ticking of the mantle clock filled the room. I took a deep breath and whispered, "I don't hate you."

"Thank you for saying that," he said from the closet.

I sat up, leaned on the headboard. "Come here, Erik."

"I can't."

"Yes, you can."

"No, Olivia. I cannot."

"Come here, please. For me."

The closet door opened a bit more and then a little further. A shadow approached. I'd never seen Erik move so slowly. He came to the side of my bed and stood at the edge of the light, looking down.

"Does this look like I hate you?" I pulled down the blanket to reveal his red velvet cape scrunched up next to me where I'd held it and cried.

He gasped and covered his mouth. "Oh, God. You *don't* hate me."

"Come here." I held my arms open. He hesitated for a second or two before he threw himself into them.

"You don't hate me."

"No, Erik. I could never hate you."

He let out a little sob and held me tighter. "I so regret ruining your birthday. I'll make it up to you. Whatever you want, I'll get for you. Anything at all. I promise you shall have anything you desire."

"I want you to kiss me."

He held perfectly still within my arms. He didn't even take a breath. An eternity passed before he whispered, "I don't know how."

"May I?" I gestured toward the mask for permission to lift it.

"Wait." Erik had reached across me and turned out the lamp before he removed his mask. He gave me a tender, tentative kiss—as though he expected me to push him away. He paused and then gave me a sweeter, longer kiss.

"Oh, Olivia."

They were the sweetest, most beautiful sounding words he'd ever spoken to me.

Chapter 27 The Violin

ERIK:

I needed to apologize to Olivia before she left Paris, but I knew she would be hysterical if I showed up in her room after what I'd done at the party. I decided to soothe her beforehand—the only way I knew how.

Music.

I brought my violin with me. I reasoned if I kept her in a light dream-state she might listen long enough to hear my apology. That is all I meant to do.

It started to work. I deducted she was in a sleep trance except—she broke through.

I obeyed with reluctance when she asked me to come closer.

Olivia had slept with my cape in her arms. My heart stopped and jolted awake again. She would not have done such a thing if she found me a loathsome creature. Earlier when she wept, it was into its velvet folds her tears fell. *My cape. Mine.*

I rushed into her arms full of unadulterated relief. She would be neither angry nor frightened of me when she boarded the ship to the United States. I would go to my grave a better man.

Olivia embraced me, holding me close and then—she asked me for a kiss.

Her birthday wish? My kiss. For a second, I thought her request had to be a joke—an elaborate hoax meant to humiliate me in a most torturous way. Even my own mother had adamantly refused to kiss me.

Olivia asked for permission to remove my mask. It was at that moment, I believed she was sincere. Olivia knew what was under the mask. She'd seen my face, seen my lips. Yet, she desired to touch them with her own—the most cherished of all gestures. I turned off the lamp, removed my mask and kissed her.

During that kiss, her sweetness rushed through me. I worried she might have a last minute change of heart, so I was careful not to ply myself too eagerly upon her. However, she did not attempt to stop me. I kissed her again.

If my soul contained nothing but darkness and shadows, then I must've borrowed illumination from her bright spirit because I felt bathed in light. That moment of shine changed me. I was no longer a man who had never known a kiss.

Long ago, I suppressed my desire to make love to a woman. I understood I would die never knowing the joys of the flesh. I sublimated my sensuality into creating art. My canvas, my stone, and my musical scores became my lovers. Then, I found myself sitting on Olivia's bed in the dark where she kissed me with passion.

My familiarity with eminent rejection caused fear to leap from the shadows of my past ready to clamp its razor sharp fangs on the jugular of my joy. I could not survive the pain of such a terrible reality if she pushed me away. But, she did not.

My desire proliferated into a need. I longed to lay with Olivia. She'd found a speck of trust in me which had not been smothered by brutal anger. Her kiss freed a ravenous hope which enveloped me. Somehow, she'd coaxed the human from underneath the shroud of shame.

I ran my hands through her long hair which hung loose about her shoulders. Just as I'd wanted to do since our first night in the carriage, I touched her face. Closing my eyes, I stroked her cheeks, nose and forehead. I explored her features as I would a piece of marble or stone. I wanted to know the contours, the shape, the texture of Olivia. I'd never dreamt anything could be so soft and warm. In that moment, nothing else existed. Lost in the exploration, I dwelt in my hands and the sensation that travelled through them.

My breathing came fast from my lungs. I wanted her more with every stroke, every caress. My eager hands travelled down her neck and continued to her shoulders. When my fingertips brushed her lacy neckline, I pulled back and wondered why she had not stopped me sooner.

"What's wrong?" She leaned forward and cupped my cheek with tenderness.

I leaned away from her.

I didn't have on my mask! She shouldn't touch…

"I'm sorry. Does this bother you?" She pulled her hand away.

Bother me? No, your touch feels extraordinarily good.

Before I could answer, someone tapped on her door. I immediately slipped into the closet.

"Yes? Who is it?"

"Cousin Olivia, it's me. Can I come in?"

That boy infuriated me. How dare he interrupt? I wished he would run away with that obtuse girl and be done with it. The impertinent fool.

"Just a minute, Raoul. Let me get my wrap."

She turned on the gas lamp next to her bed and then shrugged into a dressing robe. In my haste, I'd forgotten my mask on the nightstand. A wave of nausea soured my stomach. My mother had made sure that I always felt exposed, vulnerable, and anxious whenever something wasn't covering my unsightly mess.

The closet door opened. I threw my hands over my face.

"Here."

My heart rate slowed as soon as I took the mask from her hand.

She'd crossed the room and unlocked her door. "Come in, Raoul."

"Christine and I are leaving in the morning. Philippe will be looking for me by noon. Please, try to hold him off for us. We have to get married before my brother finds out."

"Raoul, are you sure you want to do this? You could be left penniless."

"I know what I chance to lose. There isn't enough money in the Bank of Farce to keep me from marrying Christine."

"You are passionate, cousin." She paused. "In the name of love, I have changed my mind. I will help you."

"You will?" Raoul's voice broke like a blemished adolescent's.

"Tomorrow we shall tell Philippe I begged you to take me to Spain before the operation. We'll set out in the morning just as you planned."

"You will come with us?"

"No, rent me a room in a hotel across town. Don't worry. I will have plenty to keep me occupied."

"Are you sure? You won't need us?"

"Raoul, I'm a grown woman. You keep your secrets. Let me keep mine and tomorrow you will marry your love."

The boy almost choked with excitement and gratitude. Hiding in the dark corner of the closet, I smiled at the irony. I had almost killed the youngster. Yet, as it were, I couldn't have been more grateful to him for providing an excuse for Olivia to come stay with me. Perhaps the spoiled little idiot had his usefulness, after all. My envy of him waned. I was in love and even he could not ruin the best night of my life.

Chapter 28 Nightmare

OLIVIA: Raoul took me to the Hotel Debonair where he'd registered under a false name. At the door to my room, he kissed my cheeks. "Thank you, cousin. I shall never be able to repay you for this."

"Go on." I smiled at him. "She's waiting."

"Yes, she is." Quick as a flash, Raoul rushed down the hall to rendezvous somewhere with Christine. When he reached the end of the corridor, he jumped up to touch the high arch for no other reason than to express his exuberance. "Thank you!" he shouted before he turned the corner.

At dusk, Erik's driver waited in front of the hotel. He didn't ask any questions. He simply followed Erik's instructions without needing input from me.

We drove around until darkness fell. At the appointed location, he unloaded my bags. Without a word, the driver remounted the carriage and hurried away.

I waited near the river with suitcases at my feet. The water lapped at the shore. A night bird called a haunting melody from a nearby tree. Far from streetlights and storefronts, I could not see a thing. I almost called out for someone to rescue me. I shivered with fear; my teeth chattered in the cool night. *What am I doing all alone in the dark?*

Erik came from behind me and slipped his arms around my waist.

"You are so beautiful in the moonlight, Madam Weston."

I leaned my head back onto his shoulder and closed my eyes with sweet relief. He held me for a moment before he said, "We should go now."

*****

Erik helped me out of the boat. He took my arm and we began walking up the path to his front door. "What about my bags?" I glanced behind me at where he'd left them on the shore.

"I'll get them later. Are you worried someone will steal them?" He chuckled.

"You're right. It's unlikely. Don't you get lonely down here, Erik?"

"I think safety is a fair trade for loneliness, don't you?"

"Safety from whom? From what?"

He didn't answer me. Instead, he opened the front door. With a sweep of his arm, he welcomed me to his home once again.

Giant bouquets and sprays of flowers in every color created a gorgeous, fragrant path to the guest room. Petals covered the carpet all the way to the door.

"They're beautiful. Where did you find so many flowers?"

"In a far, far away place."

"Where are we? Where is this underground fortress you've created?"

"When you are not here it is the depths of hell."

"You frighten me when you speak that way. You shouldn't take such liberties when speaking of hell or the devil. There are very real demons out in the world."

"Indeed there are, Olivia. However, I don't fear demons. Far more wicked than any demon might dare dream, you'll find the depraved deeds of man."

"That's horrible, Erik. Don't say such things. That sounds like blasphemy."

My sharp tone startled him. He dropped his head, looked at his feet.

"I didn't mean to upset you." I picked up his hand. His head snapped up. For a second, duplicity clouded his eyes. *Who is this man?* I was far from anyone who could help me should I need it. Even if I screamed, no one would hear me. We'd travelled deep underground. No one in my family knew my whereabouts.

"What's wrong, Olivia?" He tightened his fingers around my hand.

"I don't care to lie to you. Agreeing to do this is the most reckless thing I've ever done. Maybe I should go back to the hotel."

"You've changed your mind?"

"I wonder if staying at the hotel isn't the prudent thing to do."

"Perhaps your instincts are correct." He sounded as though I'd dashed every dream he'd ever had. "Shall I take you back?"

The heartbreak in his words tore at my conscience. "Well, I'm here now. No rush to leave. We can enjoy a nice visit, can't we?"

He paused for a moment before closing the guestroom door. "Of course. Would you like a cup of coffee?"

We sat on the sofa and set our teacups on the new, low table in front of us. I wondered where he got his fine furnishings. He certainly did not have them delivered to his door.

An awkward silence settled around us.

"I'm sorry if I upset you with my change of plans, Erik."

"I'm disappointed—but disappointment and I are well acquainted. I'll live. Olivia, if you worry about. . . If you believe I had assumed we would . . . I didn't bring you here so we could . . . ." He cleared his throat, adjusted his necktie and sat up straight. "I assure you, I have my own sleeping chambers. I would never visit yours uninvited. My intentions toward you are principled and moral."

"I believe you, Erik." I wanted to change the subject in order to chase away the somberness of our visit. "Where is your bedroom?"

"Back there." He gestured behind me with a toss of his chin. I turned toward the long, dark hallway.

"Why is your bedroom so far from the rest of the house?"

"Not so much distant as separate..." He shrugged and did not meet my eyes. "...and not anymore separate than need be."

*****

Erik and I sat in front of his carved marble fireplace where he asked me about my family. The most mundane pieces of information, especially about my childhood, fascinated him.

What was attending school like? How many students were in your class? What games did you play outside in the schoolyard? His questions were very odd, but he leaned forward and listened to every word.

"Did your family celebrate Christmas when you were a little girl?"

"Of course. Aren't you a Catholic, Erik?"

"No." He flicked his wrist in a dismissive gesture indicating he did not care to discuss religion any further.

"But, I thought you said—"

He leaned toward me. "How? Tell me how you celebrated. Was there a Christmas tree? Were there presents?"

"Yes, of course. Didn't you have Christmas at your home?"

"I had neither Christmas nor a home." He stared into the fire with a faraway look in his eyes.

I shivered when I realized he asked questions because he lived vicariously through my simple girlhood stories. The childhood Erik experienced obviously differed vastly from my own.

He turned toward me with excitement in his eyes again. "Tell me about presents."

I wanted to learn about him as much as he wanted to learn about me. "How old are you, Erik?"

"I only claim to estimate my years. I believe I am forty-four. Generally, in that area."

Estimate his age? A strong curiosity continued to build in my mind. *What kind of life has he known? No birthdays? No Christmas? No home?*

"The presents. What did you receive? Were they hidden in your stocking? What else does one find in a stocking?"

I swallowed the lump in my throat. "In the stockings, let's see, an apple in the toe and hard candy, a shiny nickel, a spinning top or skipping rope and always a peppermint stick."

"Which one was your favorite?"

"I found my favorite presents under the tree not in my stocking."

Since he adored stories, I told him about my childhood Christmases in narrative form. By the time I finished, tears moistened his eyes.

"That is grand. I should like to have Christmas one day."

I threw my arms around him. He stood up and embraced me.

"Oh, Erik! You shall. You'll have a most festive Christmas this year."

The hours went by as I continued to tell him about my life using different anecdotes of which he never seemed to grow tired. His fascination increased and he'd ask for more.

"It's late. I'm a little tired."

"Oh, forgive me. I lost track of time. I shall take you back at once." He hopped up from his chair.

"Considering the hour, I'd prefer to retire here for the night if the offer still stands."

"Madam, my home and my life will always be open to you. Always."

"Perhaps tomorrow you will share with me stories from your own life."

He sighed. "Ahh, stories from my own life. How can I do that, my lady? My life began when I met you."

*****

I'd settled in his guest room but, heard piano music coming from the parlor. The soft soothing melodies helped me sleep.

I dreamt Erik and I waltzed at a masquerade ball. At the end of the night, at the unmasking, he removed his mask. I waited with excitement because I was certain the doctor had been correct. He wore one mask on top of another. I put my hands on the sides of his face and pulled off the second mask.

To my horror, I realized I'd pulled away his flesh. I held his pale skin in my fists. Erik screamed out in pain, slapped his hands over his face, and dropped to his knees. Blood dripped between his fingers as he fell to the floor. Still covering his face with his blood-soaked hands, he asked, "Why? Why, Olivia?"

I woke up screaming. Erik was pounding on my door. "Olivia? What's wrong? Let me in! What happened?"

With shaky hands, I turned on the lamps next to my bed just as Erik entered.

"What's wrong? Are you all right?" He switched on the dresser lamp and hesitated near the door. "Olivia?" He quickly looked around the room to see what was amiss.

"I...I...had a bad dream."

"Are you all right now?"

Barefaced, Erik still wore his white shirt, black trousers and boots. He approached me.

In his left hand, a knife dripped blood onto the carpet; his cuff stained brilliant red.

Breathing hard with terror and shaking from the residual abject fear from the dream, I jumped out of bed. “Get out! Get away from me!” I backed into a corner and held my hands out in front of me. “Go away!”

He continued forward instead of retreating. “Olivia?”

“Don’t come near me. I said go away!”

He dropped the knife by his feet, pivoted and rushed out of the room.

I came forward to pick up the blade. Instead of a bloody weapon, I found a fountain pen dripping red ink. The nightmare faded and I realized what I’d done.

Carrying a lamp, I went in search of him. I stopped at the door of the music room. Several lamps and candles burned brightly; the room had plenty of light. Erik sat at the organ with his back to me using a piece of cloth to wipe off red ink from his hand.

When he heard me approach, he jumped up and turned around. “Are you ready for me to take you back now?”

“Oh, Erik.” The score on which he worked contained nothing but notes written in red. “I’m so sorry.” I tried to embrace him, but he stiffened and took a step back.

“Get your things. I’m taking you to the hotel at once.”

“But I—”

“I told you to get your things.”

“I’d rather not.”

“You misunderstand me, Madam. I was not asking for your opinion. I was not asking if you'd rather." He stared at me with menace. "I shall not repeat myself."

I tried to think of something to say. My mind went blank.

"Leave me!"

I jumped at the volume of his voice. He'd turned his back to me and banged his fists on the keys of the organ. "Go!"

I ran to my room and threw the few things I'd unpacked into my suitcase. I put my cloak over my nightgown before slipping my feet into shoes without stockings.

In my haste, I tripped over my small valise and fell into a table. A marble statue crashed to the ground. I fell forward, hitting my head on the wall.

Upon hearing the clamor, Erik came from the music room. He paused in the doorway for a second before he knelt at my side.

"You're bleeding. You've cut your forehead." He cradled me in his arms, carried me to the parlor and laid me on the divan. Crimson droplets had fallen onto my white nightgown and splashed onto my lavender cloak.

Erik hurried away.

He came back with a wet cloth—which he tried to apply to my forehead. I pulled the towel from his hand. I held the cloth to my wound and waited for the bleeding to stop.

Sitting on the edge of the cocktail table in front of the couch, Erik met my eyes and then looked away.

"Do you have a mirror?"

"Pardon?"

"I'd like to see what I've done."

"The one in my bathroom is the closest." Erik showed me to his fancy, tiled bathroom. An elaborate gold, full-length mirror stood in a corner. Over the apex, a fringed piece of fabric hid the top portion. A person of Erik's height would not see his face—only his perfect attire. A knot tightened in my stomach. I checked myself in the mirror as Erik waited by the door. After I washed my face and hands, I turned to leave. I found myself alone.

Erik waited on the sofa with shoulders slumped; he cast his eyes downward when I entered. "I apologize. I shouldn't have raised my voice to you. And, I should have helped you with your bags."

"I'm quite all right. I wasn't careful and tripped. Nothing you could have done to prevent my clumsiness."

"Except catch you before you fell. However, I doubt you would have wanted me there. No, that's a lie. I *know* you wouldn't have wanted me there."

"I apologize for my behavior. I had a bad dream and I—"

"You didn't want to invite the monster of your bad dreams into your room. I understand." Erik scoffed.

"I never said you were a monster."

"You believe me to be one though."

"Why would you say such a thing?"

He jumped up from the sofa and pointed with anger toward the guestroom. "As soon as I advanced, you looked as though the angel of death approached."

"You startled me. Can I help that?"

"Your being startled is not the problem. The problem lies in your telling me I do not frighten you, but screaming in terror because I entered your room."

"I told you. I had a nightmare. I wasn't in my right mind. Anyone who came into the room would have elicited the same alarm."

Erik laughed. "You don't believe that any more than I do."

"You cannot know for sure what caused such a reaction."

"If you speak the truth, Olivia, tell me. What was the subject matter of your nightmare?"

I didn't answer. I *couldn't* answer.

"You cannot fool me. I've seen that expression too many times to mistake it for anything else. *I am* your nightmare. Admit it. Don't lie. It's beneath you."

Trying to respond to Erik's conundrum was too complex and pointless. Instead, I tried to redirect him. "Why were you up so late? Don't you sleep?"

"I was working on my opera. Everything had been going rather well until my houseguest screamed as though the demon host tried to lay with her."

Furious, blood rushed to my cheeks. "How can you say such a thing? How dare you! You, you…"

"Go ahead, Olivia. Tell me what I am."

"Stop it. You are trying to goad me into saying something I'll regret. It's as though you wish me to say the thing you fear hearing. Well, I won't play your game."

"I know what you wanted to say."

"No, you don't."

"I *am* a monster. You will not tell me anything I don't know, Madam. I've been told I'm a monster since the cradle. You won't shock me with such a revelation. One gets quite comfortable in the roles assigned to him."

"You are not a monster, Erik."

"I am. Maybe you don't realize you *should* fear me. Perhaps your intuition has not led you astray. You should scream." Without raising his voice, he said, "Please, allow me to take you back to the hotel now."

"Tell me right now. Should I fear you? Tell me the truth."

He closed his eyes for a moment before he took a deep breath. "I could never harm you. Never."

"What haunts you so, Erik? What keeps you from resting your head at night?"

"Countless reasons keep me from slumber."

"You are running from your past."

"Please, Olivia, don't pry into my past. I beg you. Let me be who you want me to be."

Chapter 29 Empathy

ERIK:

I'd just laid the finished score atop the organ with immense satisfaction when Olivia's scream shattered the tranquility of the night. Jumping up from the organ bench, I'd knocked over the inkwell onto the completed score. Instinctively, I tried to right the well, but a massive red blotch had soaked the paper and enveloped all the notes. The ink had spilt over my hand and wrist. It dripped off my cuff. At that moment, I didn't care.

In my haste to reach her room, I had turned the corner too sharply and slammed face first into the wall. The blow knocked my mask askew. I tossed the mask aside just to get it out of my way.

I recognized the look she gave me upon my entrance.

As a boy, when my keeper exhibited me in a cage, I'd tried to become numb to the expression of horror. At first, the audience's response surprised me. How could my face cause the ladies to scream, the children to cry out and clutch their mothers, while grown men turned away in disgust? I knew I was different, but the magnitude of the reactions astonished me.

In my child's heart, I tried to believe they might be playacting, going along with my keeper. He would whip them up into a frenzy by telling tales about *the devil's child* and the *face of death* before he unveiled the nightmare they feared.

Night after night, I dreaded the unmasking. I couldn't turn my face away because of the restraints.

Instead, I encountered a sea of terrified people staring at me—staring at a child. *They paid money to gawk at my ugliness.*

Everything seemed in slow motion. Their eyes widening, mouths gaping open in screams, heads turning away. My keeper displayed me until the last of the curious left the tent. Some nights an eternity passed before he allowed me to cover up again. Soon, he no longer needed to tie me up. I'd accepted my fate. *Where would I go even if I escaped?*

The faces of those who filed into my tent, their *reflexive* reaction, damaged my soul with every unveiling. Years later, after being exhibited in front of one of the largest crowds I'd ever drawn, something occurred to me. No one needed to instill fear into the crowd beforehand, at all. Fear of my face, my inhuman face, happened quite naturally. And because they feared me, I had power over them.

I slipped away one night and became my own keeper. I accumulated wealth from entertaining the crowd before terrifying them, but I still hated the unveiling. No. I hated *them*!

My burgeoning trust died when Olivia showed the same instinctive horror—within my own home—the place I created where no one could hurt me. Never in any packed house, in any traveling show across Europe, had I experienced pain in the deep, furtive place Olivia's reaction stabbed me. I had almost convinced myself she didn't care what was beneath the mask—until I came into her room barefaced. *Fool! Of course she cares.*

I needed to remove her from my house. Just like after each freak show performance, I craved solitude.

She tried telling me she had screamed because of a bad dream. I wanted to believe her. To be fair, I think she wanted to believe her own lie.

I appreciated the effort, but her mendacity did nothing for the cruel slashing of my hope that someday she might love me.

We were set to leave, but she stopped in front of the fireplace.

"Don't you know who I see, Erik?"

"You see something which makes you scream, Madam." I expected falsehearted words of consolation from the dear woman who'd never failed to show me kindness. I prepared myself for the next lie from her lips. Except—

"You speak the truth." She studied the carpet, cheeks turning pink.

I closed my eyes and absorbed all the pain so I would not fall weeping at her feet. Instead, I straightened my spine and held up my head. "Let's go now, Madam Weston, for I wish you to scream no more and have no nightmares from which you cannot wake."

She came towards me. I took a step back, for I didn't wish to prolong the goodbye. The sooner she was safe at the hotel, the sooner I might try to forget how close I'd come to what I prized most in the world.

"Wait a minute. I shall allow you to take me back as soon as you listen to what I have to say." She reached for my arm. I pulled away. If she touched me at all, I would break into a million pieces.

Instead, she turned and faced the fireplace so we stood next to one another in front of the hearth. "I will tell you why I screamed."

"You need not do so. I already know." I continued looking into the ashes of the long-dead fire.

"You *were* the subject of my nightmare."

I sighed with resignation. Her words tore through me. I wanted to be alone and find solace in my music. "Thank you for being truthful, Olivia. I don't care to hear any more. I would like to leave now." I turned away, but before I took a step, she grabbed my sleeve.

"I screamed because in my nightmare I took off your mask and—"

"What!?" I faced her. "Why are you telling me this? Can't you see this causes me pain? I do not wish to hear anymore."

"No, you misunderstood me. I didn't scream because the sight of you in my dream frightened me. I reacted because in that horrid dream, I hurt you. Seeing you hurt disturbed me more than I thought possible. *Hurting you* was the cause of my panic. The dream was terrifying, yes, but what terrified me wasn't your face. Horrible shame and sheer panic made me cry out because *I* was the source of your pain."

My breathing came in short bursts as I stared into her tear-streaked face.

She was not lying.

"But, when you woke from the dream, Olivia, when you were awake, you saw me without the mask. I frightened you so badly you screamed at me and fled into a corner like a wounded animal. You may have been free of your nightmare, but I had just stepped into mine."

Once again, she reached for me—and once again, I backed away from her.

"Erik, haven't you ever had a dream that was so real, even when you were awake, it felt as though the nightmare continued?"

I scoffed. "My entire life has felt as such."

"I'm sorry life has been like that for you, Erik."

"Apologies for my life are pointless."

"You needn't speak to me so sharply. I meant to extend to you a common courtesy. It's called empathy."

"I need nothing less than your empathy."

"Wrong! You need nothing more."

I desperately wanted to be alone, to hide within my music. She would leave for the United States and consider the whole experience to be a mistake in judgment.

"In my nightmare, I hurt you. You were bleeding. You rushed into my room and I saw this." She picked up my bright red hand. The ink had stained the cuff and had splattered all along the side of my shirt. Seeing this, I had the urge to laugh. It came on so fast; I didn't have time to understand what I found so humorous. She joined me in laughter while still holding my red hand palm-side up.

"So, yes, you were the subject of my nightmare and you caused me to scream when you came into my room, but not because you weren't wearing your mask. Do you understand what I'm saying? I would have screamed at anybody looking as if they dripped blood—Raoul, Philippe, the maid."

I believed her.

I had to.

Not having any words with which to express myself, I embraced her. She put her head against my shoulder, wrapped her arms around me.

After a few moments, she said, "Erik?"

"Yes?"

"I'd check your mask before you leave here again."

"What do you mean?"

"May I?" She removed it and showed me the bright red streak of ink from the temple to the cheek.

In my haste to discard my mask when she screamed, and then quickly re-cover my face afterward, I'd besmirched the leather. She tried to rub some of the ink off with her nightgown, but too much time had passed. She handed the mask back to me.

I was about to cover my face, but she grabbed my forearm. "Don't."

Panic filled my throat; my mouth dried making swallowing impossible. "I never feel whole without my mask."

She put one hand behind my neck, the other behind my head and pulled me forward. "You are not the mask. You are you."

I kissed her—wondering if my nightmarish life might have a different ending than the one I'd always pictured.

"I believe it's too late to go to the hotel now, don't you?" she whispered. "I think I'll retire right here." She'd unfastened her cloak and draped it over a chair.

I scooped her up and carried her back to bed. I slipped off her shoes. As I leaned down to cover her; she put her arms around my neck and clasped them together preventing me from leaving.

"Don't go."

"But—but . . ." I wasn't sure of her meaning.

"Shh, everything is fine." She pulled me closer until I sat on the bed.

We kissed. Her hands moved from around my neck. She slid them inside my partially unbuttoned shirt. Her fingertips caressed my bare skin. I inhaled sharply and forgot to exhale—until she pulled the shirt from my shoulders. The material fell down my back and away from my arms making me shiver.

A tinge of panic poked at my delight, but dissipated as she continued to touch me. I bathed in the sensation. She'd awakened my senses. I leaned forward and kissed her chin, her cheeks and forehead. My fingertips explored the curve of her neck and shoulders. I untied the ribbon holding her nightgown closed.

My hands travelled downward until I found the hem. With my heart beating at a pace I'd never known, I pulled the gown over her head. Short, brisk breaths escaped from me. Olivia breathed with the same rapidity. I placed my hand on her stomach, my fingers eager to experience the pleasure of her body.

She tensed up and drew back.

I leaned away from her. *Rejection*! *She can't stand the touch of your hands upon her. No one can.*

"Your hands are cold." She giggled.

My heart restarted with a jerk that reverberated from my head to my feet. "I'm sorry," I whispered. "They're always cold."

"Don't worry," she said. "They'll warm up."

I'd unfastened my trousers and abandoned them on the floor. She held the blankets back and allowed me to slide under them.

A lifetime of constrained carnal desire burst free and intoxicated me with anticipation. Savoring every touch, every stroke, I discovered a splendor so grand I could scarcely catch my breath. Touching her with gentle yearning, I learned the secret contours of a woman. Extraordinary stirrings of passion pleasured my mind. Vibrant physical sensations swathed my body. I never knew such a state of living existed.

The discovery of physical intimacy made me recognize the utter defenselessness of my soul. Giving completely of oneself meant surrendering to the possibility of total devastation. Instead of fretfully protecting my heart, I succumbed to complete vulnerability. I was hers to either cherish or destroy. I had to give Olivia something I'd never given anyone—my absolute trust. When I let go of my innate preservation instinct, her energy, her spirit connected with mine. Her sweetness quelled the anxious compulsion to separate myself from the rest of humanity. Her complete trust in me gave me security. Her desire gave me confidence.

I produced a symphony of harmonious physicality only love could create. My unbounded creativity elevated her to every pinnacle she wished to ascend. I led her to places that made her sigh, groan and whimper with euphoria until we had an overpowering need to connect our bodies.

Amid a surge of masculine confidence, I experienced a powerful *crescendo*—one I didn't realize any mortal man could ever reach. From there, I floated down as if in a dream. The experience left me feeling profound peace. At last, I was alighted and warmed by the flame of human dignity.

I would never again be the same. The life I lived before disappeared. I had a chance to begin again. This time not as a solitary entity. Now I belonged to Olivia.

Chapter 30 Missing

ERIK:

I'd kissed Olivia on the cheek and covered her sleeping form with the quilt before I slipped out and went straight to work on my opera. A smile never left my face as I composed with swiftness and conviction. The music jumped from my head onto the page with ease.

I was on my way to the costume room to get materials for a new mask when Carlotta shrieked. "Ahhhhh! I am robbed! I am been robbed!" She hit notes she usually failed to reach in her performances onstage. Agitation always made our prima donna's Spanish accent thicker and her tantrums more severe—thus, she became far more entertaining.

Once, she had been in a particularly foul mood and had been frustrating the entire cast with her thoughtless demands. I couldn't take her spoiled behavior anymore. As she opened her mouth to sing in front of a packed house, through my mastery of ventriloquism, I made her croak like a toad. Twice. During the tantrum following such humiliation, she'd stopped speaking French for forty minutes.

This time, as she squealed in dramatic dismay, I turned around within the wall to find a mirror. I wanted to witness what was sure to be an amusing floorshow of my own creation.

Carlotta screeched out a string of Spanish curse words which merged with the insane yapping of her annoying poodles. Her dressmakers rushed from the corner where they'd been gossiping. Her makeup woman came from down the hall. "What is wrong, Señora? Tell us what has happened."

"This! This!" She flung open the double doors to her dressing room.

The women scanned the room. "What's wrong, Señora? Nothing is amiss."

The infuriated diva had dropped her dog and pointed into the room. "Are you crazy? You no notice what is wrong? Are you blind to what they take from me?" She took a step back onto the paw of one her poodles. The canine yelped and then snapped at one of the dressmakers who tried to comfort him. Carlotta picked up her dog, turned on her heel and marched to the manager's office with a colorful mixture of Spanish and French curses emanating from her lips.

"What is wrong, Señora? What now?" Firmin asked.

"I have been burgled! Oh, me!" She put her arm to her forehead as though she might swoon.

"Did they take your chairs, prima donna?" Armand asked as he steadied her.

She snapped upright fully in charge of her faculties again. "Chairs? Bah! No! My flowers. My beautiful flowers, Monsieur. They were stolen in the night."

"Your flowers?" Armand lifted his eyebrows.

"All of them?" Firmin asked.

"You suppose I notice one flower missing or two flowers gone? Of course not! All of them. Those dozens and more of bouquets. All the giant sprays. The many big vases of roses. All the flowers of my adoring fans. Gone! Not a petal left." She stamped her foot grazing the other poodle. He yelped and moved aside.

Armand, Firmin, the makeup woman, the dressmakers and the yapping canines followed Carlotta as she complained in Spanish the entire way back to her dressing room. She flung the doors open even wider. "Every flower gone!"

They all peeked into the dressing room from the hallway.

"How in the world does one make off with a room full of flowers without being seen?" Firmin asked.

"Monsieurs, it was The Phantom." The dressmaker nodded heartily.

"Don't be absurd, woman. What would a ghost do with a room full of flowers?" Armand rolled his eyes.

"This is a mean thing someone does to me." Carlotta sighed. After pushing everyone out of her way, she entered her dressing room and threw herself on the pink velvet fainting couch.

"Ahhh! Dios Mio!" She bolted upright and pointed to the empty space in front of the couch. "Someone also take my new cocktail table."

I had seen enough. I feared I'd find myself laughing if I lingered any longer.

After gathering materials for the mask from the costume room, I headed back into the wall. Before I made my exit, someone behind me screamed, releasing bolts of alarm through my body. My muscles stiffened with surprise.

Whipping around, I found Christine Daae shaking in her spot. Hands covering her mouth, her eyes were wide and fearful.

With a swish of my cape and some distracting black smoke, I disappeared into the walls from whence I came.

I lingered behind the secret door for a moment to hear her account. She screamed until poor Firmin and Armand huffed and puffed their way to her.

"What is wrong, mademoiselle? Why are you screaming?" Firmin asked.

Armand inhaled sharply. "The child is as white as a ghost."

"He was here." The young woman's voice shook with fear. I moved to the closest mirror to watch the scene.

"Who?" Firmin and Armand asked.

Carlotta and her entourage now stood to the side watching.

"He was right here." Christine pointed to the place where I'd stood a minute before.

"Who, dear?" Armand asked.

"The Opera Ghost!" Christine slapped her hands over her mouth.

The dressmakers, the makeup woman, and Carlotta gasped.

Armand tried to soothe the child's nerves. "There's no phantom here, my dear. Perhaps a shadow of one of the stage hands—"

"Yes, he's right. These hallways are dim. Perhaps a scene mover taking care of the set." Firmin smiled awkwardly.

"No, it was *him.*"

"What does he look like?" the makeup woman asked.

"Was he in formal clothes?" One of the dressmakers wondered.

"Was he tall and thin?" the other inquired.

Carlotta pushed her way to the front. "Who cares about that? The question is this: Was the fiend carrying flowers?"

Christine shook her head. "No flowers. He wore a black suit. Not eveningwear. Just a very nice suit."

I rolled my eyes. Of course not. It was morning. I wore appropriate clothing for daytime. What did they take me for?

Christine addressed the managers. "He had a cape and a wide brimmed hat, but the face! Oh, the face, was so horrible."

"A mask?" her impromptu audience asked all at once.

"No, I would have thought so, except—blood ran down the side of his face. Monsieurs, I swear to you. He was bleeding."

Carlotta swooned into the arms of the managers as she had threatened to do earlier. I left them to do their fawning over the overbearing soprano.

A terrifying thought occurred to me. *Why is Christine Daae at the opera house? Shouldn't she be with Raoul on their honeymoon? If that bungling, nitwit boy has boggled my chance for some time with Olivia, I shall kill him.*

After I returned home, I tapped on the door to the bathroom. "Olivia?"

"I'm almost finished, dear. I'll be out in a moment. I'm getting dressed now."

To get rid of some nervous energy, I put on a pot of coffee and set the table. A few minutes later, Olivia emerged looking radiant. She smiled at me as I stood next to the table. I couldn't contain my excitement. I rushed to her and took her in my arms.

"Put me down, you fiend." She giggled.

"Never."

"Then carry me to the table if you shan't let my feet touch the earth."

"As you wish." I cradled her in my arms.

"You must do something about your mask, my dear."

"I shall. I need to tell you something first." I set her down in the chair.

"Tell me what?"

"Christine and Raoul did not run off together."

"No, you're wrong. They left after he dropped me off at the hotel." She poured a cup of coffee.

I sat across from her. "No, Olivia, they haven't run away. She's still here."

Her eyes scanned the room as if Christine lurked in a corner. "Here?"

"I meant, well, what I meant to say—earlier today, I noticed she was still at the opera house."

"You were at the opera house today? Already?"

"I-I…had some business to attend to and I—"

"Erik, no! Why didn't I see the connection before? You are the Opera Ghost, aren't you?"

I wanted to disappear or find a dark corner somewhere. The lights in my house seemed intolerably bright. I focused on my empty teacup.

"What are you doing? Why did you…? Are we under the opera house? Is that where we are?"

I closed my eyes before I answered her. "Yes."

The mantle clock counted out each elongated second as she stared at me. My face burned under the mask.

Her brow wrinkled. "Why?"

"Why what?"

"Why do you scare them so? Why did you cause—"

She stood, shoving her chair back so hard it fell over behind her. Her eyes widened with terror. "You killed that man. She slapped her hands over her mouth as if she might scream or take ill.

"No, I did not!" I slammed both fists on the table making the china cups clink in their saucers. "I most certainly did not kill that man. He took his own life. They blamed me for his death—the same way they blame every unfortunate thing that happens in the opera house on me."

Her hands came from her mouth. She held them at her sides in tight fists. "I don't understand. The night I fell when everyone rushed out, you told them who to cast. You told them you'd do terrible things if they didn't obey you. People were hurt in the chaos. I was injured."

"You don't know how terrible I felt about that."

She stood frozen, staring at me. I must've been a sight in the 'bleeding' mask.

"Please, Olivia, let me explain. You don't understand."

"Why are you down here? What purpose do you have scaring people who only want to do their jobs? You don't have the right to…" She was silent for a moment. "You take money from them, as well. Philippe told me how the Opera Ghost demands money or people will die. My God, Erik! What kind of man are you?"

"Apparently, a very bad one."

"Indeed."

"May I explain myself now or would you like to continue to make assumptions and hurl accusations?"

She went to sit down, but never took her eyes off me. Since the chair had fallen behind her, she ended up on her backside sprawled on the floor. I rushed forward to assist her.

"Stay away from me. I don't need your help."

"Shall you blame me for this, too? Did The Phantom pull the chair out from under you?"

"No, but The Phantom pulled the wool over my eyes."

"Begging your pardon, Madam, but I don't understand your idiom."

"You fooled me. You made me think you were one kind of man when, in fact, you knew you were quite different than the person you represented."

"Exactly, how did I do that?"

"You pretend to be an honorable gentleman—an artistic genius. When, in fact, what you are is an extortionist."

"To be fair, you're partially correct. I may have pretended to be honorable, but I never 'pretended' to be an artistic genius."

"All this—" She gestured around the room at its opulence. "—is from ill-gotten gain."

"Once again, your idiom?"

"I think you know what it means. *Vous êtes devenu riche en accumulant la maladie de la graiss.*"

"What did you say?"

"I said, '*Vous êtes devenu riche en accumulant la maladie de la graisse.*' You've amassed your wealth through ill-gotten gain."

Unable to control my amusement, I chuckled. "Madam, you just informed me I became wealthy by accumulating the disease of greasiness."

The corners of her mouth turned up as she fought her smile.

I'd righted the chair and helped her sit. The fact she didn't refuse my assistance relieved me.

"Please, listen to me for just a minute. I have—" I chuckled. "—neither amassed my wealth by accumulating diseases of any sort, nor did I become rich by 'ill-gotten gain.' I was an incredibly wealthy man long before I began extorting money from the opera managers."

"So, you admit it is extortion."

"Oh my, yes. Nothing but."

"If you are already wealthy then why do you terrorize these people?"

I shrugged. "Sheer boredom, I suppose."

"That, my dear Frenchman, is the worst excuse I've ever heard."

"That, my dear American, is not an excuse. It's the truth. I provide some service with the payment. Truly, I do. The fools who run my theatre are always making mistakes that I need to fix wthout their knowledge. I can't tell you how many accounting errors alone I've corrected. If it were not for me, they would have been out of business by now. Their casting is atrocious. They possess no talent for staging. I must insist they take direction from me in order to preserve the integrity of the opera itself. I believe I earn my keep."

"I suppose you use your magic?"

"I use whatever means necessary."

"You told me you were a contractor and an architect. Is this true?"

"Yes, I helped build the opera house."

"And then decided to occupy it?"

"To be quite honest, I was here first. Think about it. A building is constructed from the bottom up. I created my home down here during the early stages of construction. The opera house was built on top of *my* residence."

"And…you aren't responsible for all the horrible things that are attributed to the Opera Ghost?"

"No." *Not all of them.*

"All right, Erik. I believe you. Somehow, I fear I have merely scratched the surface here."

"Nevertheless, we must take care of another matter of urgency."

"What? Oh! Christine and Raoul! Something must be wrong. If my cousin returned and found me missing, I don't know what he might do."

If that vain fashion slave involved the police, no telling how this could end.

"I should go," she said.

"Let's put together a plan first, shall we?"

Chapter 31 Christine

OLIVIA: Erik couldn't risk taking me out through the tunnels into the street during the day, so he took me through the labyrinth between the walls of the opera house. I started to ask him questions, but he swung around and put a finger to his lips.

I trailed after him as he moved through the walls with finesse. Almost all the mirrors were, in fact, windows through which Erik could watch the world.

He showed me what lever to pull in order to get into Monsieur Armand's, office. "You know what to do?" he whispered.

"Yes. I'll slip in after you create a diversion outside to lure him away."

"Perfect." He kissed my hand, turned his back and scurried through the narrow passageway.

A loud crash sent Monsieur Armand rushing from behind his desk. I pulled the lever and stepped inside.

Poor Armand almost had a spasm when he came back and found me seated in his reception area.

"Madam Weston, you gave me a start. I thought I'd seen a ghost." He chuckled. "All this nonsense about the Opera Ghost is starting to get to me. To what do we owe this great honor?"

"I was searching for my cousin, Raoul. Is he here?"

"Why, no, Madam. I have not seen him. Did you check with Mademoiselle Daae?"

"Please, take me to her, Monsieur. I'd like to visit with Miss Daae."

"Certainly." He offered his arm and took me to Christine.

"Mademoiselle Daae, I would like to introduce to you a relative of our patrons. This is Madam Weston."

"How do you do?" She curtsied and gave me a smile.

"Monsieur, may I have a moment alone with the young lady?"

"Of course." He bowed and left Christine and me in the privacy of her dressing room.

"Have you seen Raoul?" I asked, speaking French.

She slumped down at her dressing table and sobbed into her handkerchief. I put my hand on her shoulder. "What's the matter?"

"His brother, Madam, he's taken him away so we cannot be together." Christine, realizing the weakness of my French, spoke slowly and sprinkled a few English words into our conversation. Soon we'd established a means to sufficient communication.

"The Count will not let us marry. He's taken Raoul away." She dabbed at her eyes. "Raoul told me he confides in you."

"He does."

"Will you help us?" She sniffled.

"I'll try, Mademoiselle."

The miserable child threw herself into my arms. "Thank you, Madam."

"First, you must do what I ask, Christine."

"Oh! Anything. Anything at all."

"I'll need you to accompany me across town to the Hotel Debonair."

"Yes, of course. I'll do anything you ask."

We hailed a brougham to take us to the hotel.

I inquired whether I had any messages using my assumed name. The front desk clerk handed me a sealed envelope. I took the note outside to read in the sunshine.

Dear Cousin,

I have told Philippe you ran into an old friend who offered you a visit to her home. I will be back for you on Friday. I fear if Philippe doesn't hear from you by then, he will become suspicious and our plan will be ruined. Christine and I had to postpone our wedding. Philippe has insisted I accompany him on business.

I will meet you here Friday.

Your cousin,

R

Once we'd returned to the opera house, I accompanied Christine back to her dressing room where I was to wait for Erik *alone*.

"Mademoiselle Daae, would you mind getting me a cup of tea?

"Oh, of course."

As soon as she walked out, I scribbled a note on stationary from her desk saying one of the Chagny servants came to fetch me home.

Erik entered by moving a large mirror on some sort of pivot.

We hurried through the corridors behind the walls until we came to his home. Again, we went through an odd mirrored room. Erik kept his head down the whole time. I wondered why a man who hated his reflection had a room filled with mirrors. When I asked him, he dismissed my question with a shake of his head and a curt gesture which told me he did not care to discuss it.

Chapter 32 Sleep

OLIVIA: Erik led me into the music room. "I said yours would be the first ears to hear my opera and I am a man of my word." He gestured to a seat next to the piano.

"You finished your opera?"

"Yes. At last."

"I'm honored to be the first to hear *Don Juan*." I took my seat. "I can't wait."

"I changed the title from 'Don Juan' to '*Don Juan Triumphant'*. He kissed my hand, his eyes never leaving mine. "You, my lady, are my inspiration, my motivation, and my muse."

From the moment his fingers hit the first chords, his music kept me spellbound. The music started out sad, so tragic—I found myself crying. The middle portion filled the air with unusual, but beautiful sounds. Many of them contained an intense rage and haunting confusion. The ending began with sweet longing and advanced to cheerful melodies, but the last few arrangements burst forth with the joy of triumph, the pleasure of a quest fulfilled.

Marvelous music filled the room. He possessed the perfect reach on a piano as though God made his fingers to dance across the keys with grace. His hands fascinated me as he played with confidence and elegance.

He gave everything to the notes and ivory keys. The music consumed him. I would have wagered he didn't remember I was in the room. In his mind, he traveled through the keys into the wires and hammers of the piano and became the music. The transformation kept me enthralled.

I appreciated his deep desire to produce and capture beauty. I understood why Erik didn't allow anyone to see his work. He put his spirit into each piece and tried to protect his art from the world—a cruel world from which he felt the need to retreat. The man who wrote the music, painted the painting, or sculpted the stone, lived inside each creation. Each piece required defending—a fierce lover's protection.

Erik exuded passion. Now I was the beneficiary of his blazing, fervent love. To be the recipient of such allegiance was a privilege.

When he finished playing, his hands fell to his lap. His head bowed with exhaustion; perspiration dampened his hair and shirt.

The ingeniousness of what I'd witnessed left me breathless. He swiveled toward me. He didn't need or want my approval. Our eyes met. *I understand; I understand exactly what your music expressed.* He'd allowed me into his world, showed me a piece of his soul. In doing so, we created a bond which could never be broken.

I stood and opened my arms to him. "Come here." He rushed forward still breathing hard from his performance. I held him until his breathing returned to normal.

After I let him go, I began gathering the crunched-up failures covering the floor. I tossed a handful of scores into the fire. The flames roared up and spit a few tiny pieces of paper onto the grate. My gesture moved him to tears.

"Oh, Olivia." He stared at me from behind his mask. "You complete everything," he whispered.

"Thank you for allowing me to experience the beauty of your opus."

"Why should you not hear my music? This opera belongs to you." He embraced me. Despite whatever tragedies transpired in Erik's past, at that moment he was happy. He rocked me with gentleness as I leaned into his chest.

I broke the embrace and held both of his cold hands in mine, giving each one a kiss. The acidic odor of ink remover still lingered on his fingers.

He swooped me up in his strong arms and carried me to the guestroom. After he'd placed me upon the bed, he turned off the lamps and blew out the candles. He tossed his mask onto the nightstand.

I caressed his cheek, but he pulled away. "Does it hurt when I touch your face?"

"Your touch could never cause me pain."

"You know what I mean."

"Certain places. Nothing to worry about, my love."

"Certain places where?"

He didn't answer. Instead, he gave me a passion-filled kiss. All questions left my thoughts. I let the magic of Erik's love-making take me to a secret place of his own design—a place that didn't exist until he created it.

*****

Once again, I woke up alone. How I wished he'd hold me in his arms until morning. In all the days I'd stayed at his house, he'd never slept in my room. He waited until I fell asleep and then drifted away.

The next morning, I'd find him wearing the same clothing as the day before. I'd assumed Erik kept late hours working on his music or art. After we ate breakfast, he'd go to his bathroom, bathe and change, but he never opened his bedroom door.

I turned on the bedside light and carried a candle to the mantle in order to read the clock. *Where could he be at four thirty in the morning?* I set out to find him.

A slight rustle of papers came from the corner of the music room. Erik lay on the divan behind the piano. He rested on his side, his legs hanging over the edge of the couch as though he'd simply fallen over from exhaustion. In one hand, he clutched a pen and the other, a piece of music.

I didn't see a quilt or throw anywhere with which to cover him. In the corner, a purple velvet drape covered the top portion of a mirror just as I'd seen on the one in the bathroom. I yanked the material off to use as a blanket.

I gasped, my stomach tightened.

In the portion of the mirror, where he would've seen his face, Erik had marred the glass. Deep scratches and an angry series of slashes evidenced a moment of utter despair and self-loathing. I stared at the destruction. The back of my neck turned hot with anger at a cruel world that tormented a man as talented and sensitive as Erik.

I placed the drape over him.

Before I blinked, he'd yanked me off my feet and thrown me onto the divan. I hadn't even caught my breath before Erik held a knife to my throat.

In the second of recognition, he dropped to his knees next to me. He tossed the knife aside.

"Olivia, forgive me! Are you injured? Did I hurt you? I didn't know it was you."

Everything transpired so fast; it took me a moment to come to my senses. "What happened?"

"Are you all right? Did I hurt you?" Erik's voice shook with concern; fear shot from his eyes.

"I'm not sure. Did you throw me down?"

"I did. I apologize. I reacted before I recognized you. Do you need medical help? Can you stand? Did you hit your head?" He felt all around my skull before he picked up a lamp and peered into my eyes. He pulled each eyelid open in turn. "Look up. Look down. Can you focus?"

"No."

"You can't? We may need to get you to the hospital."

"Erik, I couldn't focus *before* you threw me."

Tears wetted his eyes. "Please, Olivia, be serious."

"I'm fine. You just knocked the breath out of me."

"What were you doing in here?"

"Looking for you. You were asleep and I wished to cover you. This room is rather drafty."

"I *was* asleep, wasn't I?"

"Yes, you were."

"I fell asleep," he said. "I slept." He sat next to me and shook his head in disbelief.

After a few seconds, he grabbed my hands. "Are you sure you're not injured?"

"Erik, when was the last time you slept?"

He laughed. "About a minute and a half ago."

"I meant before that."

"An eternity." Upon noticing the velvet drape crumpled on the floor, he asked, "You covered me?"

"Yes, I told you. The air is chilly down here." My intent to protect him from the cold seemed to amaze him.

He blinked a couple of times. "You've given me a second chance," he said.

"A second chance at what?"

"Life."

I thought he was teasing, so I giggled, but he didn't join me.

"Why can't you sleep, Erik? Why did you react with such panic?"

"I don't require a lot of sleep. I never have."

"But, lately you've slept less?"

"You could say that, yes."

"Do you always sleep with your mask?"

"Unless I'm in my own bedroom, I prefer to keep it on."

"Well, come on. Let's put you to bed. You'll feel better with some sleep."

"No!" He jumped up. "I'm fine. Honestly."

"Come on." I picked up the lamp and waited. He didn't make a move, so I went back and took him by the hand.

"No, I don't want to, Olivia. I'd rather not."

He tensed up as we approached his hallway, so I led him to my room instead. "Come on."

"No, I don't think I can. I've already slept tonight. I appreciate what you're trying to do."

I pulled back the covers. Something in his demeanor told me, despite his protestation, he longed to lie down and fall asleep.

He sat on the edge of the bed. "You lie down, Olivia. It's so early in the morning. You go ahead. I'll tell you a story."

I removed his boots. He didn't seem to have the strength to argue with me. I pulled back the covers further and indicated he should get in bed.

"This won't work, Olivia."

He laid his head on the pillow next to mine. I sat on my side of the bed and scooted up next to him. "I have an idea. How about I tell you a story? A bedtime story."

"A bedtime story?" He let out a heavy sigh. "I've never been told one before."

"Maybe you can't sleep because of this." I indicated the mask.

"No." He held the sides, securing the mask in place. "It doesn't bother me."

"Try to sleep without it. If you're uncomfortable, we'll put it back on. Look, I'll turn down the light." He didn't respond. He gazed at me for a long moment before he put his hands down.

I placed the mask on the nightstand.

"Oh, Erik."

Scars from years of perpetual rubbing of leather against skin encircled his face. Red abrasions blended with raised, white ridges where his flesh had healed only to be rubbed raw again. Rarely uncovered and exposed to air and never exposed to sunlight, the jaundice skin on his cheeks, chin and forehead appeared fragile, like parchment. A crevice separated his top lip into two halves. Discolored skin surrounded his deep-set, golden eyes; the drastic, dark circles made his eyes appear set even further back. Transparent skin ended at an exposed portion of skull alongside his right temple. Slim blue and purple veins cobwebbed across his face ending at the gaping hole where his nose should have been.

I swallowed hard and tried not to cry. "Is this where it hurts?" I indicated on my own face where the edge of the new mask had chafed thin serrations into his face.

"I'm used to it," he whispered.

No human should be used to that. I rose from the bed.

"Where are you going?" He bolted upright, alarmed.

"I'm not going anywhere." I searched through my toiletries case until I found a soothing salve.

"What is that? Let me see." He held out his hand to take the tub from me as I sat down.

"Just let me do this, Erik." I swiveled away from him until he pulled his hand back and laid down again.

After dipping my fingertips into the tub, I gently applied the salve onto the hotspots. Erik watched me with wide eyes. Tears ran down his pallid cheeks. I wondered if he ever looked at his mother with the same tender expression and those pleading eyes.

Erik's light saffron irises sometimes reflected illumination in a manner which made them appear to glow. His blazing eyes and their beseeching gaze could not conceal a tragic, hopeless past.

I replaced the lid and turned back to him.

He said, "No one has ever cared for me like this. No one has ever cared for me *at all.* A thousand years wouldn't give me enough time to thank you. You heal me. Your touch relieves not only my skin or my body, but my mind." He shot up in a quick motion. "Stay with me, please. Marry me, Olivia. Anywhere you go, I'll go, too. If you don't wish to stay down here, we won't stay. We can live anywhere you want. If you so desired, I would help manage your estate in New York. Anything for you. With you by my side, I can live *out in the world.*"

"Are you trying to make an honest woman of me?" I put the tub of salve on the nightstand.

"You are the most honest, virtuous, loving woman I've ever met. I couldn't make you anything you are not already."

"Let's not discuss this now. It's too early in the morning."

He smiled and fell back on his pillow. "That was not a 'no'."

"It was not a 'no'. Now, try to get some sleep."

"Not now. I'll never be able to sleep."

"Oh, no. Monsieur Erik thinks he's too excited to sleep. What could we do to tire him out? I blew out the lamp.

Afterward, I stayed awake in order to stop him from sneaking out of bed. To my surprise, he put his arm around me, pulled me closer. Before long, his breathing became slow and steady.

"Are you awake?" I whispered. My answer came from the hushed sounds of sleep, the music of the night. I closed my eyes, satisfied and full of joy.

I decided the next day I would insist he tell me why he couldn't sleep and why he reacted so strangely when I covered him. He trusted me. I hoped he would be ready to share what haunted him. Only one more day remained before Raoul was to pick me up at the hotel.

Chapter 33 It's Yours

ERIK:

I'd awakened before Olivia. I had slept in a bed and rested my head on a pillow without horrifying nightmares. God had given me a chance to redeem myself. God had given me Olivia.

I never thought I would seek out forgiveness from a God I swore abandoned me upon my birth. I'd done such evil and despicable things. I'd pushed Him far away. I had wrapped myself in hatred, in darkness and evil, in order to forget I'd been, at one time, a child of God. Listening to Olivia breathing as she lay in my arms, made me long for absolution.

I slipped out of bed without disturbing her. A realization made me shiver. A forgotten promise to a dark master shadowed my thoughts. The evil one would never willingly let me return to the light.

Olivia's goodness had kept any iniquitous thoughts from invading my mind. I refused to think about what would happen when she left my world for hers, but it was Friday. She had to go back.

*****

We sat across from one another at the table drinking coffee. She had something she wanted to discuss with me. Whatever she wished to talk about made her uneasy. A nervous smile played on her lips.

"Tell me." I set my teacup down.

"I was not meaning to tell you anything, but ask you something."

"Go on."

"Did you really mean the opera was mine?"

"Absolutely."

"I wanted to ask if I can share this gift. Let it be performed and maybe—"

"Oh, no, Olivia."

"But, the music is so beautiful."

"They would only ruin my work." I focused on the teacup in front of me.

"What if you had creative control?"

"You mean…" I met her eyes again.

"Maybe it's time you earned your salary."

"Olivia, I told you. I earn my keep."

"Prove it." She smiled at me.

I thought about her request for a moment. *Suppose the Opera Ghost sent the managers an opera. What would they do if I demanded they perform the show? I could decide the casting, the stage direction….*

"You are thinking about it, aren't you, Erik?"

*****

I lingered in the darkness of an alleyway as the driver pulled away from the curb. He carried everything that meant anything to me inside that carriage. With a flip of my cape, I returned to the tunnel.

The last place I wanted to be was the lonely house on the lake. I decided to spend time in the opera house instead. I couldn't wait to see what they would do with notes I'd written them. The night would be long and restless.

The next morning, they didn't disappoint me.

"Armand, tell me this is not the most absurd thing you've ever heard."

"The whole thing is ridiculous, Firmin. We cannot give-in to this lunatic's demands anymore. His own opera? What next? Will he demand to be the soprano?"

They laughed.

"I hate to ask, but is the music any good? Can you tell?" Firmin asked.

"I don't know. Let's find Maestro. We'll let him take a look—I mean for curiosity sake. I don't intend to take orders from a ghost. Who is this man that signs his letters O.G. for Opera Ghost? I mean, really."

"Indeed. Who is the O.G.?" The two of them walked side by side to find Maestro. I walked parallel with them within the walls.

"Monsieur Firmin, Monsieur Armand, just the two I wanted to see." Maestro's cheeks glowed red. He held my rolled-up letter in his hand. "What is the meaning of this?"

"You received one, too?"

"What is this nonsense? A spoiled specter will not instruct me. The madman claims he's written an opera. Look here, he gave me instructions on everything. The fiend has told me how to conduct my own orchestra. How dare he! This is an atrocity."

"What do you mean instructions?" Armand asked.

"For example, here." He pointed to a line on the paper I'd left with my letter. "He's told me to watch my Ligature in the Second Act. He told me to make sure his end score is in *Vivace*. Two pages of reminders and suggestions. The nerve!"

"Did he leave you a copy of the opera?" Firmin asked.

"No, the obnoxious ghoul has told me how to conduct music I have yet to see. Well, let me tell you. I can't wait to see this opera. I've studied with the best. I'd be glad to point out his amateur mistakes. The gall this O.G. has—thinking he can write an opera as though any old phantom off the street can compose. Wait until I read his mangled score and libretto; he won't be so smug then. Why, I bet he's made a grand mess of things. If he thinks I am going to stand for this nonsense, he's got another thing coming."

Firmin handed a partial stack of my work to Maestro. He scanned the sheet waiting for the right moment to pounce on any error. When he finished reading the first page, he tossed the sheet on the ground with a dramatic flick of his wrist. He read through the second page; looked at the managers, then back at the music. He discarded that score as well.

"This must be a trick," he mumbled after he read the third page. After the fifth page, he dropped to his knees and began collecting the discarded music from the floor.

"Maestro, are you telling us the music is good?"

He ignored Armand and called for his pianist to come forward. "Pierre, come here at once." He shoved the papers into the man's hands. "See what you can make of this."

The pianist shuffled the papers together to create a more orderly stack. "This says Act One, Scene One, sir." He tried to hand Maestro the score.

"I know that." The conductor rolled his eyes in frustration. "I meant for you to play it."

Pierre walked away with the sheets in his hand. Maestro shouted, "I want to hear you play the music." The pianist nodded and kept walking, his eyes glued to the score. "No, no, right now. Play the piece now."

Pierre took his place at the piano and continued reading the music before his hands touched the keys. He turned from the first page to the second. After reading a few lines, he stood up. "Maestro, whose work is this?"

"Never mind. Show us. Go ahead. Let's hear the first score."

Pierre began to play as the other orchestra members continued tuning up, talking and cleaning their instruments unaware of the Opera Ghost's newest demand. Maestro banged his wand on the stand a little harder than necessary. The musicians stopped warming up. "I demand quiet." He turned back to the pianist who had stopped playing. "Not you, Pierre." He faced the managers, rolled his eyes again.

My music filled the hall. One by one, the other musicians came forward and stood around the piano while Pierre manhandled my work. I hoped with practice he might play the score properly, perfectly. The way it was written.

When the pianist finished the demonstration, he gasped. "Where's the rest?" He was like a ravenous dog. He'd tasted greatness and he wanted more.

Firmin handed my leather satchel containing the rest of the opera to Maestro.

"I guess it's settled?" Armand asked his partner.

"I guess it is," Firmin answered. "We are going to perform the madman's opera."

"This is absurd," Armand said as they walked back to the offices.

"Yes, but think of the queue."

"What about his other demands, Firmin? We're to keep with his casting and he reserves the right to change any staging or costuming. Do we relinquish so much power to anyone for the sake of a franc?"

"Oh, no, Armand. We relinquish so much power to anyone for many, many, francs." They laughed. I didn't care to follow them anymore. They would start rehearsals at once and I needed to continue to coach the prima donna—the leading lady of the moment, Christine Daae.

*****

"Angel? Are you here?" the young soprano asked when I called her name from behind the mirror.

"It is I."

"I've missed you, Angel. I thought I'd upset you and you'd left me forever."

"Let's start, shall we, my dear? You are going to be a big star once the new opera is performed. You have a decision to make, Mademoiselle. Will you stay and become a world famous opera singer or will you go with your young suitor and marry?"

My words shocked her. Her face lost color. "I don't know."

"Yes, you do."

"What should I do? Tell me, dear Angel."

"I cannot decide for you."

"I want to do both."

I shook my head. The child had tried my patience more than once. I'd never seen such a fickle girl before. A beautiful young woman, but still a child in so many ways.

"You cannot do both, dear."

"But, I want to."

She had reached my limit for silly girl antics. My success depended on her. Should she ruin the opera, the audience would only remember her failure. They would not hear the words nor listen to the music. They would take notice of a girl whose role was bigger than her voice.

"If you take the role in the new opera, *Don Juan Triumphant*, your heart must lie only with music. You must be faithful to the opera. No one else can have your love. You must live for your music. You cannot accept any social engagements for the duration. If you cannot make this commitment, you have taken your last curtain call, Mademoiselle."

"Oh, Angel! I want to sing."

"We must get on with the lesson at once. Think of nothing else, my child. For now, this opera is your *only* love."

Chapter 34 Truth

OLIVIA: Raoul knocked on my door as I sat at the desk in my room practicing Braille. "Come in."

Without a word, he slumped into the chair by my bed.

"Are you all right, cousin?" I closed the book and faced him.

He glanced at my maid. "Shall we take a quick walk out on the grounds, Cousin Olivia?"

Soon we were out of earshot from the house and he stopped walking.

"Christine doesn't love me anymore. What did I do to fall out of her favor? She refuses to let me call upon her."

"Don't be silly, Raoul. When I was with the girl she was heartbroken. She'd worked herself into hysterics at the thought of *not* being with you."

"She's changed her mind." He handed me a note.

Dear Raoul,

Please make no effort to contact me for I will be busy with the new opera, Don Juan Triumphant. The Angel has made his instructions clear. I cannot see you anymore nor may I engage in any social commitments. If I am to star in this opera, I must put all of my efforts into rehearsal and instruction. My tutor said I must choose between you and taking the lead role in the new opera. Please, do not try to contact me.

Apologies,
Christine

"Raoul, listen to me. Young girls are easily swayed. They say things they don't mean. Don't worry. I wager as soon as she realizes what she's done, she will contact you and beg your forgiveness." I linked my arm through his and we began walking again.

"Do you believe so?"

"I'm certain. Is her taking the lead role in this opera so terrible? Perhaps this will be the last one before you are to be married."

"Yes, you're right," he said with reluctance. He lifted his head. "Yes, of course. She says she needs to study for this new role. There's nothing about breaking our engagement in here." He looked down at the letter again. A cloudy, worrisome look crossed his face.

"Is there something else bothering you?"

"Christine's singing tutor." He lowered his voice. "She believes him to be an angel. A *real* angel."

I chuckled. "She doesn't believe an actual angel is tutoring her, does she?"

"In the very literal sense. She says she's never seen him. Only heard him. He's been angry with her for the last week and refused to tutor her. That's what brought on this letter.

She will do anything he says. Even push me out of her life."

"Why would this so-called angel do such a thing?"

"Because he's jealous of me."

"Does Christine not see the ludicrousness of the situation?"

"That's the problem, Olivia. She does not. She fears him. He's a very harsh taskmaster. The angel, whoever he is, has left her disheartened. On rare occasions, he gives her praise. Yet, she lives for that infrequent encouragement."

"What do you mean?"

"For example, he left her a single rose with a note attached telling her he was pleased with her last performance. I thought she might faint. A dressing room filled with flower arrangements, but what pleased her most was a single rose. Cousin, Olivia, she wouldn't care if the audience buried her in flowers. She will only try to please this horrible angel."

"Why doesn't she listen to you about the angel not being real?"

"She says her father told her when he died he would send the Angel of Music down from heaven to look after her." Raoul scoffed. "This tutor? He is no angel. He's no more of a spirit than you or me. At first, I didn't understand. Why would he treat her so harshly? Why does he prevent her from seeing me? Now everything makes sense."

"What do you mean?"

Raoul stopped walking. "He is in love with her."

"Maybe there is another explanation aside from a man being in love with her.

"I have a theory."

"What is it?"

"The man who demands money from the managers, the fiend who insists his orders be followed; the lunatic who runs around the opera house terrorizing the employees is one and the same as Christine's angel."

"W-what makes you say that?"

Raoul didn't answer me. "I'm going to find this angel—-this phantom and when I do, he will be good and bloody at the end of my sword!" He made a violent thrust with his arm as if he stabbed his sword into the Phantom—-into Erik. The gesture made me gasp.

"Raoul, please stop."

"My apologies, Cousin Olivia, but I would not mind seeing this murderer dead." He had a fiery look in his eyes; the kind men get when they set their sights on revenge.

"What are you going to do?"

"Here's my plan. He's insisting Christine play the lead role in this upcoming opera, so, of course, he'll be there to watch her. I will order the theatre to be surrounded by the police. Maybe even armed guards stationed at all the exits." Raoul stopped walking. "Why Cousin Olivia, you are shaking. Am I scaring you with all this talk of dark angels and phantoms?"

"I'm not sure your plan is a good one. I think you should wait until the end of the opera's run. Let her be the prima donna, Raoul. She'll come back to you afterward."

He stopped short and turned towards me. "What if this madman hurts her? What if she upsets him for some reason? Suppose Christine does not do well enough to please him? What we're dealing with here is a lunatic with a colossal ego. A very dangerous man."

"I'm sure he wouldn't hurt her. He's her teacher. He wants her to excel. He wouldn't harm her."

"Don't you know, Cousin Olivia? Hasn't anyone told you about this supposed ghost? He's murdered people. There are plenty of horror stories about this monster."

"Stories?" I tried to swallow, but my mouth went dry.

"Stories about this mysterious ghost have continued to circulate between cast and crew for years. People have witnessed his lethal propensity. Do you know how this crazy man kills?"

"No."

"He murders people with an Asian lasso. The thin catgut rope works as a noose. He sneaks up on the victim. Before they blink, their necks are broken with one practiced yank." Raoul gestured a violent tug. "The victim is dead."

"Oh, Raoul, this cannot be true."

"I've heard the stories myself. Do you know who told me one such story, Olivia?"

"No."

"Joseph Buquet."

"Who is he?"

"He's the man who was found hanging at the end of a noose during Act IV. Christine says the night before he died, he made fun of the ghost in front of the ballerinas. He laughed and dared the ghost to come and get him."

"But—"

"I know what you're going to say. When I heard the tales, I thought the legend of the ghost was a figment of the active imaginations of the young girls in the ballet or actors seeking attention. However, I thought about the Buquet incident and realized his death seemed like too big of a coincidence. The same man who dared The Phantom to get him ended up hanging from the ceiling of the theatre. It's simply too convenient."

"Why would The Phantom do that?"

"Christine says he hates to be laughed at."

I let go of Raoul's arm and wiped my brow with my lace handkerchief. "So, Christine believes in this ghost as well as the Angel of Music?"

"She believes they are two different entities. Christine claims to have seen The Phantom."

"Is that right?"

"She told me he wore a black suit, a wide brimmed hat, a cape. Unlike any of the others who have seen him, she saw him without his mask."

"She did?" My voice cracked. Bile rose in my throat.

"She claims the ghost bled down the side of his face. Can you believe such nonsense? A ghost who bleeds? Ridiculous! This is no ghost. This is a man. An insane man."

"And…and this phantom killed others?"

"Indeed! Less than a year ago, an actor made fun of him. Later that week, he came screaming across the rehearsal stage engulfed in flames. The management believe he caught his costume on fire by coming too close to one of the candles, but Christine and the other girls believe The Phantom set him ablaze. There have been other equally gruesome things this crazed murderer has done. Now I think he's the same person who's tutoring Christine. Do you understand why I need to catch this man?"

"Other deaths?" My legs wobbled.

"Yes." He turned to me. "I've upset you, Olivia. I apologize."

"No, please. I want to know more."

"Let's not forget all the terrible injuries he's caused. Why, think of what happened at your birthday party."

"My party?"

"You think the poor fellow who fell down the stairs tripped? He swears not. Did you notice his costume, Cousin Olivia?"

"No, I never saw the man. The doctor took care of him while I waited in the front hall."

"He wore a Phantom of the Opera costume. He was dressed as the Opera Ghost. A black formal suit, a long black cape and a mask. Don't you see? He angered this monster and all of the sudden he's at the bottom of the stairs."

"Cousin, I'm not well. Let's go back, please." I held my handkerchief over my mouth.

"Oh, Cousin Olivia, I apologize." He embraced me. "I didn't mean to upset you so. Please, forgive me."

"It's quite all right. I think I need to lie down for a while. Be a dear and take me back."

*****

After the maid pulled the curtains closed I laid down on my bed. What Raoul said about the man who ended up at the bottom of the stairs played in my mind. Erik showed up moments after someone called for a doctor. My stomach rolled and pitched whenever I thought of him.

An intense anxiousness kept my heart racing as day turned to evening. I tried to fight feelings of utter dread. *This is Erik*, I told myself. *None of this can be substantiated. He said people often attributed terrible things to the Opera Ghost even when he had nothing to do with the unfortunate incidents.*

However, Raoul's theory made sense. Erik's inability to sleep, always being on guard, the knife at my throat. I had spent five nights in his underground fortress. I'd slept next to him. I couldn't think of Erik without my stomach reacting in swirls of nausea.

I paced back and forth in my room unable to rest. I had all four lamps on their highest setting.

The hours passed slowly. I hated to admit I missed him—my sweet Erik, my friend. Yet, I feared the Erik who could fly into a rage and lose control.

As I turned my back to the window, the lamplight lowered. Something soft rubbed against my cheek. I spun around. Erik stood behind me wearing his best eveningwear, his red-lined cape and black leather gloves. In his hands, he held some sort of toy.

I did not have a chance to reconcile the cold-blooded killer I feared with the gentleman holding a little stuffed chimp.

Erik's eyes shone with pride. "I have a gift for you." He bowed and held the toy out to me.

He moved closer when I failed to take the gift from his hands. "Here, Olivia, I made this for you." His voice gave me chills. *The voice of an angel.*

The stuffed monkey held tiny symbols and began playing a cheerful melody.

"We need to talk. Not here. Go outside," I said sharply as I gestured to the window.

His eyes showed alarm. He froze in his spot. I stood by the window and pointed again.

"Olivia, what's wrong?"

"You must leave!"

"Tell me what's wrong," he begged when I still had not given him the greeting he'd expected.

I didn't want to chance his going into a rage inside the house. "I'll meet you outside."

I hated the suspicion I had. I wanted to trust him, to throw myself into his arms and fly off to his world of make-believe and fanciful dreams. But, I couldn't pretend I didn't have suspicions. I had to know the truth.

We could not have the conversation in my bedroom in the Chagny home with Raoul upstairs where he had access to weapons.

"I will meet you outside," I whispered again.

"All right." He tossed the toy on my pillow. The chimp rolled off and landed in the space between the bed and the nightstand. I looked up and Erik was gone.

I carried a lantern and snuck out the front door. Before I reached the bottom of the front steps, Erik was at my side.

"What's the matter?" he asked.

The panic in his voice wounded me. I longed to comfort him and soothe his fear. I hated how I suspected such atrocities of him. *They can't be true.*

"Not here. We can't talk here."

"Where?"

I turned toward the meadow. The darkness stretched on and on—-a giant black void. *This is what total blindness feels like.*

I couldn't move; I stood stock-still, panic rising in my throat. Erik grabbed my arm and led me away from the house. We stopped on the other side of a hedgerow.

"Tell me what's wrong, Olivia."

I struggled to see behind him, but the world disappeared. I had never experienced such terrifying nothingness. Aside from the small glow of the lantern I carried, there was no light, no shadows; only thick darkness. The ugly truth I had fought so hard to keep hidden in the back of my mind exploded to the front. *The rest of my life will be like this.* "I can't see," I cried.

"Oh, my darling." Erik tried to pull me into his embrace.

I pushed him away with both hands. "Don't touch me."

He backed out of the measly light of my lantern. What frightened me more? Being all alone and blind, or being in the company of someone I suspected of murder.

"Erik, wait. Don't go."

"I'm confused, Olivia. Help me understand. I don't know what I've done."

Dropping to the ground, I covered my eyes and sobbed. I wanted to go home.

Chapter 35 Stolen

ERIK:

Olivia wept at my feet. Seeing her so upset tortured me, yet she refused to let me touch her, comfort her.

"I cannot see," she cried.

Her display of emotion in the Chagny garden confused me. Instead of allowing me to help her, she seemed upset by my presence. I tried not to let my imagination run wild with the thought she'd changed her mind about me.

I knelt next to her in the dark and gently tried to remove her hands from her face.

She yanked her wrists away from me. "Don't touch me."

I stood. "What is this? Why are you acting this way?"

"I know what you've done."

"What have I done? Olivia, truly, I don't have any idea what you think I've done."

"You are the Angel of Music, aren't you? Don't bother denying it. I'll never forgive you for lying to me. How could you?"

She continued to make wild accusations and berate me. We were too close to the house. If she continued to raise her voice at me, a few men from the house of Chagny would come to her rescue; their weapons all too ready to kill the monster that upset Madam Weston.

"Answer me," she demanded, but before I had a chance to say anything, she began to accuse me all over again.

My panic-driven impulses overpowered any logic; intense fear had eclipsed my reasoning. Before I realized what I was doing, I'd knocked over her lamp to extinguish the flame, clapped my hand over her mouth and scooped her up. She turned her head from side to side and tried to remove my hand.

The full understanding of what I'd done occurred to me as I hurried to the meadow with her struggling in my arms. Barnabas trotted towards me. I placed her on his back. Before she took a breath to scream, I jumped behind her, held her against me and gave the horse a good kick.

Once we arrived at the tunnel, I didn't dismount, but had Barnabas trot all the way down. At the bank of the lake I jumped off the horse. Olivia must have been too afraid to struggle while Barnabas ran, but when I tried to lift her off, she fought me like a wildcat.

"Get your hands off of me. Don't touch me."

I ignored her protestations, grabbed her around the waist and set her on the shore of the lake.

"Take me home immediately."

"I'm not going to hurt you, Olivia. I just didn't want you to cause such a commotion that you'd bring the whole household down to the front garden."

"I don't care to hear your explanations. I'm done with your lies!"

"Calm down, please. Let me explain."

"I demand you take me home right now!"

I took a step toward her. She cowered with my approach.

"Stop, Olivia! Why are you doing this to me?"

"I know who you are." She backed away from me.

"Who am I?"

I always knew she would eventually find out. I took a step closer. She put her hands out defensively. "Please, take me home. I want to go home, please," she begged.

Begged me.

She did not recognize me anymore. The woman I loved saw the monster before her. I couldn't take the begging. "Please, please."

I didn't hear Olivia's voice anymore. Instead, my victims cried out, one on top of the other.

"Don't kill me, please!"

"Have mercy!"

The voices grew louder and louder as they pleaded for their lives and begged for my clemency. The sound of their screams became an unbearable pain slicing through my skull. I covered my ears to silence them, but they only begged louder. And then—the pleas of my victims fell silent.

The cage door slammed shut with a loud clank. My keeper stomped toward me. His boots crunched over dirty hay; the tail of a whip drags on the floor next to him.

I curl into a ball to make myself as small as possible. I want to put my hands up to stop the blows, but I need to hide my face. I hear the snap—feel the force of his strength, the wind it creates near my ears. The sting of the leather tears through my skin like fire as the whip strips the flesh from my back and arms.

"No, please. Stop! I want to go home. Please, let me go."

He's laughing at me. Why is he laughing at me as I cry out?

The reason becomes clear.

He hates me.

"Home? You miserable wretch. You haven't figured it out yet? This is your home. Your own mother tossed you out as so much garbage. She is glad to be rid of you. You are mine now."

He is right. Mama hates me, too.

I silence my pleas and try to find a safe corner. I scoot away until my back hits the bars.

Trapped.

He grabs a fistful of hair and yanks up my head to prove to the other gypsies that he'd found a 'living corpse.'

I try to hide my face with my hands. He pulls my head up harder and slams my skull into the bars.

Slams my head into the bars again.

And again.

He will not stop until I remove my hands from my face. I need to protect my head, but I want to hide my face. Protect head? Hide face?

Protect head.

My hands go down from exhaustion. I wait for death.

Chapter 36 The Whip

OLIVIA: I told Erik I knew who he was. He took a couple steps toward me, but when I said I knew what he'd done, he stopped advancing. He stared at me with a dazed, far-away expression.

A moment later, he flung off his mask, dropped to the ground and covered his ears. As he had done before, he curled up into himself. Confused and frightened by what took place in front of me, I backed away.

I had nowhere to run or hide.

After a moment, Erik's head snapped up as though seeing someone tower over him. His hands flew up to cover his face.

"Please don't whip me, Monsieur. Please." He cried out in French as he winced from an imaginary beating, but never moved his hands from his face.

In the next instant, he scooted backward until he hit the side of the tunnel. He continued to cower until his head jerked back and hit the wall behind him. Again and again, he slammed his head against the stones before he dropped his hands from in front of his face.

He needed help, but at the same time I worried what reaction any intrusion might elicit. Nonetheless, I could not watch any longer.

I took a step forward, but his horse reared up in front of me, ears flat, nostrils flared. Barnabas refused to let me get closer.

Erik shrieked. “Please, give me my mask. Please, Monsieur, may I put on my mask now?” He once again reverted to his native tongue.

He curled up on his side with his knees at his chest, his hands in front of his face.

I grabbed the rope around Barnabas. Once I had the reins in my hand I talked to the horse in a soothing voice. “I’m not going to hurt him. I want to help him. Let me help him.” I rubbed Barnabas’s nose until he calmed. I continued to pat him on the neck as I maneuvered to the other side.

The sight of Erik curled up on the ground made my heart turn inside out. He’d stopped crying, stopped trembling, and now lay coiled up in silent defeat. I approached him with caution.

“Erik?” He didn’t move. “Are you all right? What should I do? How do I help you?” I knelt next to him. He didn’t acknowledge me.

Unfurling his legs out in front of him, he leaned his head back on the wall behind us.

“Erik, can you hear me?”

He closed his eyes for a moment. When he opened them, they widened in surprise to find us both on the ground. A spark of memory flashed across his face; he seemed to recall the events which brought us to his home.

He barely moved and continued to breathe heavy with apparent exhaustion.

“Are you all right?” I asked.

He reached for his mask and placed it over his face with shaky hands.

"Please, don't hate me, Olivia."

The pain in his voice made me forget our precarious situation. "I don't hate you."

"You should."

"I think you hate yourself enough for both of us."

"Touché."

"What happened, Erik?"

"I'm not sure. I'm all right now. I'll take you home." He tried to stand, but slumped back down. "Give me a minute."

Leaning his head against the rock wall, he turned toward me. "I would never hurt you. I needed to talk to you, but I didn't want your family to come outside. Taking you against your will was unwise—a rash decision made from sheer desperation."

I gave him a small smile. "For an intelligent man, you sure didn't think this plan all the way through, did you?"

He scoffed. "I can take you back now." He tried to stand.

"Erik, you're bleeding!" Blood smudged the rock behind his head. Dark rivulets evidenced where he'd hit his head several times to get away from whatever nightmare he relived.

He cupped the back of his head and then looked at his wet glove. "So I am."

I leaned his head forward. "I can't tell where the blood is coming from. There isn't enough light here."

"Olivia, listen to me. You need to get into the boat and cross the lake. Above the fireplace, on the mantle, hidden under an inlay wooden box with a carved scorpion, you'll find—"

"You aren't making any sense. We need to stop the bleeding."

"Listen to me. I'm telling you how to escape."

"You need help."

"Pick up the box. You'll find a switch that turns off the—. Turn the switch and then push the button. A door in the panel next to the bookshelves will open. The one we used to ascend into the opera house. Remember? Climb the stairs. They're safe if you turn the switch *first* to disengage the traps."

"What are you talking about? Listen to me. You need help."

"I don't want help. You must leave this place. The stairs next to the fireplace are safe, but you must turn off the trapdoors and snares. Go on, now. Row over to the house and make your escape."

"I won't leave you here."

"Just let me die."

I put his arm over my shoulder. "I can't help you stand if you don't cooperate."

"The solution is simple. Don't help me."

"I won't leave you."

"Go on. Remember, under the scorpion box you must turn the switch before you push the button."

"I cannot row over by myself. I can't see the way. If you want me to get out of here, you will have to show me."

"The house is just across the lake."

"I cannot see your home from here." I lied. "I will get lost. The boat might tip over."

In reality, his house was a blurry row of lights across the lake. I could barely make out the candelabras lining the entry. "If you want me to get out of here, you need to take me."

He put his arm around my shoulder and stood. Once he gained equilibrium, he insisted on standing by himself. We boarded the boat and he pushed us forward with the staff as hardily as he could manage.

Erik remained silent as we made our way across. The only noise was the water lapping at the sides of the boat.

On the other shore, he refused my assistance to disembark.

"Go the rest of the way, Olivia. The front path is well-lit. You can make it from here."

I misjudged the slope of the shore and ended up sliding towards the water on my backside. "I told you. I cannot do this alone."

He plucked me off the edge of the lake, put my hand through his arm and led me to his parlor.

"Right there." He pointed to the mantle.

Ignoring him, I bypassed the fireplace and walked with him to the sofa. Erik plunked down onto the cushions. "Go on, Olivia. Find the box."

"I'll be right back."

I searched his kitchen cupboards until I found what I needed.

"Why are you still here? What are you doing?"

"I'm saving your life." I ripped a clean dishcloth into bandages.

"Don't bother. My life isn't worth your effort."

Water from the bowl that I'd filled sloshed onto the carpet as I made my way back to clean his wound.

I unhooked his cape, leaned him forward and proceeded to wash the injured area. I tried to remove his mask, but he stopped me by holding the sides in place. "No, don't," he whispered.

"I need to wrap your head. Let go. Please, for me."

He dropped his hands.

I wrapped the strips around his forehead to keep the bandage in place. After I finished, I handed his mask to him.

He slipped it over his face.

"The bleeding seems to have stopped," I said.

Some innate impulse caused me to kiss the back of his head above the wound. I hadn't realized what I'd done until he jerked his head around. He searched my face with bewilderment in his eyes.

"Why, Olivia? Why are you helping me?"

"Because you need help."

"But, I've hurt you. I deceived you and I apologize."

"How is your head? Do you feel better?"

He scoffed. "That depends."

"On what?"

"On how much you know."

"Oh, Erik. Did you lie to me? Did you kill Joseph Buquet?"

He sighed heavily. "No, I did not. I told you. I had nothing to do with his death."

Afraid of his possible reaction to my questions, I eased into asking him about other murders.

“Did you push someone down the stairs on my birthday?”

“I…I…well, he had it coming. He was callous and hateful. Did you see his costume? Have you ever had anyone create a joke from your pain? This mask is not a costume. This mask is not funny.”

“I understand you were angry, but you can’t push someone down the stairs because the costume he wears is in poor taste.”

“I did not push him down. I gave him a nudge. If we’re assigning blame, gravity and inertia are just as culpable in that cad’s unfortunate accident as I. To be quite honest, his lack of decorum isn’t the only reason he took a tumble. The man’s plummet also helped distract a certain doctor from trying to steal the woman I love away from me.” He shrugged. “A demon cannot be deterred from his agenda. Quite simply, Olivia, every once in a while, the devil must get his due.”

“Oh, Erik. I wish you wouldn’t say such things. Referring to yourself as a demon doesn’t help your cause.” A moment of silence passed before I asked, “Will you tell me everything? Don’t make me pull the truth out of you. I haven’t the strength to do this anymore.”

“What do you want to know? For I, too, am tired of secrecy.”

“Are you the Angel of Music?”

“Easy question. I am.”

"I thought as much. Why are you hurting Christine and Raoul? Those two children love each other. You've made their lives hell. Why?"

"I've done no such thing."

"Don't lie to me. I read the note you forced her to write Raoul. Forbidding the deluded girl from seeing him for the sake of an opera? Do you have any idea how wrong that is? You've manipulated her into believing her dead father has sent you to teach her to sing. Doesn't the whole thing sound depraved to you?"

"Well, when you put it in those terms."

"In any terms, in any language, you know it's wrong."

"I needed to make sure *Don Juan Triumphant* would be perfect. If she were keeping late hours and meeting her lover instead of training, she risked not being able to fulfill the role. Can you try to see it that way? Your opera had to be flawless."

"I don't want the opera." I crossed my arms.

Erik sat straight up on the couch. "What?"

"Keep your opera. I don't want it."

He stared at me with disbelief. "You can't mean that."

"You are wrong. I very much mean it. If you think an opera is more important than love, then you've missed the point."

"I don't understand."

"Imagine being kept from someone you love. What if someone tricked me the way you've tricked Christine? Or, what if a man manipulated me into refusing to see you in order to benefit a personal scheme?"

He blinked a couple of times. "I would hate it. My God, you're right," he whispered. "I would utterly detest it."

I sat in silence as he worked out the dilemma in his mind.

"I will fix everything, Olivia. You have my word."

"Thank you. If she is reunited with Raoul maybe she'll sing even better. She'll be singing about love. Her song will come from here." I put my hand over his heart.

He stood and picked up his cape. "I shall repair the relationship between Christine and Raoul. You have my word. Now I'm ready to take you back."

He did not want me to ask any more questions or delve any deeper into his background. Whatever he had experienced earlier came from something catastrophic and horrifying. Everything about him cried out for love. Yet, he seemed to have lived his life without having any.

I watched him wiping his bloody glove on the edge of his fancy cape. When he held out his hand in that familiar gesture, I shuddered. His past suddenly did not matter to me. Without forethought, I rushed forward and put my arms around him.

"Goodbye, Erik." Just as he'd done the first time I'd embraced him, he tensed up and stood with his hands at his sides. I squeezed him tighter.

He muffled a sob and crossed his arms behind my back, hugging me to his chest. "Thank you, Olivia. Thank you."

I don't know how long we held each other. Time seemed to have stopped. He pulled away from me. "It's getting late. We need to leave now."

I tried to memorize everything in his parlor, his dining area. The scent of fresh flowers still lingered in the air from the many displays lining the path to my room. *My* room.

I'd been so happy in his home. I glanced toward the door to the library. Erik's Braille machine would never get used again.

My chest filled with heavy regret; my shoulders felt weighed down by deep sorrow. I wanted to go back to the United States. My mind was made up. I had resolved to leave our relationship until—I glanced over Erik's shoulder at the long, dark hallway leading to his bedroom. Something about the separation of his bedroom made me waver in my resolve.

"After you take me home, what will you do, Erik?"

"I give you my word. I will speak to Christine. I will tell her she must make her own decision and let her decide how she shall progress."

"No, what will *you* do?"

"I shall witness my opera performed," he said with finality. A resolute and dark farewell punctuated his words.

"After that," I whispered.

"Why should it matter? Come on, let's go."

"Because I care."

He turned to face me. "Don't. Once you leave here you should forget everything."

"You expect me to forget you ever existed? Pretend I never met you?"

"It is my most valid wish."

"Are you saying when I leave here you will forget me?"

He scoffed. "If at all possible. Yes, that's what I'm saying."

With tears rapidly filling my eyes, I said, "What a cruel thing to say. Take me back now, Erik. If you have any heart at all, you will fix what you've done to my cousin's life and set things right in your own life as well."

"I'm begging your pardon, Madam. I hadn't meant to be cruel. I didn't mean to upset you."

"Saying you will forget all about me shouldn't upset me? That's hard to believe."

"I never said I would forget you." He looked at me with tenderness.

"Yes, you did. I don't care to argue with you anymore."

"No, Olivia, I said I would forget you *if it were possible*. The truth is...it would be quite *im*possible. There is no way I could ever forget you. The kindness you've shown to me—" He chuckled. "Madam, you have been the one bright spot on this whole bloody expedition."

I recognized the words and replied the same way he had. "That must have been one hellacious expedition."

He smiled beneath his mask. I smiled, too.

Within those saffron eyes, wet with tears, his soul begged for help. They contained the fading hope of an injured man. Hope was not dead. "Oh, Erik. My journey to France was one hellacious expedition, but, I will always remember you with fondness. Come here." I opened my arms to him. He rushed forward and held me tight.

"You don't hate me?" he whispered.

"I told you before. I could never hate you."

"I wish I could believe you, Olivia."

"Why do you doubt my word?"

"Do you care to start this conversation over?" he said trying to make a joke.

"A very wise person once said, 'On the whole, I find once words are spoken there is nothing one can do to repair whatever damage they sought to do when the words left the lips.'"

"One thing I never claimed to be, Olivia, is wise."

"Me, either. For if I was—I would not do this." I lifted his mask and kissed him. He clutched me as though his life depended on that kiss. He pulled off the mask and tossed it aside.

Erik made me love him.

Everything I had chosen to do from the time I continued my journey to the Chagny's home unaccompanied had been unwise. I didn't care.

"I love you, Erik."

He gasped and pulled back to stare into my eyes. He didn't blink. He gazed at me with such astonishment and adoration that I said it to him again.

"I love you, Erik."

He let go of me. "Why do you love me?"

"Why I love you is irrelevant at this point. I just do."

"I love you, too! I love you so much!" He sighed deeply. "But, I need to tell you something."

Chapter 37 The Key

ERIK:

I heard *the* words. Four powerful words. In my entire lifetime, the incredible sentiment in that simple yet splendid phrase had never been directed at me. Although the one who spoke them is no liar, the words were lies. For how could she love me when she didn't know who I was? How could someone, *anyone*, love me? The most dangerous of all demons—a wickedly charming one.

With every bit of decency I could muster, I made the right decision. The ground beneath me swayed; my balance became distorted.

I was about to shatter her illusion.

The smile left her face. Her pink cheeks turned alabaster. "What's wrong, Erik? Sit down. Rest. Is your head hurting?"

From within my cloak I produced a key. My eyes stung with tears and my heart unraveled. "Here."

She turned the key over in her hand. Her brow wrinkled as she focused on the detailed skull at the handle. "What is this?"

"That is the key which will unlock the past. The key which will allow you entrance into a world you will wish you had never known. My world. My hell."

"No." She held the key out to me.

I closed her fingers around it. "I love you, Olivia. I will always love you. Go to my bedchamber and find out the truth of who I am. When you have seen enough to hate me, do as I told you before. Go to the scorpion box and let yourself out. You will never want to lay eyes upon me again."

I'd retrieved my mask from the floor and slipped it on before placing my hand across my chest and giving her my sharpest bow. "You are a lovely woman, Olivia. Thank you for trying to love me."

She flung the key at my feet. "Of all the cowardice things I've ever seen."

Never being able to anticipate Olivia's moves or reactions unnerved me. "Pardon? Cowardice?"

"You hand me a key and tell me to learn about you from something in your room? Why? You are standing right here. If you want me to know something about you, then tell me."

I picked up the key. My mind went blank.

She stood with her hands on her hips in a posture I'd come to associate with Olivia. "Don't stand there gawking at me. Let's hear the truth. What are you hiding? What makes you the demon? Tell me why you associate yourself with such darkness."

"Madam, please. I can't—"

"You won't?"

"I can't."

"Listen here, I have no desire to play these games with you. I've had enough of your showmanship. Let me see the man not the performer."

I tried to think of something, *anything,* to do or say, but I stood mute.

"You know what I think? Handing me that key is the same trick you tried to use on my birthday. You wanted me to open my present to see whether the box contained a tiger or a kitten. Well, here's the answer to your little riddle. Neither a tiger nor a kitten was in the box. The box was empty. An illusion. You, sir, are neither a kitten nor a tiger—you are neither demon nor angel. You are simply a man."

The fact that my mouth felt full of cotton and words would not dislodge from my throat didn't matter because I would *never* find the right way to tell her what she must know. I clasped her hand and tried to lead her toward the room. She yanked away from me.

Letting my troubled mind go blank, I disregarded any consequences and acted on impulse. I picked her up and carried her to my bedroom door. She fought me, but once I deposited her on her feet she didn't move. Just to be certain she would not run away, I held her by the wrist. She glared at me, but I turned from her and focused on inserting the key.

Unlocking that door sealed my fate.

Once inside, I lit all the candelabras surrounding my bed. Her sharp gasp confirmed the exact moment her eyes registered the terrifyingly ugly murals of death on my walls. I expected her to run out in hysterics.

My victims had their revenge at last.

As always, I incorrectly guessed her reaction. She stared at the nearest wall with both hands over her mouth as if to repress a scream. I backed away from her and continued to my bed. I reclined on the black silk duvet to wait for the end.

The longer the inevitable conclusion to the affair drew out, the more pain embedded in my chest. My head throbbed with defeat; my eyelids grew heavy. *If I close my eyes I will not see when she hurries straight to the scorpion box and out of my life.*

Chapter 38 The Mural

OLIVIA: I stared at the first depiction on Erik's wall. Utter shock disallowed me to speak, or scream. Instead, I simply continued to follow the dark path on which he placed me.

In the corner, he'd painted an infant lying in a cradle in a sparsely furnished, dark and foreboding room. A lady's lace handkerchief covered the baby's face. A woman stood with her back to the cradle. She held up an ornate mirror; the reflection revealed her striking beauty.

Right outside the door, an angry, violent crowd amassed. A short distance from the front garden, Satan handed out armaments to people who ran to join the crowd. Enough rocks, sticks, and knives to arm the entire village piled up in mounds at his feet.

I moved on to the next section as though sleepwalking, not fully aware of my own actions.

In a dark wooded area, under a full moon, a large man held a whip in one hand as he towered over a child. The man's muscles bulged; his eyes showed intense rage, but his mouth turned up in a slick smile as little Erik strained to free himself from the man's grasp. Erik's back and arms bore evidence of more than one brutal beating.

The man held him by the hair. He yanked the boy's head back against the bars of the cage to allow the audience to gape at his face. Little Erik groped for a rough, sackcloth mask which was just outside his reach. The crowd screamed in horror; their faces showed complete disgust. Satan watched from the woods beyond the crowd; an amused grin on his lips.

Despair emanated from the walls of the bedroom. Such incredible anguish seemed to create a physical presence. I felt as though someone or some*thing* held me by the shoulders, forced me down, and kept me from fleeing.

The next scene showed the muscular man on the floor of the cage; a knife stuck out of his neck all the way to the hilt. In the distance, an adolescent Erik ran barefoot and bloody into the night. The devil waited in the distance, arms open and welcoming. My body tensed up as I fought a wave of nausea.

I swallowed the bile building up in my throat and moved toward a two-section scene. An audience connected the two halves together. In the first part, Erik, now a tall young man, stood on a stage performing magic wearing a shiny, black cape, white gloves and a top hat. A cloth-covered stand in front of him held cards, coins, hoops and rope. Spectators surrounded him wearing bemused smiles or delighted expressions of surprise.

In the second section, Erik stood in the middle of the same audience with his arm raised holding up his mask in a dramatic reveal. The audience now clenched their fists with the ferocity of hate. Although, they were the same people in the first scene, their faces now showed murderous outrage. A violent mob wanted to rip Erik to shreds. Some of the ugly spectators held knives, rocks, and sticks in their filthy fists. In a strange twist, Erik painted his own face into that of a handsome man.

In the middle of the monstrous audience, Satan pointed one skeletal finger at Erik and laughed with delight.

I shivered in the gloom and wanted to see no more. I turned toward the door ready to flee. I discovered Erik had not left me alone in his room as I previously thought. He laid on his narrow bed—on his coffin-like bed. He slept on black satin; his mask lay beside him on the pillow. I turned away from him. As if I were in a trance, my feet moved forward. I continued onto the next scene.

Erik stood at a building site as the sun set behind a half-constructed palace in the desert. He held rolled up architecture plans in his fist as builders and craftsmen toiled all around him.

In the next scene, he performed magic within a palatial, domed antechamber supported by carved columns. A muscular man with a beard and wearing a Persian headdress stood with his arms crossed, blocking the door behind Erik. Several sentinels wearing identical uniforms and carrying long swords blocked the other exit. A young man wearing purple robes and a bejeweled turban lounged on an ornate, golden chair, his feet propped up on the back of two prostrate slaves. The shadow of a demon standing in front of a window obscured the prince's smile.

In the next scene, a queen with no facial features rested on a throne made of human remains. Erik knelt in front of her on one knee, head bowed, holding a decorative pillow in his hands. On this pillow, he presented the sovereign with a severed head. The eyes were gouged out; its flesh torn off. A noose wrapped around its neck. Blood dripped over Erik's white gloves and pooled on the floor as he offered his trophy to the queen. I covered my mouth to keep from screaming. I remembered what Raoul told me about the type of weapon The Phantom used to kill people.

I broke into a cold sweat and wanted to flee before I learned any more. Nonetheless, my feet kept moving forward toward the next scene.

The faceless queen sat in a balcony and looked down into a yard where she watched Erik and another man engage in battle. A powerfully-built man held up a sword in one hand and gripped a giant knife in the other. Erik held a thin whip; the thin appendage coiled at his feet. Behind him lay a broken and bloody corpse. A group of women dressed in Persian clothing, a harem, turned their faces away in disgust, but the queen leaned forward in anticipation.

In another macabre scene, Erik stood in the middle of a mirrored room exactly like the one in his home. Instead of reflecting his image, menacing demons stared back, flames lapping at their feet. Because of the illusion of the mirrors, each demon had a perpetuity of demons reflected behind him. They each held a whip and clutched the severed head of a different man.

The floor beneath me wobbled. My face and neck burned, but I shivered uncontrollably. My eyes fell upon a very detailed painting of a man being held down and tortured. The victim agonizes as he dies a most gruesome death.

A young man wearing a feathered turban and jewels on all his fingers stood next to Erik. A table in front of them held a rolled-out architectural plan. Instead of a schematic for a building, the scroll portrayed a detailed diagram of the torture taking place. Erik concentrated on the scroll. He indicated a section of the drawing with his finger. The young prince at his side smiled with satisfaction and pointed at the victim.

Above this ghastly mural was a collage. The faces created an ocean of abhorrence and accusation. Enormous flames surrounded the painting. Burning, singed, and melting skin partially obscured some features, but anger radiated from each man's eyes.

Above the collage were the words: *Vengeance belongs to God; but my wrongs wait for naught to be punished. Within my blood is scorching flames of mortal castigation grieved before eternal suffering.*

I didn't want to see anymore, but found I could not even close my eyes. In the last corner, he'd painted a menacing, but handsome man seated upon an onyx throne. The blue-eyed sovereign wore a crown of jewels, held a golden trident and wore a sash that read: *Beauty*.

Wearing formalwear and his familiar black cape, Erik knelt on one knee before him. Instead of feet, the glowering man had cloven hooves.

With his head bowed in supplication, Erik held out a black satin pillow. On the pillow lay his mask splattered with blood.

My silent tears turned to sobs.

On the last wall, he had painted a replica of his bedroom. Black mourning candles surrounded Erik as he laid on his satin duvet, his hands crossed over his chest like a corpse. A music stand at the foot of his bed held a score entitled *Unholy Requiem*.

In the background the opera house was ablaze. People tried to escape the inferno. Several figures engulfed in flames ran through its front doors. The fire consumed the building from the basement to the Apollo statue on the roof.

I reached the end of his mural and found myself physically released by whatever had held me there.

I ran into the bathroom where I became sick.

Afterward, I dropped to the floor. Unable to rise, I curled up on my side and sobbed. My body shivered with shock and fright.

A murderer. Not just any murderer, but one on the grandest scale. The recurring theme of demons and hell plagued me.

After I vomited once again, I put my head down until the dizziness stopped. My mouth dried; I couldn't swallow. I tried to stand, but collapsed back into a heap on the floor. Hugging my knees, I let the tears fall as I lay crumpled on the cold tile.

I rested there waiting for enough strength to stand. I'd planned to find the switch under the scorpion box and escape from the hell to which I'd descended.

Erik was three things. A genius, a gentleman, and a murderer.

Something occurred to me as I lay there shivering. *The depiction of the opera house in flames might be a suicide plan.*

I stood on wobbly legs and held onto the tile countertop. I had taken my first unsteady step to flee when a cry of tremendous pain came from Erik's room. Distress radiated from his voice as he called my name.

The anguish in which he cried out set my heart pounding anew. I had a decision to make. *Should I leave him in such a state? Would he kill himself if I fled? Would he set the opera house on fire? What if he waited until there was a packed house?*

The high-pitched music of a violin broke the silence—a heartrending melody only an injured soul could create.

In the music, I heard *him.*

Rather than a furious, vindictive, tune, the air filled with the musical weeping of someone who was tired of fighting a world full of hate.

"*One gets quite comfortable with the roles that have been assigned to him,*" he once said.

I could not leave him in that condition. I swallowed hard and tried to disregard my fear. Had he wished to harm me at any point—even when I'd enraged him, he had plenty of opportunity, but he never touched me with anything but love and respect.

I followed the music and found him cross-legged on his bed; eyes closed, violin under his chin. He became the sorrowful music he played.

If I even glanced at the walls surrounding him, I'd flee without saying anything. I concentrated on his graceful fingers moving rapidly across the strings.

He seemed to sense my presence because he put down the violin. However, he kept his eyes closed.

Chapter 39 The Threshold

ERIK:

A presence entered my room. I didn't want to open my eyes.

My evil master had come for me.

Terror shot intense heat down my spine followed in immediacy by an eerie glacial chill. My skin prickled. He was close, ready to snatch me from my transitory mortal misery and toss my soul into unending torment. My teeth chattered. Fear stiffened my body leaving me intractable, barely able to breathe without spasms filling my constricted chest.

I drew a deep breath and opened my eyes ready to accept my fate. Except—

Sweet Olivia stood at the threshold of my door, pale and with tears in her eyes. *Is she really there?* I wondered if I'd tipped all the way over into madness—or if she had.

I closed my eyes and then opened them again just to be sure. She was not an illusion. Aggressive beats thrashed my heart. *What did this mean?* I gave her the secret behind the scorpion box, yet she stood at the door to my personal hell. I couldn't make my mouth move. If I spoke at all, she might run from me like a frightened animal.

The terror and mistrust on her face wounded me. I had damaged her for the most selfish of all reasons: I loved the way she made me feel. By getting involved with me she descended into a hell she had never known before. Instead of her elevating me to the light, I had dragged her to the dark. In doing so, I created a shadow of fear in her life which would never leave her. At that moment, I wished she would flee from me. The guilt was too great.

"Goodbye, Erik."

It was readily apparent that I terrified her. *But, why did she have tears running down her cheeks? Shouldn't she turn away from the monster and ascend into the real world? Why did she gawk at me?* My throat closed up; my jaw clenched like a vice. I remained seated upon my bed, placed my hand across my chest and bowed. I closed my eyes, hoping when I opened them she would be gone. Yet, I feared her absence more than damnation, suffering, and death combined.

"Come here," she said.

"Pardon me?"

She gestured that I should go to her. "Come out of there."

"I don't understand."

She took a deep breath and stepped inside my room. Her courage amazed me. I sat very still, unable to comprehend what she was doing or why.

She began blowing out the mourning candles. "Help me. Blow them all out. It's time to go," she said.

I'd slipped my mask over my face and began extinguishing the flames on the other side of the bed. Still confused, I held the violin by its neck and waited for her to say something.

"Erik, I can't see."

I rushed to her side and held her by the arm. *She let me touch her!*

As soon as we were out in the hallway she closed the door behind us. "No one should stay in there."

We walked toward the parlor. She pulled away from my grasp as soon as her sight increased.

"Why are you still here?" My voice refused to cooperate and create a sound any louder than a whisper.

"I couldn't leave without saying goodbye. After all is said and done, you're still you. You're the same man who saved me from my driver."

My tattered heart and shredded defenses left me helpless. "I'm not the same man. I will never be the same."

"Nor will I."

"Forgive me, Olivia. I changed you and if I could go back and do everything again, I would—"

"Leave me with my dubious driver?"

"No, I would never do that."

She smiled warily. "I didn't think so."

"I have brought you nothing but heartache," I said.

"You know that is not true."

"Why did you stay, Olivia? I don't understand."

"I couldn't leave you in there. I just couldn't."

"It's where I belong. The hell of my own creation."

"You do not belong in there. No wonder you can't sleep. No one would be able sleep in there. Use the guest room from now on. Don't go back in there. I fear—"

"You fear?"

"I fear if you go back into the darkness you will never find your way out. Don't you understand? Things can change. It's not too late for you."

"It's later than you realize. On that note, I suggest you go home."

"All right. Will you escort me home or shall I use the scorpion box?"

"If you permit me, I think the gentlemanly thing to do is to see you home. If you go up the stairs, you will find yourself in the opera house without a way back to the Chagny estate."

"How is your head?" she asked.

I found her question paradoxically humorous. I chuckled.

She gave me a tiny smile. "You know what I mean. Can you ride with your injury?"

"I promise I will get you back safe and sound."

"But, after you leave me at the chateau and you are alone, you could fall from your horse. What if you were seriously injured and had to wait for someone to help you?"

"I don't believe that would ever happen."

"You don't believe you'd fall?"

"No. I don't believe anyone would ever help me."

"I'm serious."

"So am I."

"If you are by yourself, you could get dizzy, fall off and die!"

He scoffed. "As if that would be a travesty the world could do without."

"Listen to me. We should be careful with head wounds."

"I assure you, Madam. I am well within the mental and physical capacities to see you home. I appreciate your candor and the friendship you've shown me. When do you leave for the United States?"

She thought about my question for a moment. "I should like to stay long enough to hear my opera performed. Then, I must be on my way. Look for me in the family box. And Erik—"

"Yes?"

"I will not tell. Your secret is still your secret."

Such finality. I needed to be strong for her because she had been so strong for me. I still did not understand why she stayed.

"Thank you. I shall look for you in the Chagny box on opening night. And with that, we should depart." I hesitated taking her arm. She had shaken off my touch earlier. "Do you need help?"

"I can manage well enough." She adjusted the collar of her dress. Her hands fiddled with something on the back of her neck. I watched in silent awe as she approached me. She picked up my hand, placed something in my palm and closed my fingers around it. "It's not too late to come home, Erik. Until you've breathed your last breath, it's never too late."

I opened my hand. She'd placed a golden crucifix on a chain into my palm. I stood transfixed as I held the holy article. *Nothing catastrophic happened.* I don't know what I had expected, but in that instant, I felt a strange sense of relief. However, the sensation quickly vanished.

"Home?"

"You told me you were once Catholic. Maybe, it's time you went home."

"I fear I may not be welcome. I've never been welcome in any home," I said with more bitterness than I meant to show.

"Perhaps you have not been home in so long you don't realize your Father has been waiting for you."

"It's far too late for that."

"As long as you're alive, there's always hope for redemption." She removed the gold chain from my hand and placed it around my neck.

I closed my eyes. She struggled with the clasp. Her sweet breath caressed the back of my neck. The chain touched my skin; the cross made contact with my chest. That peculiar speck of relief resurfaced. *She touched me without visible revulsion.*

After she had secured the clasp, she checked the bandage on my head. I must have seemed a giant mistake to her. What I'd put her through that night was horrid.

"Looks all right. The bleeding stopped anyway. You'll live."

"What a pity," I mumbled. Then I continued, "Olivia, before we go, may I ask you for one last thing?"

"Yes?"

"May I, uh—" Clenching my fists to keep her from noticing how much my hands trembled, I stood there, nervous and tongue-tied. I wished I hadn't said anything. *Maybe I could make up something.* I couldn't get my brain to engage. The words threatened to come from my lips with or without my will. "May I…hug you one last time?"

She stiffened, so I took a step back in haste. "Forgive me. That was forward and impolite."

Chapter 40 Examination

OLIVIA: When Erik asked me for a hug my mind flashed to the pictures at the beginning of the mural. Baby Erik under a piece of cloth. A mother with her back turned and an angry mob at the door.

Erik was a murderer. He'd taken more lives than I would have ever imagined, but when he stood in front of me with his eyes pleading and his hands shaking, he was still my sweet, kind, talented Erik. For a moment, I let all judgment leave my heart and all rationale leave my head. "Remember? You never need to ask if you desire a hug."

"I was not sure whether that was still a valid offer."

I tried to purge my mind of the horrors I'd seen an hour or so before. "Come here." He came into my arms. I closed my eyes and breathed in the wonderful scent of him. I didn't want to let go. I knew he didn't want to either. If I hadn't broken the embrace, we might have held each other until daylight.

"We better go now," I whispered in his ear.

The whole way back to the Chagny estate I agonized about saying goodbye. He kept his arm around my waist, securing me on the horse while the other hand held the reins.

He let Barnabas walk at a leisurely pace until we arrived at the Willow tree in the meadow. Erik dismounted and helped me down.

Neither of us said anything as he guided me through the darkness. He embraced me once again at the door of the chateau. After giving me a perfect bow, he disappeared into the shadows.

He will never be back.

I crawled into bed, but tossed and turned all night. Horrific images kept me from sleeping. *How many,* I wondered. *So many faces—where they all his victims? What kind of monster could kill that many people?* I could not merge my Erik with a cold-blooded murderer. The two would not come together in my mind.

Near dawn, I realized something. In all the depictions on the mural, Erik's head was down or his eyes were closed. The symbolism had to mean something. Why would a heartless killer insist on sleeping in a bedchamber with his guilt surrounding him? The pictures did not show any pleasure from killing, but quite the opposite. They were not the paintings of a homicidal beast, but the skillful art of a traumatized child. *The queen? Who was this queen? Had she forced Erik to murder for her pleasure? To fight men as some gladiator? At the palace, the doors were always guarded. Was he a prisoner? Had they held him captive?*

I bolted upright. Why had I not asked him these things? How could I leave him thinking I didn't care to understand?

I had no way to contact him. Tears streaked down my face. My heart jolted when I remembered something.

From the bottom drawer of the dresser I removed his red velvet cape. Putting it over me, I laid back on the bed. Sheer exhaustion forced me to fall into a dreamless slumber.

Hours later Anna entered my room. Confused, I sat up. "What's wrong?"

The child stared at me, turned on her heel and ran shrieking down the hall. Before my feet had a chance to move from under the covers, Raoul, Philippe, and two male servants burst through the door.

"My God! What happened? Are you hurt?" Raoul rushed forward. Philippe threw open the curtains to let in daylight. I followed his horrified gaze. Erik's blood had splattered and streaked across my blouse and skirt.

"I'm fine."

"But, Madam Weston, you are bleeding." Anna sniffled, wiped tears from her eyes.

"Shall I send the groom for the doctor?" Raoul asked.

"No!"

"Yes," Philippe answered. "Anna, send Jacques for the doctor at once."

The young girl looked from the Count to me with wide, startled eyes, unsure to whom she should listen.

"I'm not injured. I assure you," I said to her in French. She gaped at her employer.

"Go!" Philippe demanded. She pushed between him and Raoul and hurried out the door.

Raoul held my forearms. "Cousin, what happened?" He released me and stopped asking questions when the velvet cape fell from the bed to the floor near his feet.

"Brother, perhaps the rest of us should wait out in the hall for the doctor. Maybe *the lady* needs some privacy." He cleared his throat.

Philippe blushed bright red. "Oh, but of course." He indicated for the two servants to follow him.

Raoul picked up the cape. "Are you sure you are not injured?"

"Yes, please leave. I'd like to clean up." I could not meet his eyes.

He handed me the cloak. "I suggest a bit more discretion."

After he left, I retrieved a dress from the wardrobe and underthings from my dresser. I made my way to the bathroom shaking and nauseated.

No wonder the poor young maid almost fainted. My own reflection shocked me.

After I finished my toilette, I looked in the mirror again. Although I was fresh from a bath, had my hair fixed and wore a smart suit, my face betrayed me. I had not slept much since my arrival in France. I gave my cheeks a couple of pinches to give them a little color before I returned to my room.

The doctor rose from a chair near the door. The maids had already changed my linens. Folded across the foot of the bed was Erik's crimson cape. I shivered as I tried to think of a plausible excuse for everything.

*****

"Good morning, Madam Weston." Dr. Fournier kissed my hand. "I see you're feeling better?"

"Doctor, the household has panicked. I ran into a wall last night. Gave myself one terrible nosebleed. I'm sure I must have been a sight this morning. I apologize for alarming everyone."

"Have you been ill? You're quite pale."

"No, I've been fine."

"Please, sit down; submit to an exam. It will soothe the Count, give me a reason for being here, and perhaps make you feel better."

I sat in the chair. "I don't require an exam."

He proceeded to check my eyes, my throat, peek into my ears. He applied his stethoscope to my chest. "When is the operation?"

"I'm not going to have the surgery."

He stood up, stethoscope in hand, brow wrinkled. "You've changed your mind?"

"Yes, I have."

He gave my shoulder a small squeeze. "What made you come to your senses?"

"Realizing there are some things in this world a whole lot worse than losing one's sight. The risk of losing my life on the operating table did not justify my gamble anymore."

"Well, Madam Weston, if you insist you are not in need of a more thorough examination, I shall be on my way."

"Thank you, Doctor. I'm sorry you came all this way for nothing."

"Perhaps I'll find my trip out here was fortuitous. Would you care to accompany me to luncheon this afternoon?"

No excuses came to mind. A knock at the door interrupted my thoughts.

"Come in."

"Is everything all, right?" Raoul asked. I needed to throw him off Erik's trail. I didn't think he recognized the cape from the party since he and Christine were nowhere to be found for most of the night. However, he had incorrect suspicions about the doctor and me. His assumptions might work to my advantage.

"Yes, everything is fine." I smiled.

Raoul turned toward the doctor. "Is she all right?"

"Just a terrible nosebleed," the doctor answered.

"I see," Raoul said.

"Viscount, would you mind if I took your cousin out for a pleasant afternoon in the park followed by a nice dinner?"

"No, we had no specific plans today. Did we, cousin?"

"No, we haven't any plans."

"Well, this is good news. Will you do me the honor, Madam Weston?"

"Yes, an outing sounds lovely."

"I'll return for you in a couple of hours. Shall you join us, Viscount?"

"I'm unable. Forgive me." Raoul answered him, but his eyes never left the red cape on my bed.

The doctor gathered his medical things. "Good day, Madam Weston. I look forward to this afternoon." He bowed and tipped his hat before he departed.

I didn't want to cause any more trouble in the household, but I also did not want to lead Raoul to Erik.

Chapter 41 Daroga

ERIK:

I longed to get away from nonstop rehearsals. Supervising the practice performances from inside the walls and up on the catwalks exhausted me. I had to make all my changes through letters from the O.G. The arduous schedule couldn't keep my troubled mind from Olivia.

I needed some fresh air after a terrible morning of rehearsal. I pulled my fedora down low and took the alleyways to Daroga's. I didn't care if someone tried to stop me. Anyone dared to get in my way, it would be the last decision he'd make. I lived for one reason: to see my opera performed. Nothing else mattered.

*****

"I know there is something troubling you, Erik. I don't like the look in your eyes."

"Meaning what, Daroga?"

"You want me to be frank with you? You don't wish me to use word games? Fine. I'm bothered by the fact you still have not explained those items on your list of provisions."

"You are still on that? I told you I don't want to discuss it."

"One day you come to my home speaking of entertaining American Presidents; then you wish me to purchase coffee for you? Coffee, Erik? You hate coffee."

"What are accusing me of, Daroga? You suspect me of clandestine meetings with the President of the United States? Or secretly liking coffee?"

"Now for the second time you've come to my home during the day." His voice changed, became softer. "What is driving you out in the daylight? Have you become tired of living underground?"

"Just tired of living." I shrugged and looked down at my boots.

"You don't mean that."

I met his eyes. He looked away. A moment later he said, "What about your request for a lady's diamond ring? Will you tell me what that was about? I fear for your sanity. I would like to understand what happened."

"What bothers you, Daroga? Is my being in need of a wedding ring that incomprehensible to you? No one could ever love a monster. Is that what you mean to say?"

"I meant no such thing."

"It doesn't matter now."

"But, the ring? Where is she? You...you don't have her *down there*, do you?"

"Is that what you believe? I've captured some defenseless woman and tied her up in my dungeon until she agrees to marry me? Do you really see me doing that?"

"Well, no, but sometimes the craving for the company of a woman can be overwhelming. The desire to fulfill this yearning can be unrelenting. You are a healthy man, you must—" His voice trailed off.

I scoffed and stood up. "So, it's your belief that after forty-four years I've had enough of my virginity, so I've decided to resolve the 'unrelenting desire' by *taking* a woman?"

"It is not unthinkable for you to perhaps pay for—"

"I would never!"

"Calm down, my friend. Sit, please. I don't mean to run you off. I know you would never take a woman against her will or pay for her services."

I took a step toward the door, but he placed his hand on my shoulder. "Sit down, please. You must understand. It's obvious you are troubled, but you make me guess why—you oblige me to use conjecture. When I make an erroneous assumption, the blame does not belong on me, but you."

I returned to my seat. I had no desire to leave. The house on the lake grew colder and darker every day, so I stayed away as much as possible.

"I finished my opera."

"At last. That is a good thing, right? Why are you so solemn?"

"They are planning to perform it at the opera house."

"This is remarkable news. You've given your opera to the world."

I gazed out his window and mumbled, "I've given my opera to a woman."

"I thought as much," he said quietly. Then he added, "Who? Someone from the opera house? The young soprano you are coaching? Is the ring for Mademoiselle Daae?"

"No, someone not involved with the opera, at all." I clenched my hands into fists to help keep my composure.

"Tell me what happened, Erik. Tell me everything."

"It's over. Nothing to tell."

"Did you fall in love?" Daroga whispered as though he worried I could not endure hearing the word. His eyes showed genuine concern and interest in what I had to say.

"Yes, but more amazing than that…someone fell in love with me."

"Praise Allah! What happened? Who?"

I didn't want to relive any of the pain, but at the same time I wanted to tell him. If I spoke the words aloud, if someone heard them, the story became real.

"Her name is Olivia Weston. She's a widow from New York."

Daroga smiled. "An American. That explains the coffee and cookies, too."

"She will leave Paris after the opera is performed."

"So, you didn't give her the ring?"

Leaning forward, I rested my arms on my thighs. After an eternity of silence, Daroga whispered, "She refused you?"

"I never had the chance to ask her for her hand. Someone told her the opera house was haunted by a ghoulish fiend. She'd been informed that the Opera Ghost was a murderer." I scoffed. "Of course, in due time, she figured out I was both phantom and fiend—a murdering fiend. Even though she already discerned the truth, I admitted to my wrongdoing."

"She loved you before this confession?"

I rose from the chair, stood at the hearth with my back to him. I didn't want Daroga, with his keen police observation, to see the pain and vulnerability in my eyes. "You still find that so implausible?" I asked. My voice cracked, betraying the heartbreak I tried to hide.

"No," he said in his gentle way. "It is not so implausible. *You* are the one who always thought so."

I choked back a torrent of tears.

"She has refused to see you now?"

"No, I haven't been back." I swallowed hard and began again. "She seemed to understand. Or, at least, she *wanted* to understand. At first, she was horrified, but then she tried to tell me something—she tried to help me. Afterward, I took her home as I always had." I touched the gold chain underneath my collar.

"*That's* when she told you never to return?"

His words made me wince. A realization formed in my mind. "No, she did not."

A smile twitched under Daroga's mustache. "She never told you not to return, did she? You have assumed such a thing, yes?"

My mind raced as I tried to put the puzzle together.

"Did you tell her the whole truth? All of it? Did you tell her about the sultana? Did you tell her what she forced you to do?"

My breath hitched. "I told her nothing. I explained nothing."

"But, you said—"

"I am such a fool."

"You aren't making any sense. Did you or did you not tell her about your past?"

I couldn't answer him. The scene played in my head. She threw the key at me and demanded I tell her, but I refused. She was absolutely correct; my actions were cowardly. *Why had I not tried to explain? How could I leave her with so many unanswered questions?*

"Daroga, help me get her back. Please. Can you bring her here? I cannot go to the Chagny estate. If she sees me she might try to have me arrested—or she may very well shoot me with the revolver in her handbag." I smiled. Perhaps there was a slim chance I had not lost the only sunshine to touch my face. "But, Daroga, she may not do either of those things, right?"

"She carries a gun?"

"She's American." I shrugged. At that moment, my hope doubled.

Daroga laughed. "Thank you for the warning."

"Will you help me? Will you bring her here so I can explain?"

"I would have no way of doing that. A man she does not know cannot escort a lady of her rank into this part of town without arousing some suspicion. You cannot risk that. Think of what you are saying."

"I will risk everything."

"I can see as well as your conscience I will have to take on double duty and work as your common sense. You have truly gone mad this time," he joked.

"Maybe I have."

"Or, perhaps my friend is not mad at all. Love can take away one's rationale as quickly and efficiently as madness. It just feels better." He patted me on the shoulder.

"Thank you, *friend*."

We shook hands. I surprised him by pulling him into an embrace. After the astonishment left him, he put his arms around me and patted my back.

Chapter 42 Fountains of Paris

OLIVIA: The doctor and I enjoyed tea together at an outdoor café. As he talked, I watched people walk around the fountain. My mind continually returned to Erik. I wondered if he ever had a chance to experience the glory of a sunny day, the pleasure of a warm summer breeze. Had he ever stood in the plaza or felt drops of rain on his face? His memory brought tears to my eyes.

The doctor, noticing my mood change, stopped his story. "What is wrong, Madam Weston? Are you upset about something?"

"No, I have a little dust in my eyes. That's all." I dabbed them with my lace handkerchief. "Go ahead with your story, doctor. You were saying..."

*****

The past weeks had been sheer torture. Every sunset made me both hope and fear Erik might come back.

One of the servants found me knitting in the parlor by the window where the sunlight was strongest. I paused and gazed out at the grounds.

"Oh, Madam Weston, I didn't know you were home. A message was sent for you." She carried a small silver tray with an envelope on top.

"A message?" My heart beat out of tune for a moment. I tried to keep my composure. "From whom?"

"He didn't leave a name, Madame Weston. A Persian man told me to give you this letter."

"Thank you. That will be all."

I held the envelope in shaky hands. So much time had passed since that frightful night. I had tried to make myself stop thinking about Erik, but I daydreamed about him all the time. Part of me didn't want to open the message for fear of being whole-heartedly disappointed.

I stood in the parlor with the envelope in my hand. A sudden jolt of adrenaline and guilt left me breathless. *Erik had made a toy for me and I never took it from him.* I never held the little chimp or even acknowledged the gift.

I hurried to my room. Reaching between the nightstand and the bed, my fingers wrapped around the toy,

Like the madwoman I was becoming, I dashed through the hall and knocked into a couple of maids. "Pardon me!" I yelled over my shoulder.

I pulled open the door, ran into the sunshine, and down the front steps. Heading for the blurry green hedgerow, I couldn't wait to be away from the prying eyes of servants.

I was thankful for the blaze of the afternoon sun. Sitting in the grass I studied the little monkey. As with all Erik's creations the toy was perfection. I ran my finger through the tiny feather in the chimp's turban, touched his silky pants and bejeweled vest. Even his little feet had pointed shoes decorated with tiny jewels. As my fingers explored the details of what my eyes could not quite see, I found a thin chain around the chimp's neck. I gently pulled the gold chain from inside his vest.

Prisms burst forth all around me. Flashes of brilliance and rainbows colored the grass. A stunning diamond ring dangled from the end.

"Oh, Erik." Tears ran down my cheeks. I imagined his disappointment and heartbreak when I refused to accept his gift.

After a few moments, I calmed down enough to read the message I'd received. The notepaper contained perfect penmanship made with a skillful hand. Erik's imprecise, jagged handwriting slanted peculiarly to the left which I attributed to being left-handed. He was *not* the author of this note.

Dear Madam Weston,

I have been commissioned by a very dear friend to extend an invitation to have tea with me tomorrow at Café Duet. He wishes to express his remorse over the unfortunate occurrence on your last meeting. If you accept this invitation, please send word by messenger to the Café Duet today. They will forward any correspondence to me. My most talented and artistic friend will not be available at teatime tomorrow. Therefore, he shall not be joining us should you acquiesce.

Respectfully submitted,
A Friend.

I clutched the paper to my breast and realized I'd been holding my breath. Tomorrow could not come soon enough. I refolded the note and placed it in my pocket. I put the chain around my neck and tucked it under my blouse. The ring dangled close to my heart.

As I bounded up the front steps I was met by Philippe. "Cousin Olivia, you must stop disappearing like that. The staff cannot keep up with your whereabouts if you leave without warning."

"Why must the staff keep up my whereabouts?"

"Well, uh, you realize…you cannot see well. You might hurt yourself or trip and fall. I don't mean your every move must be monitored. Perhaps you will let someone know where we can find you if necessary.

Already, I am becoming 'the poor blind relative.'

"What is that you carry? A little monkey?"

A cold sweat broke out over my brow. "A chimp."

"May I?"

I handed the toy to him.

"Exquisite."

Philippe wound the musical device in the back. The chimp kept time with his symbols. "What a wonderfully made item. Is this a gift from Doctor Fournier?"

Before I answered him, two servants came into the hall. He handed the toy back to me.

"May I have a word with you in private?" He led me into the parlor.

We sat on the settee. Philippe cleared his throat before he began. "When our parents died, I took responsibility for the entire estate. I didn't have much time to, well, to be an unencumbered young man. I fear because of my situation, I have let my younger brother run *too* freely. He's a good boy, but I'm afraid he's about to make a dreadful mistake."

"Are you talking about courting Mademoiselle Daae?"

"Indeed. It's all over town and now has reached my ears once again. This match does not bode well. He will forfeit his inheritance if he does not stop such foolishness."

"Philippe, the boy is in love."

"You know more than you let on."

"What is so wrong with him finding love at his age? If the girl is in agreement, I fail to see the horrifying result you fear."

He scoffed. "I don't expect you to understand since you and your American comrades have no royal or imperial hierarchy, but this is France. Our family comes from generations of fine, established families with similar backgrounds. Now this brother of mine wants to add scandal to the name and join our ancestry with common blood. Not only common blood, but an entertainer. Unheard of."

"Although I disagree with you, Cousin Philippe, I do understand why his choice of paramour upsets you."

"Then you agree to help me?"

"Help you what?"

"I believe my impetuous younger brother may be on the verge of an elopement. I hope to circumvent this travesty by retiring to our estate in Nice for the rest of the season. He will be much more inclined to do so, if you are excited about the idea."

"Oh, Philippe, is it necessary to hurt Raoul like this?"

"I'm not hurting him. I'm saving him from years of regret."

"He won't see it that way."

Philippe lit his pipe and faced the mantel. "He will someday when he's properly married."

"Or, he'll spend the rest of his life miserable, married to the wrong person."

Philippe looked pained by my words. He wanted nothing more than his younger brother to be happy. He just had a misguided loyalty to his title and heritage. I held his hand in mine. "Let him stay to see her perform tomorrow. Give him that option. We'll all leave soon afterward."

Philippe sighed. "I suppose one night at the opera will not hurt anyone."

"Agreed." I started to leave, but turned around. "May I borrow a servant to send a message to the doctor?"

Philippe joined me at the door. "Of course. So, you and the doctor have been seeing quite a bit of each other?"

I blushed. "It seems so."

Chapter 43 The Second Truth

ERIK:

As soon as Daroga answered the door, I rushed into his flat. “Tell me everything that happened at the cafe. Is she doing well? Does she look all right? What did she say?”

“Goodness, Erik. Sit down. Have some tea. I just made a pot.”

He wouldn’t begin until I obliged, so I sat down. I noticed he’d already placed the tea set on the low table in front of me. I was not in any mood for social engagements.

“Well?” I leaned forward. He continued to pour tea into my cup and then his own. His expression did not reveal anything. I wanted to knock over the table and force him to tell me what she said. Instead, I drummed my fingers on the arm of the chair and glared at him. He never looked up. I had the impression he toyed with me. I was about to grab his lapel when he took his seat.

“What did she say? Did she ask about me?”

He took a long sip, set his cup down on the saucer with care. I wanted to seize him by the throat and force the information from him. Fortunately, for Daroga, he started his discourse.

“She asked about you, yes. I told her you are morose and miserable.”

“You didn’t!” I jumped up, angry at the pathetic way he made me sound.

"Do you want me to tell you what happened or not? If so, you need to sit down and keep your infernal temper in check."

"Do go on." I sat in my chair again, tension making my neck and shoulders rigid.

"First, let me tell you something. You could not have chosen a more beautiful and kind woman."

"Don't waste my time telling me of things I already know. Tell me what she said. Please, Daroga."

He chuckled. "The impatience of a man in love."

"Don't tease me, friend. I die a little more as we sit across from each other."

"You sent me to find out if she would meet with you. But, I—"

"Once again, do not tell me what I already know."

"What I'm trying to say is…I understood that you only wanted me to give her a message, but…I told her the *real* truth, Erik. I told her everything."

Heat burned my cheeks under the mask. Rage boiled up inside me. I had the urge to tear him limb from limb. "You ruined everything." I threw my teacup at the wall; the pieces clattered onto the floor. "Why? Why would you hurt me like this? I don't understand." I covered my mask with my hands.

"I told her because she deserved to know. You cannot pretend it never happened. Your past is your past."

Feeling the heat of fury, I yanked him up.

"Kill me, Erik! Go ahead. I'm not afraid to die. I will be reunited with my wife and son."

I dropped him into his chair. "You hate me? Is that why?" I forced out the words.

"Sit down. I will not have you stand over me like an angel from hell."

I threw myself in the chair, crossed my arms and glared at him. Nothing mattered anymore. I wanted to kill us both.

"Erik, the things that occurred with the shah and the sultana should have never happened. The two of them transferred their lust for blood to you. You did not leave Teheran the same man I escorted there. I brought them a magician of incomparable talent to entertain them. By the time you left, you were a coldblooded executioner. The shah turned you into a ruthless assassin and his mother forced you to become an architect of execution for her entertainment. If you killed before I took you to Teheran, I would wager it was only in self-defense. Am I correct?"

I shrugged, stretched my legs out in front of me and slouched back in the chair. I rested my arms over the armrests in utter defeat. *What did it matter?*

"I know this to be the truth. So do you," he said.

"What is the meaning of this, Daroga? I grow tired of you now. You told her everything and she's gone. I know how the story ends and do not wish to relive anything that happened to me before I met her."

"Perhaps due to his arrogance or maudlin mood, the greatest storyteller postulates the ending instead of letting the tale playout. Maybe he rushes the story and ruins it."

I sat up. "You are telling me it did not end that way? Are you saying she *doesn't* despise me?"

"I'm trying to tell you she sent you a message."

"What? Tell me! What message?"

"She says she found the secret hidden in the toy chimp. She bids me to tell you that her answer lies in Luke 15:11."

"Daroga, do you know what this means?" I stood, tears forming in my eyes. I didn't care if he saw them. "She would not send any message if she hated me. She would have nothing to say if she believed me to be loathsome. I must find a Bible and I dare say there isn't one here. Where can I find one? Where?"

"You are asking *me* where to find a Bible? You have gone mad."

"Is there more? Did she say more?"

"Not in words."

"Meaning what?"

"Meaning she still cares for you. Her concern is apparent in her voice when she spoke of you and the way she said your name. Go find a Bible, Erik. Find your answer."

Darkness had not yet fallen, but there were sufficient shadows to keep me hidden while I found the closest church. When I reached the giant, wooden, double doors, I wrapped my hand around the silver handle. Shame mixed with fear. *I can't go inside. I have no right.* I'd turned away from this God and damned my soul for all eternity. *Why should I defile such a holy place with my presence?* I let go of the handle and took a step back. All of the sudden, I heard the sounds of an organ and the beautiful pitch of a child's voice.

Kýrie, eléison Kýrie, eléison Kýrie, eléison

The music called me forth.

I opened the door. The sound drew me closer and closer until I found myself in the entrance hall. I hid in the shadows and listened, letting the familiar music fill my ears. As I crouched in that dark corner, a sudden wave of bitterness turned my stomach. My shoulders tensed with anger; my hands balled into fists. *Why have I entered this place? I do not belong here.*

Long ago, within the fury of my youth, I thought God deserted me. Now, as an adult, curled into a corner of a church shaking with guilt, I realized God had not turned away. I had.

I learned of the dark master's hateful deception too late in my life. The devil lied! I had not obtained any real power. I received no glory, had no revenge. The pain did not go away. None of the promises he made to me materialized.

Disillusionment filled my stomach like acid. I pulled my legs up and wrapped my arms around them. As I listened to the child's rehearsal, I let go of my defenses. When the practice session finished, I had no tears left. The setting sun shone through the stained glass. Instead of darkness, I was half-bathed in colored light.

Footsteps of the child and his mother echoed through the knave as they approached. Not wanting to cause the child any undue fear by seeing me, I backed into a dark portal and hid behind heavy velvet drapes.

A small window slid open to reveal a screen. "Yes, my child?" A man's voice came from behind the panel.

Since the mother and her son lingered in the vestibule, I was still unable to leave. "I need a minute. Excuse me," I whispered.

"Tell me when you are ready, my son. It's all right if you need to take a moment to collect yourself. You are the last one today—no one behind you."

I peeked into the vestibule just as the woman and boy rose from kneeling in front of a statue. The young mother kissed her son's rosy cheek before they pushed open the door to the street. A painful longing seized my chest.

"Are you ready, son?" the voice from behind the screen asked.

Oh! I forgot about him. "Yes, you *can* help me. What does Luke 15:11 say?"

"Aren't you going to confess your sins?"

"I need to know. Please, tell me."

"That is the story of the Prodigal Son. Are you familiar with the parable?"

"The one where the father is not angry with his son anymore?"

"The father was never angry. The son's departure filled the father with sadness not rage. He wished for him to come back. When the young man returned, the father is filled with joy."

"Why?"

"Simple. Love. You remember the son thought the father would rebuke him because of all the horrible, sinful things he'd done. He came home believing his father would send him away or make him a slave."

"But, he did *not* do that to his son."

"No, he didn't. Even after all the wretched things the errant son had done, the father still loved him.

"He still loved him?" I repeated with a shaky voice.

"Yes, of course."

"But, he'd sinned. He wasn't a good man; he'd done wicked things. His father should have been angry."

"Oh, but, don't you understand? The son no longer wanted to be that kind of man. Instead of letting his shame keep him away, he decided to return. The father rejoiced over finding his son again."

"But, he had disgraced his father…"

"Yes, but if the son continued to feel disgraceful, his feelings of unworthiness could've prevented such a reunion. Instead, he humbled himself and went home. And the father had been waiting for him all along. When he sees his son in the distance, he runs to him."

"He runs to him? Despite everything?"

"The past did not matter. Love is what mattered."

"How can the past not matter?"

"Because the son is truly repentant. He falls down on his knees and begs his father's forgiveness. The father pulls him up, places a cloak around his shoulders, sandals on his feet and a ring on his finger."

"A ring on his finger?"

"Yes, do you know what it means?"

"It means she doesn't hate me." *The past does not matter. Love matters.* "She still loves me."

"She?"

"Thank you."

"Don't you want to confess?"

"I can't…not yet."

I needed Olivia's help to get down on my knees and beg my Father for forgiveness.

"Son, are you all right?"

Without giving him an answer, I slipped from the church into the moonless night. I hurried through the streets of Paris straight to the Chagny estate.

She'd left her window open; a gas lamp burned on the ledge.

"How come I never see you enter? I waited for you." She greeted me with a shy smile.

"A good magician never reveals his secrets."

We stood at opposite sides of the room staring at each other.

"Olivia, I love you."

She *ran* across the room and threw herself into my arms. "I love you, too," she said. I closed my eyes and let the words fill me with warmth. She knew *me* and loved *me. Me!*

"Olivia, please, marry me." I dropped to one knee in front of her. Before she answered, a knock on the door sent me scurrying for the closet. That rotten Chagny boy had the worst timing.

"Cousin Olivia, we are leaving for the opera at a quarter past the hour. Will you be ready?" He spoke extra loud as if he wanted me to hear. It was very odd. When he closed the door behind him, I realized he wanted someone out in the hall to hear him.

He lowered his voice. "Christine and I are leaving tonight after the opera. She's agreed to marry me as soon as possible. I am supposed to wait for her at the stage door in the alley. I'll have the carriage ready. We're leaving right after the performance. My brother will be watching my every move. I'm glad I will be in the family box alone so I can leave early. How did you convince him to sit in the main gallery?"

"It's closer to the stage. I can see better from the front." Olivia gave him a conspirator's smile.

"It's perfect. I only need a head start. That's all I need."

"I wish you all the happiness in the world, dear, dear cousin."

Chapter 44 Acceptance

OLIVIA Using a young servant as a messenger, I'd sent a letter to Erik's friend, Daroga, giving him instructions to meet me at the premier of *Don Juan Triumphant.*

Raoul helped me into the carriage and then sat across from me. We both watched his elder brother make his way down the steps into the courtyard wearing a top hat and carrying a walking stick. When he paused to speak to his valet, Raoul whispered, "I've ordered Jacques to bring my carriage to the opera house half an hour before the show ends. I'm so excited, Cousin Olivia. This is going to work out, isn't it?"

"Yes, I believe so." I reached across and stopped his knee from bouncing with excitement. "Try to control your enthusiasm. Don't look so nervous. You're bound to get his suspicion up."

He kissed my hand. "Thanks for all your help."

Philippe stepped into the carriage and took a seat. "I guess we're off to the opera now." He smiled.

The driver mounted and we pulled away from the Chagny estate.

"Philippe, thank you for arranging for us to sit so close to the stage. I'm afraid the view from the box is just a tad too far." I smiled at him.

"Anything for you, Cousin Olivia." His eyes darted to the little toy chimp sitting on my lap. He lifted his eyebrows with curiosity. "Why are you bringing that?"

I'd refused to leave the little chimp behind when Erik and I ran away to get married. "The mechanism in the back is sticking. The doctor will be at the opera tonight. He said if I brought it, he'd take it to the toymaker to be repaired," I lied.

The count nodded and then focused out the carriage window.

"Philippe, there is something I meant to tell you earlier."

"Yes?"

"I've invited a friend to join us. I know it's short notice, but he says he's been wanting to see this opera for what seemed like twenty years."

"But, Olivia, I've only secured three seats."

"Oh, maybe I should sit in the box with him then. After all, he is my guest."

Raoul shook his head. "No, cousin, sit in the main chamber with your friend. You should be closer to the stage so you're able to see better. I'll sit up in the box. Besides, the box might afford me a better view of Mademoiselle Daae." He shot his brother a narrow-eyed glance.

Philippe scoffed.

I gave Raoul a silent chastisement with my expression. "Are you sure?"

"Positive. I'm happy to help you."

"Thank you. I'm sure Monsieur Daroga will be thrilled with our seats."

Philippe gazed out the window; clearly something important was on his mind.

I smiled and winked at Raoul. Our plan, so far, worked without flaw.

I sat back and admired the brilliant sunset. On my voyage to Paris, I had a strange premonition I would never return to New York. I had made the decision to journey to France when my eyesight worsened. Disheartened and angry, there was nothing to lose by having a risky, experimental operation. Even if the surgery killed me, I would not die blind and alone somewhere.

Then, I met Erik.

God had saved me from that other life. Erik reached out from the shadows. I wanted to guide him into the sunshine even as daylight faded for me. In return, for the rest of my years, I would be loved and adored as no woman ever had been.

*****

As soon as we settled into our seats, Monsieur Daroga read the program to me. "Paoulo Piangi is playing Don Juan."

"Piangi's voice will never measure up to the gift Erik possesses," I whispered.

"Indeed. Erik's voice is a gift from above."

"*Erik* is a gift from above."

Monsieur Daroga squeezed my hand. "Thank you, Madam Weston."

"For what?"

"For saving him." He smiled and turned toward the stage. The curtain rose and the opera began.

I marveled at the beauty of Christine's voice. After the first song finished, 'Don Juan' entered. From the moment he began singing, I knew who hid behind the Don Juan mask.

"Is that...?" Daroga whispered.

"Yes."

The audience sat riveted in their seats. Erik's magnificent voice coupled with the dramatic libretto moved the ladies to tears. Charged air surrounded me. He had the crowd in the palm of his hand.

Near the final scene, Philippe whispered, "Where is he, Olivia? Why isn't he in the box?" The Count once again searched the family's box using his opera glasses.

"He's probably gone out for air. I'm sure he'll be back."

"I had a feeling he was up to something." Philippe whispered, "I'll be right back. I'm going to find my brother." He made his way out of the row and rushed up the aisle. My heart fell from my chest into my stomach. *Oh no, poor Raoul.*

Philippe had not returned by the last scene where Mademoiselle Daae and Erik rushed into each other's arms for a climactic kiss.

"Oh, Monsieur Daroga!" I wiped away a tear. "There has never been a more beautiful performance than what we have witnessed here. It had Erik's touch. Perfection."

Before I turned back to the stage, the audience erupted in screams and gasps.

"What happened?" I tried to find the performers onstage through my opera glasses.

"The young woman ripped off Erik's mask." Monsieur Daroga bolted upright from his seat.

"She recognized his voice as the Angel," I said under my breath. "I cannot see well. Tell me what's happening."

"Mademoiselle Daae pushed him away with both hands. The other performers have fled the stage. Poor, Erik." Daroga's voice dripped with empathy. "He's panicked, Madam Weston."

"What's happening now?" I asked.

"No, don't do it."

"Tell me what's happening. I can't see."

"Erik, no," he yelled, ignoring my pleas.

"Tell me, please."

Monsieur Daroga turned toward the audience and shouted, "Don't panic. Sit down." The chaos continued. He turned to me. "Madam Weston, I can see the fright and anger in his eyes."

A sharp whistle screeched over the audience's uproar and police filled the aisles.

"Please, sirs, don't advance. Leave him alone. You will make things worse." Monsieur Daroga stepped over my feet on his way out into the aisle. "Sergeant, don't advance. Let me reason with him."

The police ignored his request and lined up on both sides of the stage awaiting the order to capture Erik.

"Raoul made good on his threat to catch The Phantom," I mumbled. In my excitement to be with Erik, I had forgotten about his plan.

"Monsieur, wait!" In my rush to reach Daroga, I bumped into several people and tripped over a lady's train. When I finally found him, I clutched his arm. "The doors are barred. The police are armed with instructions to shoot. I know this to be fact. What should we do?"

Monsieur Daroga approached the police captain. "Sir, please, the use of force is unnecessary. Let me talk to him. Don't give the word to advance. For godsakes, hold your fire."

"Move." The captain shoved Daroga aside. The patrons continued to stream out of the theatre. Daroga turned toward the audience. "Stop this madness. You're making things worse. Stop panicking. Return to your seats. Sit down. Stop this nonsense!"

Shaking and breathing hard, I made the bleary-eyed journey against the crowd to return to my seat. I tried to keep my opera glasses directly on the man that I loved, but he rushed about the stage in a frantic effort to flee, making it impossible for me to track him.

I choked back a sob and whispered, "I am so sorry, Erik. You were right. They've ruined your opera. They've ruined everything."

Monsieur Daroga clutched my arm. "Madam, he's looking out into the private boxes. Does he search for us? Does he think we've abandoned him?"

"I forgot to tell him we wouldn't be in the box tonight. I know what he sees when he looks out into the theatre. He sees an angry, murderous crowd."

"I must go to him. Stay here. It's safer. I'll come back for you." Daroga moved down the aisle against the crowd. Another prolonged whistle and the police carrying guns with bayonets began to close in on Erik.

"No!" I jumped up. "Monsieur Daroga, where did you go? Please, don't leave me. Take me to him."

Chapter 45 Letting Go

ERIK:

If I can block the majority of the police from coming closer, I might escape. There was only one thing big enough to prevent them from advancing. I rushed up the catwalks and released the counterweights holding the chandelier in place. The half-ton light fixture ripped across the ceiling before plummeting. The violent crash scattered patrons and police alike. The chandelier succeeded in distracting the authorities and thus, delaying their progression, I took advantage of the diversion and maneuvered back to the stage. Christine stood on top of the secret trap door. I had no other means to escape. I pulled the lever. We dropped below in the blink of an eye.

I forced the troublesome girl to go with me as I traveled to the house on the lake. Once on the shore, I released the prima donna. The stupid child whimpered and backed away from me. I stomped up to her. "Why Christine? Why did you do that?"

"You're not an angel. You're not a phantom. You're not even a man. You are a monster."

I turned away. *How do I find Olivia in what is sure to be pandemonium upstairs?* The knowledge that neither Raoul nor Philippe would leave her alone this time comforted me. *She should be safe in the chaos.* I needed to think of a coherent way out of the mess.

Christine huddled against the wall of the tunnel terrified. I didn't want to play the villain anymore. I wanted a new role— and I wasn't sure the world would allow me one.

The alarm in the torture chamber disturbed my thoughts. I yanked Christine up and pulled her into the house.

She protested, hitting me with her small fists. "Let me go, you monster!"

The alarm continued to ring as she yelled and struck me. I knew who was inside the chamber. That insipid Chagny boy followed me down. The egotistical youth had made his way far enough into my home to land in the torture chamber.

I thought about leaving him inside, but couldn't do it. He'd been in there too long already. I opened the door and he crawled out gasping for breath. Christine ran to him, threw her arms around his neck, toppling him over onto his side. They clung to each other.

Damn them both!

I nursed the impetuous boy back from his heat-induced stupor. He and his paramour sat on my sofa clutching each other. When the little blue-blooded imperialist regained his strength and felt man enough, he drew his sword from its scabbard. I didn't feel like playing with the child at the moment. In order to find Olivia, I needed to get them out of my house.

"Put that thing away. You'll exhaust yourself once again," I said.

The silly youth refused to heed my warning. He insisted I fight him. Ignoring his mad threats, I wrapped my cape around my shoulders. His forehead wrinkled in confusion, but he still pointed his sword in my direction. I rushed around gathering money, jewels and portable revenue, stashing them in the pockets within my cape so Olivia and I could make our escape. Raoul followed me with his weapon at the ready. I attached my own scabbard and sword to my waist.

Just as I was about to lead the lovers back upstairs, the little pest went into a fencing posture. "En guarde!"

I laughed at his attempt to be gallant in front of Christine. What a shame I would have to humiliate him instead. My patience had worn thin with his following me around my home with his sword drawn as if I were under his arrest.

"Viscount, there is no need for that. Put away your weapon and I'll let you go."

"You have haunted this opera house, stolen money and terrified Christine for the last time, you villain." He thrust his sword so close the point nicked my chin. My face turned hot with rage as small droplets of blood slithered down my neck.

His family heirloom sword was airborne and landed near my feet before he drew his next breath. From the astonished looks on their faces, neither he nor Christine had any idea how I disarmed him. They stood with their mouths agape as I opened the front door and tossed his sword into the lake.

"Now, are we to act as gentlemen or animals? Your choice, Viscount."

"Christine, stand behind me. Get away from this man—this *thing*."

"Animals it is then," I said. Before he responded, I had his wrists at the end of my whip. Banal and arrogant, the boy pulled away. My whip tightened.

Christine threw herself at my feet. "Let him go. I beg you."

"Move out of the way, Mademoiselle Daae. Let go of my legs. Look what you've done. You've smeared your stage makeup all over my trousers."

The wretched girl cried, "Let him go. You can have me as your hostage, but let him go."

"No, Christine, I would rather die than leave you here," the Viscount said.

"Listen to your lover, Mademoiselle. He's chosen death. You heard him. He's the one who came into my home uninvited, drew a weapon and insulted me." I scoffed. "Really, you two are the worst houseguests I've ever had."

"I know you're in love with Christine. You've brought her here to be your captive bride," Raoul accused. "I've figured the whole thing out. I know why you've done this. You are jealous of me. You want Christine to yourself."

I laughed long and hard over that one. The sound of my maniacal mirth silenced both of the sniveling fools. They probably thought they were at the mercy of a madman. And they were.

Christine backed away from my legs and stood. She thrust herself at Raoul. With his hands bound, he could not embrace her, so she wrapped her arms around his neck. "Let us go, you monster."

"Monster? Oh, my! I am growing tired of the discourteous behavior you both have shown in my home. Haven't you any manners at all?"

"Your home?" Raoul looked around. "What are you?"

"*What* am I? *What* am I? Oh, my, dear boy. I am the Angel of Death! The Devil's Child! The Living Corpse!"

Infuriated, I dragged him to the guest room where I tied him to a chair in order to keep him from destroying my house or trying to escape only to kill himself on one of the many snares and traps.

I need to find Olivia.

"Viscount, prima donna, if you are good children, I shall set you free when I return. If you try to escape, I promise you will find certain death."

"Mademoiselle," I gestured to the chair I'd set up next to Raoul.

She stared at the rope in my hands with terror in her eyes. Instead of sitting down, she threw herself on the floor in front of Raoul, wrapping her arms around his calves. I tried to pick her up, but she clung to him. Her refusal to release him caused his chair to fall backward. He banged his head rather soundly on the floor.

I righted the Viscount's chair. Instead of fighting with the girl, I simply tied her to his legs.

"Blood! There's blood! He's killed in this room before."

Raoul followed Christine's line of vision to the big red ink spot on the carpet. He struggled harder to pull his hands free from the chair, but once again failed.

"Quit your squirming. All you're doing is succeeding in giving yourself one hell of a rope burn. Learn some patience. I shall be back momentarily. Viscount, Mademoiselle Daae, please make yourselves at home while I'm away. I would offer you some tea, but how would you drink it?" I laughed. "Tsk. Tsk. Such a shame we couldn't have been civilized."

I exited the guest room. Before I reached the fireplace, the alarm on the torture chamber rang again.

Daroga!

He'd read over the plans I'd drawn up for the shah's secret passageways. He'd seen the plans for the traps in the sultana's palace. *My fault. A good magician never tells his secrets.*

I rushed to the chamber to let him out. Daroga wasn't inside as long as the brat, but he came out gasping, his clothing wet with perspiration.

"Daroga, you fool. If I hadn't been here to hear the alarm, you would've—"

"Erik," he said breathlessly. He steadied himself by resting his hands on my shoulders. "Why did you drop the chandelier? You kill—"

"I haven't the time for this, Daroga. I have to find Olivia." I knocked his hands off and walked away.

He once again blocked my path. "No, you don't understand." He placed his hands on his knees, still trying to catch his breath. Suddenly, the lovers began screaming.

"Is someone there? Help! Please, help us! We're in here!"

"What have you done?" He brushed passed me on his way to the guest room.

"No, Daroga, do *not* let them go. I will return for them as soon as I find Olivia."

Daroga never heeded my warnings as he should. He began to untie the Viscount.

"Leave them there," I demanded.

As he bent over to untie Raoul's wrists, I captured Daroga's hands in my whip and yanked him to me.

"Now, see what you've forced me to do? Why can't you ever mind your own business?" I pushed him into a seated position and tried to tie his hands to the back of the chair next to the Viscount. The old chief of police had some fight in him and we struggled with each other for a moment. I grabbed the handiest thing I could find. I slammed the marble statue onto his head. He slumped over and I finished tying him up as Christine continued to scream.

"Shut up, child. You're ruining your voice!"

Daroga began to stir. *He'll be okay. Maybe a headache; maybe some memory loss*. If I were lucky, he wouldn't remember who hit him. *I'll blame the Viscount*. I rushed out of the room, but I heard him say, "What happened?"

The insufferable boy said, "It's The Phantom! He's in love with Christine and has taken her to be his hostage bride."

"Where am I?" Daroga's voice warbled and he slurred. "What happened? I don't remember…"

"We're in the monster's lair. He was holding Christine hostage. I came to rescue her."

I turned the lever under the scorpion box and exited up the stairs before I heard any more ridiculous fabrications about my kidnapping Christine.

With no notice of me hiding in the shadows, medics continued to care for injured patrons. That sort of thing was to be expected when half a ton falls upon one's head. Medical teams carried a few people out on stretchers. Mostly flesh wounds. *Look at the damage that has been done to my theatre because of that rude child.*

The chaos had died down, but police still roamed the theatre.

If Piangi had not collapsed and died backstage right before the show, none of it would've happened. I had found the overweight tenor in the hall next to the dressing rooms. Piangi always had terrible timing. Dying on Opening Night is incredibly irresponsible. Refusing to allow a gluttonous boar like Piangi to ruin everything, I had made a decision. I dragged his body to the storage closet and hurried to the costume room to find suitable attire for me to replace him.

Medics and the injured audience members began to leave the theatre. A few yards from where I lurked, the only fatality of the chandelier lay under a bloody sheet. Part of her ball gown stuck out from under the cloth.

What a pity.

Seeing the Chagny's private box empty put my stomach at ease; my shoulders relaxed. *Surely, the Count has taken her home. I'll make my way there as soon as I…*

Something caught my eye on the floor of the main chamber. The toy chimp I'd made Olivia lay on the plush, red carpet near the stage—just a short distance from the corpse. I crept closer and hid within folds of the stage curtain. When it was safe, I came from behind the black velvet and pulled the toy from under broken crystals, pieces of gilt and shattered glass. *Why is this here? Had Olivia come looking for me?* An arctic sweat broke out under my mask. *Or had she been seated closer to the stage so she might see better?*

I craned my neck upward to observe the devastation where the chandelier had ripped through the ceiling before plummeting onto the first four rows. The massive structure lay in pieces all around my feet. *No! Surely, she was in the family box.*

I swiveled toward the body. The edge of a lavender ball gown trimmed in ivory lace stuck out from under the sheet. My mind went wild trying to remember what color Olivia wore when I took leave of her hours earlier. I conjured up a memory of her running to me from across the room in a pale purple ball gown. The world shrunk and turned black.

I clawed the little chimp, clutching him with extreme horror. Something moved under my index finger. A thin chain encircled the chimp's neck. At the end of the chain, tucked into the little vest, I pulled out a man's gold wedding band. Quick breaths bounced off the mask; my stomach tightened with waves of nausea. I took a few steps toward the covered victim, but could not continue. *It can't be her. It can't be.*

My mind went blank. My emotions shut down leaving me numb. I stopped caring if someone spotted me. It didn't matter if I were about to be shot or bayoneted in the back. I stood frozen, staring at the lilac piece of taffeta surrounded by a pool of red. My chest seized with pain; I couldn't catch my breath.

I'd quickly slipped the ring on my finger, dropped the toy and moved away from the victim.

Clusters of policemen throughout the theatre prevented me from returning to my home through any of the secret panels, so I exited the theatre undetected through a side door. I made my way to the tunnel and began my descent.

*****

Upon my return, I found a body had washed up on my shore. He lay face down in the black water. I turned the victim over with my foot. Philippe had drowned in one of the underwater snares. No doubt he'd searched for his reckless brother and paid for his loyalty with his life. I didn't care. Nothing mattered. I stepped over him and continued onto my home.

I untied Daroga and the lovers. Christine clung to Raoul, crying into his chest as I herded them to the parlor. They gaped at me warily as if waiting for me to do something. I pointed to the open panel next to the fireplace, but they looked at me with wide eyes, not moving.

"Go! You're free. Go now!"

Raoul grabbed Christine by the wrist and the two of them fled.

I needed to be alone. *She was wearing lavender when I left her. Or was it dark pink? Rose with white lace?*

"Erik, you didn't kidnap that young soprano, did you?" Daroga's head wound bled down his face and reddened his collar. His eyes were dilated with concussion. I did not care.

"Leave me or I will kill you where you stand."

"No, I'm not leaving until you explain. Why was Miss Daae here? Are you in love with her? Did you kidnap her? You took her as your hostage bride?"

"Leave now." I took a menacing step toward him, my whip at my side and my hand on the handle.

He glanced at my weapon and then met my eyes.

Daroga turned sharply and followed Christine and Raoul up the stairs.

On the opposite side of the mantle, I lifted the inlayed grasshopper box and turned the switch. The panel closed. There wasn't any way in from the other side except through the stone and mortar—but they'd come for me anyway.

I returned to the guest room, sat on Olivia's bed and tried to think rationally. *Was she dressed for the opera already when I came to her room? Or did she change into another gown before they left? Was the dress lilac?*

Seeing the tub of soothing salve on the nightstand sliced a new wound into my heart. And then—

A dark, hot rage filled my soul.

She cared for me. She loved me. She forgave me. Did I kill her?

I removed a candle from the stand and set the bedspread on fire. Turning to the nightstand, I set the tablecloth alight. I hurried to the music room and tossed candles into the piles of scores. I threw oil lamps onto anything that would burn.

Running my hands along the carvings of a column, I found the hidden lever. A large painting squeaked on its hinges. I glanced behind me. Flames engulfed my home. All the other beautiful things in my life were destroyed—*by me*.

I stepped through and then hit the pivot on the other side making the passage close. There was no way back inside once the mechanism latched.

I made my way through the murky, unused tunnel by feeling along the walls. I'd built the passageway during the construction of the opera house as a last-ditch escape. Even though I fooled myself into thinking I had isolated myself from man, I subconsciously must have known that one day he would chase me out of this home, too.

I exited through a manhole across the avenue. My chest still heaved from the exertion of my destruction and hurried escape through the secret tunnel. I tilted my head to the starry night sky. I didn't want to run anymore; I didn't want to exist anymore.

"As long as you're alive…" she'd once said to me, "....there's always hope for redemption."

How can I be redeemed without her? How can I live without her? She can't be dead. Not her. My feet refused to move.

I fell to my knees, touched the place where the gold cross lay against my chest. "Please, help me. Just give me one more chance. I realize I deserve nothing more than your valid contempt, but my heart cannot take this. I'll do anything…just give me back my light."

A shuffling noise and the sound of hurried footsteps aroused me from my desperate prayer. I pulled the hood further over my brow.

The black of night engulfed me as I set out to the Chagny estate.

*****

The chateau came into my view. Its stately presence gleamed in the moonlight—a scene I'd come to know so well. *Had I once been welcomed within its walls?*

No candlelight burned within her bed chambers; no lamps beckoned me to her side. The entire mansion was dark.

Pain anchored itself in the depths of my battered heart. I passed the hedgerow where I'd stolen her. *I'm so sorry, Olivia. I never meant to frighten you. I would rather die than hurt you.*

I slid over the windowsill and into the shadowy room. A soft voice called to me from the dark. "Erik? Is that you?" The strike of a match, a whiff of sulfur and the face of my beloved came into view.

Olivia held a white candle; the flames illuminated the captivating beauty of her features. I stood mute—trembling with amazement and utter relief.

"Oh, Erik. I was so frightened. I didn't know if they'd captured you. I thought it was too late..." She sobbed.

I ran across the room and took her in my arms. "It's never too late, Olivia. As long as there is breath in me, it will never be too late for anything."

The End

Thank you for reading Phantom: Edge of the Flame

Please visit the author's website:
kristinegoodfellow.weebly.com
Blog: kirstinegoodfellow.wordpress.com
Facebook: Kristine Goodfellow, Author

Other books by this author:

The Missing Chapter – A Story of Love
The Mansion on Butcher Lake
Command Performance
The Tributary
The Gift of Winter

48295616R00204

Made in the USA
Middletown, DE
14 September 2017